THE CYBORG'S RIDDLE

BOOK 3

Benoit Lanteigne

80 Mapleton Rd, Unit 11-80
Moncton, New-Brunswick, Canada
E1C 7W8

Benoit Lanteigne

80 Mapleton Rd, Unit 11-80
Moncton, New-Brunswick, Canada
E1C 7W8

https://thecyborgscrusade.com

Book Layout © 2016 BookDesignTemplates.com
Edited by Eliza Dee
Book Cover Design by 100 Covers

The Cyborg's Crusade / Benoit Lanteigne. -- 1st ed.
ISBN 978-1-7779002-1-2

CONTENTS

Do you want a free short story that serves as a prequel to The Cyborg's Crusade? Then, join my newsletter on my website https://thecyborgscrusade.com.

The next book, The Cyborg's Fortune, is available for preorder and releases on June 3, 2024.

Angel of Deception

Chapter 1

Lacdor 16, 2134, on the Nirnivian calendar

The smell of burnt grass and flesh penetrated Diabo's nostrils. Several dead bodies surrounded him, many killed by his own bloodstained hands. In the distance, his men ransacked the transport truck they'd attacked. Some of their crude jokes and banter reached Diabo's ears, but not enough for him to follow any of the conversations they shared.

The moment Diabo had recovered, he'd planned a revenge strike against Ostark. Plague had warned him not to approach the vehicles. Through fancy science that lay beyond their grasp, the mechanical freak had engineered detonators that responded to the BBR founders' DNA. As long as Diabo remained out of range, it'd be fine. If he took a single step too close, however, boom—a repeat of the previous events that had rendered him bedridden. Diabo itched to investigate the cargo himself, but the thought of reliving that horror left him cold. That fear served him well, for after a five-minute search, his underlings discovered rigged explosives.

The assault had gone smoothly despite Diabo's lack of practice. Allison had incapacitated their foes through dread, without resisting. No need to force her with that elaborate remote control Plague had concocted. As a result, instead of losing consciousness, the telepath sat on the ground trembling and whimpering. A better fate, all considered, or at least it served BBR's purposes. When she cooperated, they could use her again sooner.

After a shake of the head, Diabo groaned and paced around. The battle spiked his adrenaline and had proved too short for satisfaction. He craved more action, and having to wait while others completed the work failed to satisfy that need. Frustrated, he twiddled his fingers while mumbling curses. Then he heard a wail and turned his neck. A ravaged Ostarkiran soldier crawled on the soil. Legs shattered, he'd lost his ability to walk, and instead he inched forward on his forearms. Crimson stains soiled his face, making his features indistinguishable. Diabo doubted he'd recognize the guy anyway. They'd probably never met. Otherwise, the poor fool would be dead already.

When the unexpected survivor realized Diabo had spotted him, he gasped and attempted to change direction, clawing away. With a chuckle, Diabo crossed his arms and watched his pitiful attempt at fleeing. For a minute or two, maybe even five, Diabo stayed immobile and observed in silence. Then he approached the Ostarkiran and said, "Hey, pal, where are ya goin'?"

The broken man glanced at Diabo, terror filling his eyes. His lips moved, but instead of words, they produced meaningless sounds. The injuries he had suffered ravaged his jaw.

"Ain't gonna get far like that. How about I give ya a push?" On that note, Diabo lifted his foot and brought it down on the soldier's back. The sound of shattering bones echoed. "There ya go."

Diabo exhaled in relief. That had quenched his thirst. Then he noted a silhouette in his peripheral vision and clenched his fist, ready to pounce, but the figure ended up being a BBR ally carrying a metallic suitcase.

"Hey, boss, we found this strange thing in there." He pointed at the truck. "Ain't got no idea what it is. We thought you should take a look."

Intrigued, Diabo bent down and studied the container, a nondescript box except for three triangles arranged in a circle with their points touching and a menacing skull in the middle. Clearing the cobwebs from his mind, Diabo recognized the Ostarkiran biohazard symbol. A smile formed on his mouth as he rubbed his chin. They might've stumbled on potential material for a dirty bomb. Suddenly, his plans for revenge attained greater heights than he had dared hope.

***

"Sorry to disappoint, boss, but we ain't making weapons out of these." On the screen, Plague brandished a sealed cylindrical vial half-filled with bright orange goo. Much like the suitcase they had come from, the glass was branded with a red symbol formed of triangles and a skull.

Dejected, Diabo produced an annoyed growl. His excitement had spiked at the possibilities when that goon had presented the metallic container. The instant he'd returned to the camp, he'd set up delivery for Plague and instructed him to consider the study of the contents a top priority. While he'd waited for results, Diabo's enthusiasm had reached a ludicrous height as his imagination had run wild. At first, he'd dreamed of a bomb causing hundreds of fatalities, but this had increased to thousands, tens of thousands, and so on. Soon, he'd contemplated the possibility of unleashing a disease upon Ostark so devastating and cruel it'd annihilate the population to extinction. Now Plague had dashed his hopes. At least the decrepit mutant had obeyed orders and delivered his reports quickly, preventing Diabo from indulging in his fantasy for longer than necessary. Living with that vision for months only to have it snatched away would be heartbreaking.

"You sure 'bout that?" Diabo asked.

"Yeah." Plague tilted the transparent capsule left to right. Inside, the gelatinous substance followed the motion.

"Hmm... I guess they ain't dangerous, huh? That beautiful symbol let me down."

"Oh, I never said that." Though Plague's bandages concealed his facial expression, Diabo imagined a grin under them. "They're Alcharia samples. Deadly disease, but too random for a bioweapon. It's easy enough to catch it. Freak, roughly forty percent of the population has it. Thing is, it often remains dormant for decades, and for most patients, it doesn't"—he continued with finger quotes—"wake up before something else kills 'em. If we directly injected the stuff into someone's veins, we'd get results, but other than that..."

Diabo roared in frustration. He knew about Alcharia. Regardless of its low fatality rates, people feared the virus due to the dreadful symptoms it imposed on its rare victims. After his initial infuriation, Diabo rubbed his chin. Based on reports, Doctor Death had shown an interest in Alcharia. BBR information tended to be unreliable, so until then, Diabo couldn't vouch for the accuracy. However, those samples confirmed it. They were likely destined to the mechanical man himself for his research.

"Plague, why would the Doc need that whole bunch of Alcharia? Think he weaponized it after all?"

With a chuckle, Plague dismissed the notion with a wave. "Nah, I doubt it. If anybody could, it'd be that bastard. But there ain't no way. There's plenty of nasty stuff he could create kick-ass bombs with. Don't know what he wants with Alcharia. Maybe a cure, but if that's it, I don't see why he's focusing on something that kills four people a year. I guess he likes the challenge. He enjoys mysteries."

Diabo shrugged. "I'll be damned if I understand that twisted asshole. What a freaking letdown."

Chapter 2

Lacdor 19, 2134, on the Nirnivian calendar

Don't ask me what happened, but for a while, I couldn't find my minicomp and that sucked. I mean, Janice had gone to the trouble of getting me a gift, and I'd lost it. Besides, it had a few games on it that were decent time killers. I thought I'd left it on my bookshelf, but I couldn't find it there. Then, that evening, I noticed it was under those shelves. It must have fallen and somehow got pushed under. Relieved, I fished it out.

—Thoughts of James Hunter, Hocmar 28, 2134, on the Nirnivian calendar

Since he'd located his minicomp, James decided to play a few rounds before going to sleep. After a yawn, he lay on his mattress, turned on the machine and slid out the stylus. For a moment, he studied the game selection. Though he considered continuing the story-heavy adventure game he'd started a while back, James soon concluded he'd rather enjoy lighter entertainment. In the end, he chose a simple puzzle where you matched colored shapes.

Despite his lack of recent practice, James retained his skills. He slipped the pieces around at a quick pace and accumulated a fair amount of points in a short interval as he hummed along with the cheerful tune. Of course, the first few levels proved easy, so things might change later. He'd never find out, for when he'd almost reached the fifth stage, the screen on his minicomp flashed, then turned black. Frustrated, James grunted and dropped the gadget on his bed. Ah well, he was growing tired anyway. He stretched before grabbing the device, intending to put it in a safe place, when a monotone robotic voice echoed.

"Hello, James. I sincerely apologize for the inconvenience."

James gasped. On the screen, the cybernetic man appeared. How? Janice claimed NISDA had ripped out the networking parts of the minicomp. Though not a computer expert, even James understood that rendered outside communication impossible. Once he'd recuperated from his shock, he shook his head.

"Goodbye," James said as he pushed the power button. A smirk spread on his face while he imagined Doctor Death's reaction, but it vanished in an instant. The minicomp refused to shut down. "What the hell?"

"I am afraid getting rid of me is not that simple. Did you expect I would not anticipate an attempt to turn me off?" The electronic emoticon on the mechanical man's visage showed a laughing animation before returning to its default display. "In any event, I merely ask for a minute of your time. I swear I have your best interests in mind."

It wasn't what he said... I barely heard him. I'm not sure what it was. I'm not sure why I didn't just shove the minicomp in a drawer, or smash it, or run out to Rose. I think it was his remaining eye. There was something in that deep blue eye, like a glimmer of truth and compassion. Whatever the reason, it doesn't matter. The important part is that I listened to him. He didn't talk much, but his words shaped the future.

—Thoughts of James Hunter, Hocmar 28, 2134, on the Nirnivian calendar

"Do not worry, I shall be brief. I mentioned previously that Rose Ricdeau and her followers are lying to you. This is an absolute truth, but I understand that without concrete proof, you will never believe me, and I do not blame you either. Exposing all her deceptions would be an arduous task. However, I hope that if I can reveal one measly little lie, it might open your mind to the possibility there are more."

"You're taking too long for my liking," James said as he glanced toward his watch.

"As you wish, I shall expedite. I suppose Rose already told you about a previous 'visitor' who appeared in Nirnivia. As unlikely as it seems, he came from Earth, and ever since your arrival, he has been referred to as the first human. Rose stated that he reacted badly to his sudden teleportation; that he panicked, and a child died in the aftermath, which is why humans are hated. Am I correct?"

James scratched the back of his head. "Um, yes, that's right."

"Excellent." The cyborg nodded. "Am I also correct in assuming that Rose affirms she never met this peculiar character?" James acquiesced. "What you have been told is inaccurate. The first human lived in Nirnivia for years, and Rose met him. In fact, they spoke on several occasions. He never, ever harmed a child. That I am telling the truth can be proven quite easily."

A part of me always thought their story about the first human wasn't right. For one thing, the people's reaction felt too extreme. There were also holes, like how did they know the 'visitor' was a human? I was a bit suspicious, but I rationalized that they had no reason to lie. My doubts didn't change the fact that I didn't trust the Doctor and preferred not to give him the pleasure of seeing that I might believe him.

—Thoughts of James Hunter, Hocmar 28, 2134, on the Nirnivian calendar

"Oh yeah?" In an attempt at false bravado, James crossed his arms and attempted a sneer. "How about you do that, then?"

The Ostarkiran president shrugged. "Ah, but there is no need, since you already have the proof at your disposal. It is tucked away somewhere in your underused brain. Think about it and you will discover the solution, eventually."

"Um, really?" Confused, James blinked twice. "So, you go through the trouble of contacting me and that's all you got?"

The mechanical man replied in the same monotonous tone as always. Conveying emotions vocally was impossible for him, after all. Still, somehow, James detected a touch of malice in his synthetic voice, maybe because his emoji turned into a furious frowning face.

"Perhaps I would do just that, James, if you had not so rudely terminated our last conversation. I have feelings too, even if I appear to be a machine. Do not concern yourself. You can figure it out alone. Rose blatantly exposed her lies herself. You should have realized this a long time ago. If it motivates you, consider this a test—a way of determining whether or not you are worthy of my help. Goodbye, James."

"Wait!" But it was too late. The Ostarkiran president cut the transmission.

I decided he was bullshitting me. Rose warned me he'd try to manipulate me if I listened to him. Better to forget it for now and tell Rose what happened in the morning. At least, that's what I told myself, but... Doctor Death's riddle, if we can call it that, remained stuck in my mind. I spent a good part of the night searching for the answer. What did he mean, she had exposed her own lies? The simplest explanation was that she'd said something that had let the truth slip... I tried remembering our past discussions, but there were so many of them it was impossible. From what I recalled, I couldn't find anything suspicious. What if the freak used a psychological trick so I'd imagine something existed when it didn't? I tried convincing myself that was it, but my doubts kept haunting me.

—Thoughts of James Hunter, Hocmar 28, 2134, on the Nirnivian calendar

***

"Are you sure you've told him enough?" Evelyn asked the Good Doctor while exiting the shadows. The president took pity on her confusion concerning his so-called deus ex machina and let her assist to the transmission provided she didn't interfere. To be frank, the conversation had increased Evelyn's perplexity rather than quelled it.

"Absolutely. Uncovering Rose's mistake by himself will have a far greater impact."

Evelyn scowled. "I think you're overestimating him. I don't see what you meant at all."

"And that is perfectly normal. James has knowledge beyond what you possess. Do not be concerned. I will give him a clue if necessary."

I wasn't convinced. That James didn't look bright. If I couldn't figure out the riddle, I doubted he would. Then again, I didn't understand the Good Doctor's plan. I still had no idea why he bothered with that human. He was insignificant.

—Thoughts of Evelyn Losier Hocmar 28, 2134, on the Nirnivian calendar

Chapter 3

Lacdor 20, 2134, on the Nirnivian calendar

After that call from Doctor Death, I couldn't sleep. I spent the night tossing and turning, wondering what he meant and trying to figure it out. Not that I succeeded; far from it. Morning came, and I could tell that even though I needed rest, I'd be awake for the whole day, so I went out to grab a quick breakfast. I bumped into Rose and Brucie as I exited my room. They were going to the gym, and Rose asked if I'd hang out with them while she worked out. I didn't want to, since the Doctor had given me a lot to think about. Still, I worried it'd seem weird if I refused, so I said yes.

—Thoughts of James Hunter, Hocmar 28, 2134, on the Nirnivian calendar

Once she finished a session of lightweight training, Rose shifted to her cardio regiment. Brucie's guidance proved as merciless as ever, and James noted a heavy dose of perspiration soon stained her clothes. Along with her exercising, she often spoke to him, attempting to start a chat, but he mumbled short, dismissive sentences in response. The questions Doctor Death had put in his mind weighed on him like a shroud. James feared talking would drag his worries into the light, revealing his communication with the mechanical man. No doubt the fact that he had hidden the intrusion would displease both Rose and NISDA, and what then?

Terrified by the prospect, James almost lost his nerves and disclosed what had happened to Rose. Except that posed several problems, so he resisted the temptation. The whole ordeal with the first human had sounded fishy even before Doctor Death's warning. Now that further shade had been thrown on the issue, he needed to investigate, whether he liked it or not. Keeping in touch with the Ostarkiran president granted him an alternate source of information. Not that he trusted the cyborg, not one bit. Then again, while he hated to admit it, his faith in his new friends might be misplaced. But what would deceiving him about the first human accomplish? Why would exposing the lie benefit the Doctor? Nothing made sense...

Those conflicting thoughts wrecked James's brain, and Rose's chattiness complicated matters. The prophet babbled about random subjects as she exercised. Though Brucie scowled at her distraction, so far, he'd stopped short of intervening. Despite her prattling, she kept up with his regimen.

"You know, Hunter, between the strike and the euthanasia protests, I haven't done this in a while. I feared my forced break would dull my senses, but I'm on top of my game. That's a relief."

"Mm-hmm."

A frown spread on Rose's face. "What's wrong?"

"Uh?" James shrugged. "Oh, nothing."

After a sigh, Rose stopped her jumping jacks and sat beside him. "Don't lie, Hunter; you're lost in thoughts."

"She got that right, man!" a frustrated Brucie shouted as he stomped his foot. "Wouldn't be my business, but you're messing up my routine, bro. Come on, Rose ain't focusing cause you're all freaking moody, ya know? How 'bout ya go to your room and let us finish here?"

With an annoyed groan, Rose presented her open palm to interrupt the bodyguard. James actually appreciated

Brucie's interruption: it allowed him to ponder his next move.

"Um, it's nothing. I'm just homesick, that's all. Nadia's been on my mind. I worry about her." In truth, due to the recent events, his home and girlfriend barely registered as a concern these days, and that shamed him.

"I understand," Rose began in almost a whisper. "Anything I can do?" James shook his head. "Thought so."

James contemplated her words. Perhaps she could help. In theory, she possessed answers he lacked. If the Doctor's claims were accurate, the question posed a risk. However, he doubted he could sort it out without additional information, and her reaction itself might be an important clue. "Rose... can... um, can you tell me more about the first human?"

If nothing else, I surprised her. She gasped and sat there in shock for a minute. To my eyes, it looked like she'd rather not say. Was I imagining it? I had no idea.

—Thoughts of James Hunter, Hocmar 28, 2134, on the Nirnivian calendar

"I'm afraid not." Rose's lips twitched. "I never even met him." She rubbed her nose. "There were armed security guards where he appeared. They tried to communicate, but the human was too startled." After a pause, the prophet rested her hand over her mouth. "It ended in tragedy. He took a child hostage and the child died, but I always felt the poor soul was just scared and accidentally killed that girl. Why are you asking about him all of a sudden?"

"I don't know..." James's irises darted up. "I guess it's because he's from Earth, so I'm curious. Is that crazy?"

"No, that sounds perfectly normal. I can't promise, but maybe we can find someone who can tell you more about him. I'll see what I can do."

"Thanks."

Rose offered assistance so eagerly. She wouldn't want me to speak with anyone else if she was hiding something. Or would she? What if she provided a false witness so her story appeared more legitimate? All those conspiracy theories gave me a headache. So far, Rose had been the nicest person I'd ever met. Why would she lie about that guy, anyway? It wasn't even the fact that she might've lied that bothered me. Everybody does! I just couldn't see any reasonable motive. It had to be one of the Doctor's tricks, and yet there was something nagging me deep inside.

—Thoughts of James Hunter, Hocmar 28, 2134, on the Nirnivian calendar

Chapter 4

Lacdor 21, 2134, on the Nirnivian calendar

That evening, I played Kuhard with Rose in the garden. As expected, I didn't stand a chance. She was a far better player. I doubted I'd ever win. Besides, I wasn't in the mood for games. Rose made great efforts to stay with me because I pretended I felt homesick. While her sympathy was touching, I didn't want to play, but I didn't dare refuse either. That might have seemed suspicious.

—Thoughts of James Hunter, Hocmar 28, 2134, on the Nirnivian calendar

"And Kuhard! Sorry, Hunter."

"No problem. I, uh, learn with every loss. And with that knowledge, someday I'll last longer than ten minutes."

"You're not a sore loser. I appreciate that!" Rose giggled. "The one time I played with Brucie, he threw the board." Both laughed at their impatient friend's expanse while starting another match. "Hunter, you're not yourself. You're barely talking."

"Yeah, sorry." As he replied, James attempted to ponder his move, but the conversation left him rattled and he failed. He lowered his gaze. "Like I said, I'm homesick lately, but you're helping."

"Good! By the way, Kristina tracked down one of the security guards who were present when the first human appeared. He'd be happy to meet you."

A mix of excitement and nervousness filled James. Conflicted by a desire for information and the fear of being discovered, he reached for his mercenary and dragged the figurine on the board. He put no effort into the move and expected it to be worthless. The way Rose wrinkled her nose confirmed that fact.

"Really? Great!"

"Hunter, you're my best friend." Rose stared at James, who almost jumped out of surprise. "We met not that long ago. That you're my best friend is pathetic, I suppose. I never had much luck in that respect due to these wings." Her eyes watered. "The thing is, I realize you don't feel the same way, at least not yet. You're a normal person with friends who have been around since childhood." After a sniffle, Rose grabbed her berserker. "I'm been unfair, but your distrust still hurts." With a gulp, James froze. "That another human visited this universe is a big deal from your point of view. These days, you've been wondering if I've been hiding information, or even downright lied."

James swallowed hard, and perspiration covered his brow. If Rose found out that...

She smiled. "Don't be so tense, I'm not mad. You are trapped here with strangers and don't know if we can be trusted." Relief filled James, and he let out a discreet exhale. "To be honest, we can't be sure you deserve our trust either... though I believe so. You have every right to be suspicious, but I would never harm you. I'd rather drive a knife through my own heart." Rose scowled. "To be fair, I didn't help my case. While I don't recall outright lying, Hunter, I hid information in the past, like my role on the Council."

"Rose—"

The prophet ignored James and went on. "Hunter, because of my position, I have access to secrets concerning national security. Perhaps in the future, I'll have to lie. But

I promise, even if that happens, it will be on subjects that don't concern you. Everything we said about the first human is the truth. It's okay if you don't believe me. We haven't given many details. There's not much to say."

"Listen, Rose, uh..." James took a deep breath. "Rose, in this world, you are my best friend." The winged woman beamed. "Someone from Earth was here. Maybe it's meaningless, but to me, it's important. You saved my life twice. You've been nothing but kind. I trust you!"

"Hunter, it's okay. You don't have to explain. I'm sorry for being difficult."

She seemed sincere. For the moment, I'd avoided a potential crisis. Yet I worried. How long could I continue this charade? How long before Rose figured out that Doctor Death had contacted me again? Sometimes she read me like an open book. If she was an enemy, I was outmatched.

—Thoughts of James Hunter, Hocmar 28, 2134, on the Nirnivian calendar

Chapter 5

Lacdor 24, 2134, on the Nirnivian calendar

The setting sun blinded James, causing him to squint at the water rushing through the sharp rocks. To block the annoying rays, he attempted to shield his eyes with his hand, with limited success. Too bad he lacked sunglasses. Despite the protective railing, Bruno Arnold, the security guard Rose had organized a meeting with, recommended that James stay at a distance from the edge to avoid falling down Pelona's Falls. In truth, James doubted there was any danger of that happening, but he obeyed. Though he noted several picnic tables, suggesting a tourist attraction, no one else walked around. They were alone.

"Yeah, that's the spot," Mr. Arnold almost shouted, a necessity in this environment. The waterfall presented a majestic view, but its thundering roar assaulted their ears, rendering conversation difficult. "The railing wasn't as high back then. They increased the size afterward."

I nodded, eager to hear more. Mr. Arnold seemed like a nice guy. He provided all the information I'd requested. I felt he'd rather not be there, though. The events that had happened here scarred him. That was too bad. Penola's Falls was a beautiful place.

—Thoughts of James Hunter, Hocmar 28, 2134, on the Nirnivian calendar

"Why did he take that kid hostage?"

Bruno shrugged. "Because we screwed up." The ex-guard averted his gaze and rubbed his chin as he recalled the experience. "I was patrolling the area with a new guy, Henry Kist. The human appeared like magic. He looked disoriented. We aimed our guns. It was a reflex. I swear we didn't mean to shoot without provocation. 'Visitors' are unpredictable, and some are dangerous by nature. The man panicked. He grabbed a girl, put a knife to her throat and ordered us to drop our weapons. I tried to calm him and told him we just wanted to talk." Tears formed in Mr. Arnold's eyes. "He might have listened, but my partner shot him in the shoulder. The human recoiled, tripped on the railing and fell, bringing the kid with him."

James considered the account in silence. It corroborated what Rose had revealed earlier. While a sad story, he still deemed the hatred and terror he'd witnessed on his arrival unjustified. The mob had almost torn him apart, for crying out loud.

"Um, I'm sorry about what happened, and I hope I don't sound insensitive, but I don't get it. When I got here, people wanted to kill me because I'm human. I never saw such rage before."

"I don't know about humans, but Gorumars care deeply for their young ones."

"So do we!" James scratched behind his ear. "But, um, the guy didn't murder the girl. He shouldn't have taken her hostage, but it's not like he slit her throat. He was just scared..."

"I agree." Bruno nodded. "But it's how people are. They exaggerate facts. Myths about humans grew, and our media played up the tragedy for ratings. Crazy rumors spread and some believed them. To make matters worse, the girl in question was the daughter of a councillor." After a sigh, he went on. "This mess had more repercussions than the two deaths and your species' reputation. My partner's life was ruined. Poor Henry never forgave himself and quit. This place was a popular attraction. Now nobody comes here. Too many bad memories, I suppose."

Then I noticed a huge hole in his story, big enough to drive a truck right through it. Screw that, ten trucks side by side would have fit.

—Thoughts of James Hunter, Hocmar 28, 2134, on the Nirnivian calendar

"Wait! How come you know he was a human? He never said that..."

Though James had expected a reaction, Bruno remained calm and collected. "Oh, the police found his body and a backpack filled with various things, in particular magazines and books. They were soaked, but readable. It's weird, we could understand the human when he spoke and read his language. The important part is it was determined that the man came from Earth and he was a member of the human race. Now, James, the multiverse is vast. Maybe there's another universe with beings calling themselves humans and a planet Earth, but it's probable you're from the same place."

Well, that filled up the hole. Even if I had exposed a lie, it couldn't have been linked to the Doctor's "puzzle." He'd mentioned something Rose had said. Not long after we left, I thought about everything Mr. Arnold had revealed. He'd addressed most of my concerns, and he seemed so sincere that I figured he told the truth. The Doctor's "riddle" still worried me, but I guessed he was only playing around with me. I had no idea why, though. According to Rose, he was a genius and would manipulate me if given the chance. I decided she was right and that I'd never speak with him again. I considered admitting he'd contacted me to Rose and Daniel, but I feared they'd suspect me of wrongdoing, so I kept my mouth shut. Anyway, I managed to get the incident out of my head. More or less...

—Thoughts of James Hunter, Hocmar 28, 2134, on the Nirnivian calendar

Chapter 6

Lacdor 27, 2134, on the Nirnivian calendar

How to use the Alcharia virus samples they had stolen came to Diabo in a dream. That disease obsessed Doctor Death, and it would be his downfall. Such a simple plan, he should have thought of it on the spot. The moment he woke up, he organized a video conference with Plague and Stalker, eager to share his vision. Hours passed as he waited for the appointed hour, but at last, it arrived, and containing his excitement required effort.

"Hey, Plague, didn't ya say if we injected that orange goop in some guy directly, he'd get sick?"

"Yeah, it should. Ain't gonna do much for us unless we find a way to jam a syringe in every freaking Ostarkiran soldier."

"Yeah, but let's say a bunch o' people caught Alcharia. Do ya think the Doctor'd show up?"

Half a second after he pronounced the words, Plague's blank eyes widened in comprehension. Stalker, however, kept the same scowl and opened his mouth, confirming his obliviousness. That was one of Plague's best qualities, his sharp mind. You didn't have to explain anything twice. Too bad his broken body limited his potential.

At any rate, the decrepit mutant lifted a glove-covered finger. "Boss..." He coughed and then cleared his throat. "You can't mean..."

"Freak yeah, I do." Diabo grinned, followed by a wink. "Here's how it goes. We break into a hospital, infect a bunch o' patients. Ya can bet Doctor Death will hear 'bout that. There's like five, maybe eight victims a year? This ain't ever happened before. He'll be curious and he'll check it out. Too bad fer him, we'll steal his trick and have the building filled with bombs. His metal body's damn tough, but mine's tougher." He snapped his fingers. "When things go boom, he'll be dead."

A mix of anticipation and dread overcame Diabo. While he wished to hear his colleagues gush about his brilliance, somehow, he doubted that would happen. Both lacked strength and determination these days. They grew weak and complacent, preferring safety over victory, and so he expected pushback. The intensified frown on Stalker's face and his clenched fists confirmed Diabo's assessment of the elusive man. As for Plague, he hopped to his feet and paced while rubbing his chin. He had memorized the layout of his office to the point that he could navigate the area without the help of a cane.

"Interesting idea, but there's a flaw." Plague groaned. "Doctor Death fears Allison. He'll never leave the telesthesia blockers' protection. That means if we infiltrate a hospital that's not covered by telesthesia blockers, he won't come. This limits our choices."

With a smirk, Diabo dismissed the complaints with a wave. "That ain't no problem. I picked out a perfect target: the Halford's Children Hospital. Halford is a small city, no freaking soldiers there. Turns out part o' the clinic is on the edge of a telesthesia blocker's field by dumb luck. Allison ain't a threat there. 'Sides, Doctor Death always had a soft spot for kids. He won't let that damn virus kill a bunch o' them. The bastard will be there for sure."

A resonant bang echoed through the speakers. After straightening due to surprise, Diabo noticed Plague's palm resting flat against his desk. "Diabo, have you gone mad?" The tension in his muscles proved so great he trembled. As a response, Diabo crossed his arms and stared into his white globes devoid of irises. Despite being blind, the zombie sensed the glare, and with a brief twitch, his shoulders fell.

"I'm sorry, boss, but I can't stay silent. This won't work. Boss, please think it through." He sighed. "Doctor Death isn't a dumbass. He won't fall for it. He knows one of his Alcharia virus shipments was lost and that we have it. As soon as he learns about the outbreak, he'll smell a trap. Especially since it happened at the most convenient location from our point of view. He won't show. Worse, he might reverse the trap on us and we won't have Allison's power to save our butts."

"Have a little faith, won't ya? The freak will be there and he'll die like a rat." Diabo grinned at the screen. "What's wrong, Plague? Ain't got the stomach to blow up a kiddie hospital?"

A short pause came from Plague and then he shrank back. "Hmmph, I'll admit that's something I'd rather not do, but don't doubt my resolve. I want him dead as badly as you. I'd blow up a hundred hospitals, but this plan won't work."

"It will!"

Stalker harrumphed. "Boss, I'm with Plague. It's madness. You're too reckless. We should lay low for a bit, slow down."

A terrifying growl escaped Diabo's lips. Even though they weren't in the same room, Plague and Stalker cringed. "This ain't no democracy! I'm the boss. I decide. Unless you two wanna challenge me?" Both men shook their heads with exaggerated eagerness. Diabo had anticipated as much. They were cowards, which, in this current situation, suited him fine.

After a moment of hesitation, Plague said, "Boss..." He flinched. "Maybe you'll at least listen to this advice. I think we should keep Wrathchild out of this one."

With a moan, Diabo considered his suggestion. These days, Wrathchild had developed a bothersome sense of morality. That wasn't accurate—she'd always had it; she simply followed it more now than before. Diabo trusted her loyalty, but infecting a bunch of kids with a virus and blowing up the building would push it beyond comfort. She had endured a rough childhood and empathized with children because of it. Besides, she disliked explosives due to a horrific experience, and working with them might ravage her concentration, increasing the risk of error.
"Yeah, you're right. Wrathchild's outta this one. All right, boys, time to prepare!"

Chapter 7

Rose was caught in a weird dilemma. She wanted company but needed to read her "fan mail." Since she didn't get out of Valardir anymore, she made a point of keeping in touch with her followers as best she could. That's why she let me and Brucie hang out in her room instead of having him guard the door outside. Rose didn't talk to us much, so we had to figure out a way to entertain ourselves. Brucie exploited my boredom and tricked me into playing a game of Red Hand. Accepting had been a huge mistake on my part. The bastard was fast and strong. Out of mercy, he allowed me to slap him first. I missed, but he never did. Red Hand indeed.

—Thoughts of James Hunter, Hocmar 28, 2134, on the Nirnivian calendar

"AAIAAAAAYAA!" James screamed in pain after another brutal blow. "I hate you, Brucie. I really hate you!"

"Ah, man, don't hate! Ain't my fault if I kick ass at this game, ya know."

Rose took her eyes off the letter and gave her friends an annoyed look. "Guys, keep it down, please. I'm reading."

A shrug came from Brucie. "Don't ya blame me, I ain't making noise." Then he smacked James's hand once again. His lips twisted, but with great effort and tongue biting, he remained quiet.

Rose sighed. "Maybe you could, I don't know, play this outside?"

"But I'm comfortable here!" the bodyguard said in a whining tone. "Admit it, gal, it ain't the freaking noise, it's my hot and sexy muscles that distract ya."

"Oh, please, your muscles have no effect on me. Hunter's screams, though, they are distracting."

"Um, sorry!"

Rose didn't answer. Instead she grabbed another envelope and opened it. Brucie slapped James once more. A burning fire spread through his limb. With a hesitant peek, he noted his skin tone had morphed to a crimson tint. While he managed not to yell, he couldn't take it any longer.

"Okay, that's enough! I give up! You win."

"Already?" After a disappointed groan, he shook his head. "Dude, you got no pain tolerance. Don't ya agree, Rose? He's a wuss, ain't h—" Brucie never completed the sentence. He turned toward Rose, and the sight swallowed the rest of the words. The color had drained from her, and she pressed her fingertips to her temples. The alleged prophet inhaled and exhaled at a rapid rate, putting her at risk of hyperventilation. Apprehension filled James, and he took a step forward while a gulping Brucie asked, "Are ya okay? You're like all freaked out."

A few seconds passed before Rose replied. When she did, her voice broke. "Guys, I want to be alone for a while."

"Um, Rose?"

"Don't worry, Hunter, I'll be all right."

Brucie clenched his fist and gritted his teeth. "What's going on?"

Still silent, Rose offered him the letter. Though reluctant at first, he accepted the piece of paper. "Go outside and guard my door. Read it, you'll understand. Please, guys. I'm sorry, I want to be left alone now." A little more, and she'd be begging.

With a nod, Brucie wrapped his arm around James's shoulders and led him toward the exit. "All right, come on, dude."

***

Once James and Brucie were gone, Rose sat on her bed and held her forehead. Memories from several years ago rushed through her mind. How she wished to forget, but she recalled every single detail, every single sight, every single sound, and even every single smell. Back then, she'd lived with Miguel and they'd formed a happily married couple, unaware of the upcoming tragedy.

***

With a splitting headache, Rose opened her eyes and groaned. She ran her tongue around her dry mouth, feeling as if she hadn't brushed in a week. The sofa hurt her back, which was why she hated falling asleep there and avoided it like the plague. Though the act demanded several additional moans, Rose sat up and rubbed her brow. Not that it helped reduce the migraine.

Once Rose recovered enough senses, she glanced at the clock. That late... she stifled a curse. An unfortunate incident had landed a councillor's spouse in the hospital, and Moderator Thomson had canceled a meeting out of sympathy. That gave Rose a rare afternoon off, and she'd planned on using this opportunity to prepare a meal for Miguel. He enjoyed her cooking, or at least he claimed to. Too bad she seldom had the chance to do so. In fact, on the occasions when they didn't eat at a restaurant, he almost always whipped something up, not her.

When she'd arrived home, Rose had rushed to the kitchen and rummaged through the cupboards for a recipe.

He loved her targo, so she considered making that. The problem was, she had forgotten the correct order of the steps. Soon, Rose had located the desired instructions and fished out the required ingredients, as well as a large pot. That done, a sudden weakness had assailed her. Her drive, so powerful seconds before, had vanished. In truth, that did not surprise her. She had been so fatigued lately. Prey to somnolence, she lay on the couch to rest her eyes and succumbed to slumber. At least she had woken before Miguel's arrival, but she lacked time to finish the food. As if to confirm her assumption, the door opened and her husband entered. A warm sensation filled Rose as she watched him grab a hanger and remove his coat. People swore that intense passion disappeared after a year or two, but so far, it remained with her. Those blue eyes still melted her heart.

"Hi, honey!" she said with a wave. "Hard day at work?"

Miguel approached and gave her a soft, tender kiss before answering. Her eyelids closed as she savored his lips against hers. Too soon they parted, but then again, it'd always be too soon, even if it lasted for hours. "No, not that bad. Busy, but I've been through worse." He winked. "Besides, being with you chases my weariness away. How about you?"

"Oh, I've had the afternoon free, actually." Rose sighed. "I'm sorry, Miguel, I wanted to cook a special meal. I dozed off. This cold sapped my energy. We'll have to order out, again."

If the news disappointed Miguel, he shrugged it off. "Don't concern yourself with such trifling matters. The important thing is that you get better, my love."

"I still feel bad, I haven't cooked since..." She counted on her fingers. "I can't remember."

"Now, now, that is quite all right. I didn't marry you to have a chef." He kissed her again as if to prove he didn't care.

"Yeah, you married me for the sex."

"Rose, that's unfair." He caressed her face and then peered into her eyes. "You have so many wonderful qualities. I married you for much more than that..." He adopted a charming smile. "Believe me, food and sex, that's at most ninety-five percent of my reasons."

With a giggle, Rose pushed Miguel back, crossed her arms and tilted her head. "I hope the other five percent is important to you, because after that joke you're not getting any sugar for a month."

"The powdery kind or the carnal one?"

"Neither!" Then she stuck out her tongue.

Miguel grinned and was about to counter when she erupted in a bout of coughing. "Rose, that cold isn't going away." A frown formed on his brow. "You should be cured by now. And you are pale. How about we go to the hospital so they can run tests?"

That was a request Rose had heard before, and while the cold had turned out to be resilient, she'd rather not visit the hospital. It gave her the creeps. Miguel deemed that quirk to be so silly and kept reminding her that fearing a place meant to heal was illogical. Though she agreed, she couldn't help it.

"I'm fine! I'll order some food. Alfredo's okay?" Miguel nodded, and Rose walked toward the phone. As she reached for the receiver, her vision blurred and she stepped backward. A gasp escaped her lips while an invisible weight crushed her shoulders and her stomach churned. Then Rose's legs turned to mush. Weakness, such weakness. Unable to stand, she collapsed. A loud thud echoed through the house, followed by Miguel's worried shrieks.

"Rose? Is everything all right?"

Though she mouthed words, no sound came. So cold... She trembled. Why was she so cold? Her husband rushed toward her with such speed he almost stumbled. Once by her side, he crouched.

"Rose!" Then he gulped and rubbed the area above her upper lip. She wondered why, but when he retracted his finger, she noticed a red stain... Blood! Her blood. How? She hadn't struck her nose. Nosebleeds happened, but somehow she had a bad presentiment and trembled. Miguel kissed her forehead.

"Everything will be all right, my love; everything will be all right." With that, he grabbed the phone.

Chapter 8

That morning, when Anya arrived at the lab, she discovered Tania already at her desk. However, instead of typing at a rapid pace, the pink-haired sibling slumped over her bureau while holding her forehead with both hands. Since the posture suggested discouragement, Anya walked toward her. Once near enough, she caressed Tania's shoulder. "Tough night?"

"You betcha. This is impossible."

"You mean the chemical compound the Good Doctor wants you to synthesize?"

Tania sat up straight in her seat, then nodded. "Uh-huh. Whatever that stuff is, there's nothing close in Ostark. Since it's plant-based, I decided I'd look for the closest matching plants, DNA-wise, and use that as a base. I've tried the six best matches, and none of them produced decent enough results for the Good Doctor." After shaking her head, she sighed. "Frankly, I don't know what do to anymore."

"Oh, I see." Anya stifled a chuckle. Based on her sister's personality, she had an idea of how to improve her mood. "Maybe you need a break. How would you like working on the skins test trials for a while? We can ask the Good Doctor to switch."

As she dismissed the notion with a wave, Tania laughed. "You crazy? That's so boring." She rubbed her chin. "Yeah, my experiment isn't progressing, but it's thrilling. I've done nothing like it! The possibilities boggle the mind." Then she got to her feet and paced around. "What if... no, that won't..." She shook her fists in excitement. "But I could try to pinpoint the best aspects of each of my plants and combine them. That'll give me days, or even weeks of exciting science!" With those words, Tania hopped on her chair and spun it for one full circle as she pumped her fist. "Yahoo!" With that, she began typing. A large smile formed on Anya's lips. Mission accomplished!

Chapter 9

Once outside the room, Brucie read the letter in silence. When I asked him what was wrong, he said not to worry. I pestered him for more info, and he promised he'd explain during lunch. That was soon anyway. He wanted to get Janice and her father to eat with us so he could tell everyone at the same time. Turned out Janice was available, but not Mr. Ricdeau.

—Thoughts of James Hunter, Hocmar 28, 2134, on the Nirnivian calendar

The three of them sat at a table. Though they bought meals, only Brucie showed any interest in eating. The bodyguard chowed down his food at a rapid pace while the other two looked at him. Behind Brucie, James caught a glimpse of Patricia, Nathan and Gareth with his impressive scar chatting. No signs of Charlie or Dylan, however. At any rate, James wondered when Brucie would reveal details about the letter.

As for Janice, she grew sick of waiting. "Hey, big guy, how about telling me why I'm here?"

He shrugged. "Sorry 'bout that. Gotta fill up on proteins, ya know."

"Whatever. This better be important. You pretty much forced me to come." Janice giggled. "Not that I mind the company."

Then she gave James a quick sideways glance. Perhaps his imagination played a trick on him, but he sensed Brucie tensing up and thought he saw the corner of the bodyguard's mouth twitch. At any rate, Brucie reached for a piece of paper and waved it.

"Yeah, so Rose got a letter..."

Janice shrugged. "Only one? Oh boy, that's a downgrade. Anyway, what's so special about it? Bad news?"

After nodding his head, Brucie rubbed his chin. "Sorta... well, I guess more like sad news, ya know. Some kid, I'd say 'bout seven, wrote this." His voice became serious as he read the text. "Dear Holiness, me and my mommy and daddy are very sad. My four-year-old sister Tessa is sick. The doctor calls it Alcharia. Mommy and Daddy think Tessa will leave us forever. I'm scared. I don't want her to go away. Mommy and Daddy said you could help by praying with us. They say you won't do it, but I'm sure they're wrong. You're a nice lady. Please come and save my sister." Brucie then laid the paper on the table. "It's signed 'Anita.'"

By Janice's expression, she understood the situation, which wasn't my case at all. Well, a little girl was dying from a terminal disease, and that was awful. I also figured Rose would love to go pray with the kid's family, but it wouldn't happen since she couldn't leave this place. But as heartbreaking as it was, it didn't justify Rose's reaction. I mean, she'd seemed terrified, to the point she'd almost hyperventilated.

—Thoughts of James Hunter, Hocmar 28, 2134, on the Nirnivian calendar

"Poor girl..." Janice lowered her gaze. "This is terrible. Rose must be devastated."

"Yeah, these ain't gonna be happy days."

The group fell quiet. Nobody made a sound. Soon, James grew tired of the mystery and asked, "Uh, what's Alcharia?"

Brucie grunted. "A freaking disease, dude."

"Yup!" A scowl formed on Janice's brow as she nodded. "There's no cure. Either the victim gets better by pure luck or they die. At first, it's like a simple cold." She enumerated on her fingers. "Some light coughing, a sore throat, maybe headaches, nothing too scary. Because of that, it takes a while before people seek medical attention, but it doesn't matter. Chances of survival are almost zero, and early detection doesn't help. After a while, the sickness worsens. The patient suffers intense muscle pains, and it becomes harder and harder to move, starting with the legs." The tone Janice adopted reminded James of a schoolteacher. By her manner of speaking, he assumed she studied medical texts. "Severe nosebleeds are also frequent, and over time, lesions appear all over the body. In the final stages, the patient loses consciousness." A shudder overcame her. "This always happens. There's never been an exception. From that point, there can be two outcomes. In rare cases, they'll wake up within four days and survive. If that doesn't happen, they'll be dead in a week at most."

Impressed by her explanation, James's mouth gaped for a few seconds. Once he recovered, he said, "You sure know a lot about that disease!" Janice gritted her teeth and tensed up, but she stayed quiet. As such, James deduced she wasn't so informed out of interest, and he gulped at his faux pas. "So..." He scratched the back of his head, desperate to break the tension. "Nobody ever woke up after four days?"

Brucie shifted on his seat. "Was one miracle case."

"Oh? Who?"

"You're slow, eh? What do ya think? Dude, it was Rose! She used her holy powers to fight the virus and stuff, ya know. Not the Melkar my ass... pure bullshit!"

Whenever something interesting happened around here, Rose was involved. It was getting a bit annoying.
　　—Thoughts of James Hunter, Hocmar 28, 2134, on the Nirnivian calendar

"Brucie, this is terrible. Rose must be devastated. She'll want to pray with that family, but we can't let her."

"Yeah..." A touch of sadness tainted his normally jovial voice. "Rose gets that. She ain't gonna do anything stupid, don't ya worry. It's just gonna bring back bad memories."

"I'd say. They're already coming back for me." She winced. "Do you remember? Her beautiful face... covered in blood. She couldn't walk by herself. My little sister... it broke my heart."

I didn't understand Janice. When Rose was around, she barely looked at her. She acted so distant toward her. Yet she seemed so concerned for her too.
　　—Thoughts of James Hunter, Hocmar 28, 2134, on the Nirnivian calendar

"Ain't gonna fo'get that. I thought she was dead, ya know. Everybody did. Whole freaking nation was mourning."

Silence fell over the table again. No one ate or talked. It was as if a weight crushed them. And then James jumped to his feet and, with a determined expression, walked away.

"Where are ya going, man?"

James stopped and glanced toward Brucie. "I don't know Rose as well as you two, but I know her enough to realize right now she's torturing herself over this. She, uh, said I'm her best friend. Well, what kind of best friend would I be if I left her alone?"

"Got a good heart, dude, but she won't let ya in."

"I don't care. At least I'll try."

***

With a sigh, Brucie watched James leave the cafeteria. The whole story had sapped his appetite. Still, he needed his nutrients and should force himself to eat. Muscle mass like his demanded it. Janice beat him to the punch on that front. She already nibbled at her food, though she adopted a slow pace that betrayed a lack of enthusiasm for the meal. At any rate, Brucie followed Janice's example, cut off a piece of meat and stuck his fork into the cooked flesh. About halfway to his mouth, he dropped the utensil and a click echoed as it touched the plate. "Hey, you're Rose's sister. Maybe you should go too?"

Janice shrugged, then closed her eyes. "Eh, James can handle it."

"Sometimes I don't get ya."

Chapter 10

Concerning the sick child, Rose understood what she had to do. Still, for some strange reason, she sat before the mirror, studying it. What did she hope to accomplish? She had already decided. Unpleasant memories of the last few conversations with her reflection filled Rose's mind, and she shuddered. With a gulp, she glanced at the bed and debated lying down next to Ms. Penny the doll instead. Despite her apprehension, she groaned and returned her focus to the glass.

"Can I help her?" Of course not. Modern medicine stood powerless before Alcharia. Why should Rose triumph where the best doctors had failed? She lacked any special talent, except for extra body parts due to an unusual mutation. Though her followers valued those wings, the appendages served little purpose.

In the mirror, the reflection shook her head. "Impolite as always, not to mention imprecise."

"The sick girl who caught Alcharia, can I help her?"

"A healer, are you now? I do not believe you can cure the ill."

Rose groaned in frustration. Sometimes her subconscious proved so finicky. She had to be careful with her choice of words since her other self took things too literally and missed the subtleties of figurative speech. To be honest, the whole process was tiresome. "I mean: if I pray with her family, could it change anything?"

"Her fate belongs to the gods. Asking for their help cannot cause any harm, but would it save her? Maybe, maybe not. The truth is unclear."

At least the doppelgänger offered a straight answer instead of the convoluted riddles she favored. "I see, thank you."

On that note, Rose almost left her chair, but her likeness continued, "Why do you wish to save her, anyway?"

Confused, Rose frowned. "Isn't it obvious?"

"No. You survived against logic. A miracle allowed you to trump fate. Would you pretend that was for the best? Your prolonged existence has been a curse for you and everyone else."

"That's enough!" Rose slapped her desk, producing no effect except a resounding bang. A turn of her head would end the torture, but somehow she failed to do that.

Her reflection kept talking. One by one, lesions slashed open over her face, dripping blood. "Perhaps the girl is supposed to die. If so, why wish her to live? To have someone else feel as miserable as you? Years ago, you should have died from the same disease. Was it so good to cheat death? Maybe you want that child to suffer also?"

"No, that's not true!"

"They say misery enjoys company. Maybe you want her to burn with you!"

"Enough! Leave me alone!" After that furious scream, Rose at last averted her gaze. Tears of rage and sorrow ran down her now-pale cheeks. Again, her thoughts drifted toward that dark period of her life.

***

A burning sensation spread inside Rose's throat as she retched. In a quick motion, Miguel seized the bucket they had prepared for such occurrences and handed it to her. Given she had hurled three times since her arrival at the hospital, they'd prepared themselves and it had served them well. Once Rose had secured the pail, he held her hair so it wouldn't interfere. About a minute later, she finished, grabbed a tissue and wiped her lips. Then she lay again on the mattress, exhaled and adopted a weak smile.

"That must really make me giving no sugar for a month painful."

Miguel forced a laugh, but she noted the uneasiness. No doubt he worried about her condition and was in no mood for jest. Still, he sensed her joking served as a defense mechanism and reacted accordingly. In truth, Rose shared his apprehension. She'd presumed she had caught a cold due to her early symptoms, but the nausea and vomiting suggested a more serious disease.

As soon as they'd arrived, the hospital had given them priority. Less than half an hour later, Rose found herself in a room, surrounded by doctors running a battery of tests. If something happened to her, not only would they lose the woman deemed the most important person in Nirnivia, but they might receive the blame. Such was the burden of having a fake prophet as a patient. While Rose appreciated the eagerness with which they treated her, a lump formed in her throat whenever she considered the poor souls enduring delays because of her presence. Some risked their lives as a result. How unfair and shameful.

Miguel stayed with Rose through her whole stay, though he barely uttered a word. The shock and fear vanquished his usual eloquence. While the nurses asked Miguel to remain outside so Rose could rest, he refused and Rose was thankful. Even as a nervous wreck, having him near helped her relax. Besides, she'd rather not face this ordeal alone.

They waited several hours before a doctor entered the chamber. His disheveled hair and sweat stains sent a shiver down Rose's spine. The man opened his mouth yet remained silent. Rose swallowed hard. He'd prefer the news he intended to deliver be forgotten.

Oblivious to the tension, Miguel stood up. "Do you have the results? What's wrong with my wife?"

The medic winced. "Her Holiness caught the Alcharia virus."

For a second or two, shock paralyzed Rose. Her brain attempted to comprehend the severity of the announcement, without success. Then understanding came. She closed her eyes and whimpered. When she opened them again, Miguel glared at the doctor and gestured emotionally.

"No! That's impossible! You made a mistake! Redo the tests this instant, you incompetent buffoon! If you fail again, I will see that—"

With difficulty, Rose sat up. The motion caused her head to spin, and she reached for the bucket. In the end, she recovered. An almost inaudible whimper escaped her lips.

"Miguel, please calm down. Just because you don't like the diagnosis doesn't mean he's wrong. You have no reason to doubt him."

Miguel gritted his teeth, and a few tears dropped on his cheeks. "You... you're right, my love." Again, he faced the physician. "I apologize for my unacceptable behavior, but Alcharia..."

"It's okay. I couldn't believe it either, but I rechecked three times, and several colleagues verified my work. Trust me, I wouldn't give such a dire diagnosis to the Melkar without being sure." His voice faltered, and he lowered his head. "I'm so sorry."

Overwhelmed, Miguel stumbled into a chair, held his forehead with both hands and wept. "No... that can't be. There has to be something we can do!"

"You know as well as anyone there's no cure for Alcharia. The most we can do is ease her pain."

"But we can't let Rose die!"

"Some people survive." The doctor scratched the back of his head. "There's always prayer. That's what I'll do."

When the physician was gone, Rose started crying. She held back the tears because she realized her apparent strength helped others confront tragedy with confidence and faith. Terror overwhelmed her to the point that all she wanted was to break down, but she kept a brave face on for the sake of everyone else. Miguel often mentioned that was one of the many reasons he loved her.

"I'm going to die... Miguel, I'm going to die!"

Between sobs, Miguel grabbed her palm and squeezed. "Don't say such a thing. You're not dead yet, baby. You're not dead yet. You will live, somehow. I don't know how, but I will do anything. You will live."

Though he mustered a surprising amount of false bravado, Rose noticed he didn't promise. Miguel never, ever broke a promise to her. That he wouldn't give her his word in a situation so grave meant he doubted his own claim. Put simply, he lied, but she couldn't blame him. He wanted her to feel better. How she prayed he ended up being right anyway, but her heart told her there was no hope. She owed the gods a death, and they were cashing it in. No resistance could change her fate.

Chapter 11

As she indulged in reliving the past, the doorbell echoed, pulling Rose out of her reverie. Afterward, the interphone broadcast James's voice. She opened the door, and they both sat on the bed.

"So, Brucie explained everything?" Rose asked as they rested on the mattress. In a quick motion, she grabbed her doll, Ms. Penny, and caressed her hair.

"Um, yeah..." James scratched behind his ear. "I figured this must be difficult for you, so..."

A grateful smile formed on her lips. "You're a good friend. Alcharia..." Rose's voice trembled. "It's a frightful disease. Just hearing the description is bad enough, but you don't understand how horrific it is until you've experienced it firsthand. Everything hurts and burns as if you're engulfed in fire. So many lesions covered my body, I was drenched in blood. Hunter, I was like a sight from a horror movie. And I couldn't do anything. I needed help for even the simplest task." Recollections flooded Rose. Miguel carrying her to the bathroom, since she couldn't stand. How her husband manipulated the utensils during meals. Though swallowing was her only chore, that proved harder than expected and irritated her throat. "I wouldn't wish that cursed illness on my worst enemy, least of all a four-year-old girl! What a tragedy."

James swallowed hard. "Um, yeah."

"Since I've read that letter, my memories have been rushing back." Rose sighed. "Anita wants me to go pray with her family. Such a simple request, but I can't, Hunter.

I want to, but I can't leave here." While rubbing her chin, she reconsidered. "No, that's a lie. I'm not a prisoner. I can leave if I choose to. Dad would be furious, but he couldn't stop me. I've been through this before. If I go, it creates an opportunity for Doctor Death. Should he find out, I'd be putting myself at risk. I can accept that, but I'd also be endangering Anita and her family. That's unacceptable." Rose gave James a sideways glance.

"Except I've been stuck in here for so long, the Doctor won't expect me to leave. Maybe we could fool him, but he wouldn't make that mistake twice. In other words, it would be a one-time deal. I receive letters like this every week, and I ignore them. Now it's different. I feel sympathetic toward Tessa because I once suffered from the same disease." She scowled.

"If I try to help that little girl, wouldn't I be a hypocrite? Is that so good? So bad?" A moan escaped Rose as she caressed her brow. "I don't know anymore. I'm so tired. The worst part is, I enjoyed meeting my followers and comforting them in their moments of need. We'd pray, and I'd guide them spiritually, confess them—whatever they wished. Such simple gestures brightened their day. Though my role as the Melkar has been a trial, I loved that part. It made the rest tolerable. Now even that is gone."

"Um, Rose"—James swallowed hard as if hesitating—"if you want to do this, why the hell not? Anyone accusing you of hypocrisy is an asshole. Four years old... that's too young to die."

That statement puzzled Rose, and she wrinkled her nose. "Too young to die? What a strange saying."

"Why?"

"Oh, you don't believe in reincarnation. When taking that into consideration, I understand. It's different for us.

We live many lives. Each is an opportunity to learn from our suffering and better ourselves until, eventually, we earn a place in the afterlife. In our society, someone dying at age one isn't any sadder than someone dying at age one hundred and twenty. Everyone lives several times: sometimes for a short while, sometimes longer. In fact, strictly speaking, death itself isn't bad. Death is rest for the soul. Existence is full of hardship. After such sorrows, we need respite so we can reflect on our experiences and prepare for the next iteration. In that way, death teaches us to live better. A prolonged existence can bring devastating effects. It can push one to commit atrocious acts they'd normally never consider, which in turn steers them toward nothingness." After a sigh, Rose rubbed her chin. "There are moments when I think I need rest myself."

"Somehow, I doubt that kid's parents see things that way."

Rose nodded. "No one does. Not even me." Then a derisive laugh escaped her mouth. "I'm still struck with grief due to war casualties, and I still mourn Miguel. Several of my decisions as a councillor were intended to save lives. I even feel sorry for the Ostarkiran soldiers dying in this futile war. Considering my position, I should know better, but I can't stop myself. What I said before, that's the theory, but in practice, death is hated and feared. I guess in part because it's hard to recover from the loss of a loved one, and also because, despite our faith, doubts linger in our minds."

"My people are the same," James whispered. "If we follow our religion, death is supposed to give us a perfect life, yet everyone fears death."

"Well, with the threat of eternal punishment, I can't blame them..."

"Sure, but nobody thinks that's going to happen to them. Everyone assumes they're righteous and going to heaven, even if they're complete scumbags in reality. But we fear death anyway. I guess deep down, we understand we're not that good."

Rose chuckled. "I have my flaws, and I have sinned. I cannot judge anyone for being less than virtuous." Then she smiled at James. "That was quite a tangent! We got sidetracked, but I enjoyed it. Thank you for cheering me up, Hunter. You're a great friend."

"Um, have you decided what to do?"

"I decided as soon as I read the letter."

"So... that means?" Rose acquiesced. For a moment, she noticed James's irises darting up as he tensed up. "Rose, I hope you don't mind me asking, but about Alcharia—did you really wake up after four days?"

Rose bit her lip. Ever since what had happened when Hunter had discovered her role as a prophet, she feared revealing anything that made her seem special in case those dreadful events repeated themselves. However, he was already aware, so she lacked options. Besides, he seemed stable compared to back then.

"Yes. Don't ask why, as I have no idea. I woke up on the sixth day. News of my miraculous remission spread in an instant. My people's faith strengthened as a result. They were certain Ulgorack had saved me. I didn't think my followers could become even more fanatical, but I was wrong once again..."

"Uh, I can understand why. You're the only one." James shuddered. "I mean, I almost believe now."

With a groan, Rose crossed her arms. "Stop right there! I'm not a prophet, I'm just lucky!"

"I said almost!" He lifted his palms in the air as if shielding himself from harm. "But still, Rose, it was a miracle."

Indeed, and that left her uneasy. As much as Rose wished to deny it, the possibility that God had rescued her remained a valid hypothesis given that none other existed. While she considered that notion, a few tears dropped. She turned to conceal them.

"Um, I think you're making the right decision." James's voice trembled. "I mean, it's not like a prayer would save the girl's life. Besides, you can pray from here, can't you?"

"Yes, but prayers are more effective in groups. And having anybody there won't do. When praying for someone, the effectiveness is increased when those assembled truly love the person. I will organize praying sessions, but they won't be as valuable as if I joined the family."

"So? I mean, the family will form their own group, right?" Rose acquiesced. "Would your being there make a difference?"

"It's hard to tell. Our doctrine isn't clear about that subject. Some believe the Melkar joining a praying group increases the usefulness of the prayers; others don't. If I'm only a winged woman, then my presence, or lack thereof, changes nothing."

"Then don't sweat it, Rose. It doesn't matter."

She understood James's attempt to lighten her mood, and he was correct, but even if her attendance ended up futile, at least she would have tried. A wave of sadness crashed into her. Hunter's efforts had succeeded to some degree, but she was filled with sorrow. He couldn't send it all away. Rose trusted that he would stay and listen to her plight all day if she desired, but he had done enough.

"Hunter, I'm okay now, thank you. I appreciate your company, but I have a ton of work to finish."

A grimace formed on James's lips, showing she'd failed to fool him. Despite this, he said, "All right. You're probably not hungry, but you should eat."

"I'll get someone to bring something here. Don't worry."

"If you need to talk later, I'll be there."

"Thank you."

As instructed, James left. Rose hadn't lied; she had plenty of work. She tried focusing on those tasks but found herself unable to. Instead, her thoughts drifted toward the past again.

***

How long since Rose had entered that wretched hospital? She failed to answer the question. Alcharia had rendered her body paralyzed. The smallest attempt at motion spread an unsupportable ache through her muscles. She stayed in bed, counting on others to carry her should movement be required. In this dilapidated state, concepts such as hours or days and nights served little purpose, and so she stopped keeping track of time.

The worst aspect was that her condition deteriorated at a rapid pace. It seemed every few minutes, a new lesion opened somewhere on her body until no part remained untouched. Then again, it was possible her mind exaggerated the speed at which the disease progressed. Either way, the gashes ravaged her, and she couldn't stand her reflection in the mirror. Should any children witness her current appearance, the poor souls would run away screaming. At least the bruises didn't bleed a lot yet, but still, they turned Rose's hospital gown into a red-stained mess. The staff changed her often to compensate, but despite the effort, she wore soiled clothes for most of her stay.

Beyond Rose's own suffering, her health concerned her followers. She received a multitude of letters, flowers, and gifts. Rose appreciated the gesture, but she lacked the strength to check her mail. On occasion, Miguel read aloud the wishes for a prompt recovery, but concentrating on the words proved difficult. The TV stayed off. Every channel ran stories about her sickness and kept showing people mourning her before death. Rose grew well aware of her impending doom without the need to be reminded.

Through Rose's torments, Miguel stood by her side, and that ended up being her only solace. He never left—except for bathroom breaks, but she couldn't blame him for that. When a nurse informed him a folding bed wouldn't fit in the room, Miguel swore he'd sleep on the floor, and he kept true to this vow. At first, the administration tried convincing him to leave after the visiting hours passed. Soon, it became clear that calling the cops would be the only option to get rid of Miguel. They preferred avoiding that, given his status as the Melkar's husband, so the administration offered a separate chamber, but he refused. Miguel wanted to be near Rose every second. He deemed even a folding bed in the hallway unsuitable.

The surprising part was that they could be together and enjoy comfort. Usually, Alcharia patients didn't stay at the hospital. No treatment existed, and contagion posed low risks. Why waste money and deprive patients of the coziness of their own homes given the situation? However, Miguel considered that unacceptable too and insisted Rose live at the clinic so the physicians could run more tests and figure out a miracle cure. It was futile, but she supposed Miguel sought hope wherever he could. Under normal circumstances, his request would have been denied, but since she was a prophet...

Rose missed her house and wished to return there. If she conveyed her desire to Miguel, he would consent, but she didn't feel like taking away what hope he had left. Without her husband's permanent presence, this would be a nightmare. With him, the pain became bearable. Too bad that took its toll on Miguel. Between the enormous bags under his bloodshot eyes and his pale skin tone, he'd earned the appearance of a chronic insomniac. Rose prayed he would go rest for his own well-being.

Thinking of this, she said, "Miguel, go back to the house and sleep. You look terrible." The raspiness of her voice gave her a shiver. Should she survive, Rose wondered whether her throat would recover.

Miguel played with his hands for an instant and then shook his head. "No."

"But, it's all right. The nurses will take care of me. Go get a decent night of sleep. Please, you're hurting yourself."

"Sorry, I can't." Miguel lowered his neck and exhaled. "There were times when I could've been with you and foolishly decided otherwise for selfish reasons. There were occasions I wasted." Tears formed in his eyes. "These might be our final days together. I won't miss any of it."

Rose turned toward Miguel to see him better. This simple action caused discomfort, so she winced. Nevertheless, she forced a smile. "Now that's touching. If only we could make this moment truly special." A sad laugh escaped her lips. "Though I mustn't be very attractive anyway."

"You are the most beautiful woman in the universe, and no amount of blood can change that fact." Miguel groaned. "It's so unfair. Not long ago, you were full of life. Now experts say you're dying." Frustrated, he formed a fist. "How are you so calm at a time like this?"

"It's okay. I've accepted my destiny. I don't want to die, but I can't stop fate."

"Rose... I can't go on without you."

The shock of hearing those pessimistic words made her sit up. Or at least it would've, had the ensuing pain not caused Rose to drop back on the mattress.

"Don't say that! Ever since we've been together, I've relied on you. I needed your support so my burden wouldn't crush me. You've always been the strong one. Don't weaken on me now. You never depended on anyone before and faced everything without fear."

"That used to be true, but I'm not so certain anymore..."

"Miguel, you'll find someone else. Surely a woman will fall for those eyes."

"Can't you understand that I don't want anybody else?! Rose, how can you be so calm?" he asked again. The tone Miguel adopted rested a notch below the level of a shout.

Since Rose had met Miguel, he'd displayed complete control over his sentiments. Through obstacles and confrontation, he kept a composed demeanor and solved problems using rationality. In fact, he often criticized Rose for being too emotional, not rational or logical enough. And now she witnessed him broken and in tears.

"Miguel, please. I can accept death, but I have to know you'll move on. Don't waste your life by mourning forever. Please, I want you to live. Won't you live for me? Tell me you will be all right, and move on! Lie if you must."

Miguel averted his gaze, and then his jaw tightened with determination. "I will be all right, but I won't move on. There won't be any need because you will live. I won't let you die."

"Miguel, you're a special man, but you can't beat death."

"I won't let you die." He clenched his fists. "I promise."

Shocked, Rose blinked twice as her mouth gaped. Her ears tricked her. Miguel never, ever broke a promise made to her. On occasion, he went to an extreme length to ensure it. But he had overstepped his limits. What power did Miguel wield against the Alcharia virus? None, of course. Luck would determine Rose's destiny.

"If I were to die now that you promised otherwise, you'd blame yourself. I'll give you a special chance: take it back. Just this once, please take it back."

"No! When I first asked you on a date, it wasn't exactly a resounding success. Do you remember your response?"

Rose did, and recalling her answer made her blush out of a sense of foolishness. "Yes, I said you were a pompous arrogant ass and that I'd rather date Brucie."

"Your memory is flawless. Love, you meant every word, yet I persevered, and I seduced you. You assumed it was impossible. I proved otherwise. You'll be cured. That you doubt me is of no consequence once it becomes a fact."

"Miguel..." Rose murmured. Her husband had grown accustomed to victory. Things usually ended up going his way. He was good looking, had obtained an amazing job where he'd excelled and married the woman of his choice. But he had to realize, just because life had offered him such generosity didn't mean life wouldn't take it away. He had to realize he couldn't perform miracles. He had to accept she might die. Otherwise, it would exacerbate his grief should tragedy strike.

"Miguel, I love you so much. Promise me that when I die, you will find happiness again."

"I can't promise, but I'll try. Rose, you're the world to me."

Overwhelmed by his devotion, joy and sorrow combined in a strange mixture. Perhaps sensing Rose's dilemma, Miguel caressed her hair. With her body so ravaged, the touch brought agony, but she relished in it without complaining.

"Listen, Miguel, right now, you think you can't live without me, but with time the wound will heal. It's not like we were the perfect couple."

"Only because there's no such thing. Still, we were as close as possible."

"Oh? It's easy to remember the good parts, but we shared plenty of bad ones too. Didn't you often say you were better off before we married? Once, you even wished we'd never met."

Tears rolled down Miguel's cheeks as his lips quivered. "Those words were spoken in anger! There wasn't any truth to them. You claimed you understood that and accepted my many apologies."

"Oh, love, no. Don't misunderstand. Listen, back then, you felt like marriage was a mistake, but you were wrong. Now you think you can't go on without me, but you can! Be strong, Miguel, for my sake." After a short pause, Rose grinned. "Hey, remember that fight? At least, you won't have to endure anything like that once I'm gone."

His scowl, not to mention his shudder, confirmed that Miguel remembered. Torment and anger flashed in his deep blue eyes. What a quarrel... Rose had yelled at him for several days and then they hadn't spoken for a month. Both had contemplated divorce, but they'd reconciled somehow.

"Oh, I won't forget that. In the grand scheme of things, it's irrelevant. I suppose it's a cliché, but the fights, the bickering, the ugliness we went through... it was worth it. I'd rather spend the rest of my life in marital dispute than be without you."

"My dear, that's beautiful." Rose's voice choked up. Once she recovered, she giggled. "I'm afraid that, should I survive, you'll regret those words. I'll use them against you in every future fight."

"Is that so?" Miguel chuckled. "I guess I can't blame you for using ammunition I generously provided. Well, then, I implore you, do make me regret them. The alternative seems far worse to me."

Chapter 12

Again, Stalker called Plague in the evening. Ever since they'd started work on Diabo's plan, the master of camouflage had discovered a need for venting and contacted Plague every day for this purpose. No question, infecting children to lure Doctor Death troubled him, and Plague shared his disgust. Making matters worse, the asinine scheme lacked any chance of success. Still, in Plague's estimation, when faced with a crisis, panicking rarely produced a valuable result. That was why, when Stalker fumed in a frantic fury, he kept a cooler head and attempted to find a solution through logic and rational thoughts.

"Diabo's gone freaking insane!" Stalker said as he waved his arm in an erratic pattern. At least, so Plague assumed. His poor eyesight prevented him from distinguishing the details, but that was what the animated blob on the screen suggested to him. "Look, we're all murderers, but come on!" He grunted. "Bad enough we might have killed kids when we blew up a goddamn apartment building, but this? No, that shit's too low even for me."

"Same here, but it'll be all right."

"Oh, yeah?" Stalker let out a derisive laugh. "How? Diabo's kinda messed up to begin with, and he ain't getting better."

With a sigh, Plague shook his head. "Yeah, I'm aware. Try to relax, I'll handle it."

"Really?" He scoffed. "Sorry, pal, but I doubt it. You're always babbling about how we can control the jackass once he calms down, but don't you dare tell me it's working this time."

"Oh, I agree that he ain't gonna calm down. That's why I'm preparing plan B."

"And that is?"

Plague leaned forward. "We'll trick him."

Chapter 13

Lacdor 30, 2134, on the Nirnivian calendar

Due to a minor emergency, Rose and Kristina met at her office. A councillor was dealing with an unexpected family issue. As such, Doug Thomson had postponed a planned reunion to accommodate their unfortunate colleague. While Rose considered the gesture appropriate given the circumstances, it caused a small difficulty. The replacement date chosen conflicted with one of her sermons. No doubt the political engagement possessed a greater priority, so she needed to reschedule her speech. Though not a catastrophic situation by any stretch, her calendar proved crowded, and finding a spot ended up being a bigger challenge than expected.

As a result, Kristina swiped through the agenda application on her minicomp with her stylus in search of any potential free space. Since no simple solution presented itself, she now shuffled appointments around in an attempt at creating the time slot they sorely lacked. Over half an hour had passed since the two of them had started this mission, and so far, success eluded them.

"Hmm..." Rose rubbed her chin as she contemplated the grid displayed on the screen. "How about the day after at one?"

Kristina shook her head. "No good. You're free, but the crew isn't."

"Oh, that's too bad."

"Rose, I..." The assistant twitched. Sensing her hesitation, Rose offered an encouraging smile. "This isn't my business, but I don't care what people feel about that girl. You're right, and I support your decision."

"Uh?"

"I mean the kid who caught Alcharia." Kristina scowled. "The news spread through the complex. Everyone's talking about it. Nicky said you should go pray with the family, and many agreed. They say we can fool Doctor Death, since you haven't left for so long. That may be true, but as far as I'm concerned, you're making the right call. You're the Voice of God. You're too important! You can't risk your life to comfort one family. It might seem cruel on the surface, but if something happened to you, Nirnivia would never be the same." She bent her neck. "I know it's not like my opinion matters..."

As her smile widened, Rose patted her shoulder. "Your opinion matters far more than you think. I appreciate your support. Through the years, you've been indispensable. I'd be lost without you. Kristina, you're an intelligent young woman filled with good ideas. Everyone realizes how brilliant you are except you."

A blush reddened the blond woman's cheeks. "Maybe."

Kristina's words stuck in Rose's mind and sent her down a spiral of thoughts. More precisely, she reflected on the part about comforting the family. That was what it was about in the end. Whether praying could save Tessa was debatable. Rose had faith in prayers, but that didn't mean she was right.

On the other hand, having the Melkar by their side would help the family cope. As much as Alcharia tortured Tessa, those who loved her endured similar pain. If the child died, her torments would vanish, at least until her next life. Not so for the others. Her parents, her sister, her friends, they would remember her and miss her forever. For the living, death brought scars that sometimes never healed.

***

Too great a crowd packed the room beyond its capacity. Small in size, the chamber rendered Miguel's extended stay troublesome, so having Rose's whole immediate family there demanded some cramming. The number of people caused the temperature to rise, which made breathing difficult. Alcharia had left her throat a burning mess, and that already posed respiration problems. With everyone there, the issue was only exacerbated. Not that Rose would ever consider sending them away. This might be their last chance to enjoy each other's company.

Janice kneeled beside the bed with her head resting on the mattress. Tears streamed down her cheeks as she sobbed. That was a rare sight. On a mere few occasions had Rose witnessed her weeping; she could count them on her fingers and have more to spare.

On the other side of the bed stood Daniel and Madeleine, her adoptive parents. Her mother stroked Rose's hair while praying. As for her father, well, he presented the strong facade a military career demanded. Still, between the twitching muscles in his face and the way he clutched Madeleine's hand for comfort, Rose sensed his raging emotions beneath the surface. Through both childhood and adulthood, she had never seen him cry. However, this was the closest she recalled. A bit more and he'd shed manly tears.

Last remained Miguel, present as always, though distant. Her dearest husband stayed far from the group, rubbing his chin, silent and with a permanent frown. How unfortunate. They should cherish every precious second, but with him like this... of course, Rose understood why he was lost in thought. No question, Miguel searched his mind for any potential knowledge, no matter how insignificant, that might help combat the disease. A foolish endeavor, she presumed, but one he had to pursue, lest he regret missing a crucial possibility.

"Sis"—in the middle of her sniffing, Janice caressed Rose's hand, staining her own red—"is this a nightmare? We can't be losing you."

With a searing ache spreading through her muscles, Rose lifted her arms. The movement demanded a ridiculous effort, to the point that she almost gave up. In the end, Rose succeeded and grasped Janice's palm in what she hoped was a comforting gesture. Then she turned her head, attempting to look at her sibling. During the motion, blood dripped into Rose's eyes, and she winced as she closed them. Those annoying lesions went beyond ravaging her appearance and bringing pain.

"It's going to be okay," Rose whispered in a hoarse voice that reminded her more of an animal's growl than her own soft, feminine tone.

"Not if you don't open your eyes again!"

With a sigh, Madeleine nodded. "Indeed, the loss of the Melkar will be a tragedy."

Infuriated, Janice hopped on her feet and glared at her mom with crossed arms. "I don't care about the Melkar!" Madeleine gasped, and Rose's jaw tightened. Why should there be any confrontation now? She prayed Madeleine wouldn't escalate the conflict by accusing Janice of blasphemy. Such a response would be beyond tone-deaf, but given her role as head priestess, she might fail to contain the rebuttal. "I care about Rose! How can you be so cold when your daughter is dying?!"

Rose mouthed Janice's name, but no sound came.

"Oh, my dearest Janice, I assure you I am devastated. This is without question the toughest trial I have faced in life. While I understand your anger, this is so much bigger than us. I cannot forget that the whole country is saddened as well. Everyone is prematurely mourning the holy prophet, and I am afraid to imagine what will be if Rose does not survive this twisted sickness."

"Mother, please"—a few coughs interrupted Rose's sentence—"I just want to spend time with my family while I can."

"Of course, my child, I apologize."

Silence fell over the room. A few minutes passed and Daniel said, "Princess, I'm a lucky man: I've been blessed with two wonderful daughters." A sniffle later, she finally saw her dad cry. Strained by the emotion, his voice broke. "Melkar or not, you're a gift from Ulgorack." Daniel clenched his fist. "If only he'd done the right thing and shown up."

"I wish I could have seen Laurence again too, so I'd know he's okay after all these years. But his absence doesn't surprise me. He hated me."

"It took days, but I tracked him down. I sent a message through a friend." Daniel groaned. "Laurence wouldn't meet me in person. I figured that, given your disease, he'd admit the error of his ways, but the little bastard is stubborn as ever."

"Dad, please, stop. Don't speak ill of Laurence today. Yes, he hurt me, but he's still your son and my brother."

Daniel nodded and offered a soft smile. "You're right, princess. I shouldn't waste my last moments with my daughter grumbling about the past."

Then steps echoed as Miguel approached. Once near enough for his purpose, he rested his palms on his hips and stared at the group, alternating his gaze from one person to the next. Fury radiated from his deep blue eyes. "I can't believe what I'm hearing! You're acting as if her death is inevitable! Rose is still alive! Some have survived Alcharia, as she will!"

"Don't you think we want her to?" Janice screamed. "I'd give anything to save my sis!"

"Really? Then why abandon hope so easily? I can't help but wonder if your premature grieving shows a hidden desire. What if deep down, you're so jealous of Rose, you're hoping she won't wake up!"

Rose shuddered. Such cruel, mean-spirited words coming from the man she loved. She admitted Miguel could occasionally be too blunt and hurt people's feelings, but that wasn't intentional. This time, he meant to upset her sister. Filled with sudden anger, yet lacking the energy to intervene, Rose fumed.

Not to worry, however. Janice didn't rely on anyone for protection. With a terrifying glare, she pointed at Miguel. "Say that again, I dare you."

A trembling Miguel burst into tears and Rose exhaled in relief. "I'm sorry. Janice, I'm sorry. Please understand that for me, there's no greater horror than losing her. The thought crushes my heart in a million pieces. When you all talk as if she's already gone, I—" He grunted and dismissed the notion with a wave. "Pessimism is pointless. I won't let Rose die!"

"I'm afraid that's impossible, my boy," Daniel said. "You have to accept the reality of the situation."

"Bah, you should have learned not to underestimate me by now, Dad."

Had she not been in intolerable agony, Rose might've had to stifle a giggle. Since their marriage, Miguel had addressed Daniel that way. Though he chose not to complain, her father found that strange, and it made him uncomfortable. Whenever the term of affection escaped Miguel's lips, she recalled Daniel's reaction when he'd first heard it.

"Ah, you have a point there!" Daniel admitted after a laugh. Then his expression grew somber. "But I'm afraid that, in this case, you're outmatched. As much as I hate to admit it, you can't save Rose from Alcharia."

"We'll see about that."

After a nod, Daniel approached Miguel and patted his shoulder. "Miguel, I'm not your dad, and we've had our differences in the past, but I've always respected you. The occasional friction between us doesn't change the fact that you're far more resourceful than I'll ever be. It's not a secret I didn't believe in your marriage with my Rose. It wasn't personal. I just didn't feel you two were a good match. I didn't meddle because it was her mistake to make, but I was sure the whole thing would end in a bitter divorce. My boy, you proved me wrong, and I couldn't be happier. You're a wonderful and loyal husband, better than me." Daniel winked at Madeleine. "But, if Rose dies, you must let go. I know it sounds impossible. I don't know how I'll do it myself. But we have to, or we'll go insane, and Rose wouldn't want that."

A sudden urge to throw up overcame Rose. She tried asking for the bucket, but her mouth refused to work.

Thank God the expected vomit didn't come, though her nausea worsened.

"I've always respected you too, sir, but I disagree. I won't have to let go, she will live! I'll do anything to make it so."

Rose's vision blurred as a splitting headache assailed her. Unable to express her discomfort, she endured it in silence.

"And what will you do if you're wrong? Fight death itself with your bare hands?"

"As illogical as that is, if it were a possibility, I'd attempt it without hesitation. Tell me, why is the only atheist present the one displaying the most faith? How can you maintain your God is so cruel, he'd take away the holy prophet he sent in such a pointless manner when you claim he loves you? It seems... Rose? Rose!"

Miguel yelling her name was the last thing she heard before the darkness.

***

"Rose? Did you hear me?" Kristina's voice brought her back from her daydreaming.

"Uh? Sorry, I got distracted..."

"I just said, how about next Wednesday at two?" Rose studied her agenda. The date seemed fine, and so she agreed.

Chapter 14

Lacdor 34, 2134, on the Nirnivian calendar

After a cough, Stalker grunted and surveyed the area. BBR had set up operations in an abandoned building near the hospital. The place had been deserted for years and was filled with dust. Although they had cleaned up during their stay, it remained filthy, and the dirt did a number on his sinuses. That only exacerbated his miserable mood.

From the start, Stalker had hated Diabo's plan. Adding insult to injury, he'd implemented most of it. Some other BBR goons had helped him out, but given his status as the ultimate infiltrator, he had taken the largest share of the work. Diabo himself was ill suited for such a mission. His large, clumsy body defied any attempt at discretion. Beyond that, the red-shaded skin Ostark's experiments had bestowed upon him drew attention. One foot in the hospital and he would have been discovered. That was why their boss stayed behind, barking orders and insulting their competence, while they dirtied their hands. And so Stalker had smuggled the bombs inside, then wired them. As much as it disgusted him, he'd even injected several IV drips with the orange fluid provided by Plague. Good thing the explosion would never come, or the decrepit mutant's effort would have been in vain...

As he paced around the room filled with antiquated mechanical equipment, Stalker wondered how long until Diabo realized his scheme had failed. Given the crimson beast's stubbornness, probably a while. Enough time had passed since they'd finished their preparations for symptoms of Alcharia to show. Day and night, Diabo stayed at the window, watching the hospital through his binoculars. Occasionally, he shook his head and mumbled a curse, or blamed his underlings for the fact that the Doctor hadn't appeared yet. Stalker kept his distance. Between Diabo's temper and his own sourness, any verbal exchange risked ending in a fight, and he doubted the outcome would favor him. At any rate, Diabo still had plenty of waiting left before he admitted defeat. Or at least that was what Stalker assumed, until the boss pumped his fist and let out a victorious laugh.

"Here comes the bastard. Told ya!"

For a second, Stalker's heart stopped and he staggered backward. Once he recovered, he gulped. Incredulous, he rushed for the window and grabbed his own binoculars. He held them to his eyes. At first, he only noticed a crowd of soldiers, but soon, he spotted the cyborg's glimmering body among them. The group walked toward the hospital at a brisk pace. Shocked, Stalker's mouth gaped and he dropped his binoculars. They hit the floor with a crashing sound, the lens shattering. That made little sense. Doctor Death was too smart to fall for this crap. Besides, Plague had said... had he been lied to?

***

Filled with glee, Diabo rubbed his hands together and grinned. After all the criticism and doubting, he'd proved the naysayers wrong. A rush of adrenaline flowed through his veins, causing such excitement that he almost feared a heart attack. Stalker still stood there dumbstruck, his mouth gaping. Perhaps, at last, he and that fool Plague would learn not to question his leadership.

As the Doctor entered the hospital, Diabo grasped the detonator resting on the window's edge. His finger caressed the button. The temptation to push it grew inside him. Gritting his teeth, he resisted. Due to limited resources, his men had used a minimal number of bombs, so the explosion should only destroy the wing hosting the infected children. If his impatience bested him, the plan would fail.

While he giggled like a schoolgirl, Diabo turned his head to the left and fixated on the monitor they installed there. Besides explosives, Stalker had prepared a camera, so they'd know when their target arrived within range of his doom. Tension filled Diabo's body as sweat covered his brow. To calm his nerves, he counted the passing seconds. One... two... three...

Before he uttered the next number, the mechanical man appeared on the screen. With a demented chortle, Diabo slapped his knee.

"Doctor Death, you're now Doctor Dead!" A cheesy line, he admitted, but it reminded him of the crappy old action movies he'd relished as Pierre Garland. With a large smile on his face, he pressed the button with his thumb. Nothing...

Perplexed, Diabo frowned and tried again and again. Still nothing. After a furious roar, he threw the detonator to the floor and it shattered, the cracking sound of plastic echoing. A series of expletives escaped his lips before he forced himself to stop and take several deep breaths. Then he glared at Stalker.

"You freaking idiot!" He seized the master of camouflage by the collar and lifted him off the floor. "You messed up!"

Stalker whimpered as his feet moved in the air. "No, boss, I swear it ain't like that. They knew! They found the damn bombs and disarmed them."

"Ain't no way the bastards—" Diabo growled and threw Stalker on the floor. "I'm gonna storm that place and crush him with my bare hands!"

With a gasp, Stalker struggled to get back on his feet. "Are you crazy?" He almost fell but stabilized himself at the last minute. "That ain't..." He never finished his sentence, as shattering glass interrupted him. Perplexed, Diabo turned toward the source. Strange canisters broke through the windows and now landed on the floor, causing metallic clinks. Then they hissed and emitted a yellowish gas. In an instant, the haze filled the whole chamber.

Though his men yelled and coughed due to the sudden smog, they didn't seem as affected as Diabo. Even before he breathed it in, the fog scorched his skin. Once it reached his nose, his throat and lungs burned as his eyes watered. Such pain. He stumbled forward in search of a safe spot. A migraine assailed him and his vision blurred. Weakened, he fell. Then he heard the blast of firing guns and bullets strike two of his goons. Bloodied, they collapsed with a scream. He tried calling Stalker's name, but his voice vanished. Desperate, Diabo looked around and saw his colleague, unconscious and foaming at the mouth. Whatever the toxin they faced might be, it had poisoned him quicker.

Soon, Ostarkiran soldiers approached, yelling for them to surrender. The sight stoked Diabo's fury, and thanks to that extra motivation, he forced himself up and sprinted toward the nearest enemies. Once close enough, he seized one and jammed the soldier's back against his knee, cracking his spine. Then Diabo spun around and punched another fool who'd attempted to sneak behind him, sending him flying into a wall. All the while, bullets ricocheted off Diabo's armored body. Despite his debilitated state, they posed little danger. Since he'd used the last of his strength, he stayed immobile as the projectiles struck him while trying to catch his breath.

At that moment, a towering shape popped in front of Diabo. He blinked twice, not believing his eyes. That wheel-mounted triangular machine... it was a WarBot, a rare sight. In fact, he assumed them to be experimental Ostarkiran technology untested in combat. Maybe his foes had made greater progress than anticipated. A single red lens appeared in the middle of the contraption, probably a camera. More concerning were the two machine guns attached to the sides.

With a gulp, Diabo realized he needed to take care of that threat. He gathered what remained of his energy and hopped to his feet, only for the WarBot to fire an intense flow of bullets. Though they didn't penetrate his skin, they bruised him. The impact projected Diabo backward, and he crumpled while vomiting. This time, he was down for the count. Soon, a metal leg landed next to his ear.

"Ah, my dearest enemy, it would seem you will never understand the subtleties of a proper strategy."

Chapter 15

Not long after supper, Daniel rang Rose's doorbell and she let him in. Once he stepped inside, he presented her with a brown bag. As instructed, she grabbed it, then turned toward her desk and rested it on the wooden surface.

"How are you holding up?" Daniel asked as Rose performed the gesture. Local news stations were following the story of Tessa, and according to them, the child had lost consciousness three days ago. Either she'd wake up before the following morning, or she'd remain in her coma until death. No doubt Daniel understood this proved to be a difficult moment for Rose. While he had come to deliver a package, she expected he also used this as an excuse to check on her.

"I'm all right." She paused. "Emotionally shaken, but all right."

After a nod, Daniel walked toward Rose and laid his hand on her shoulder. "Princess, you won't change your mind at the last minute, will you?"

Rose sighed. "No. It's too late for that now."

As she uttered that response, Rose looked in her mirror standing above the desk. The reflection laughed and then mouthed the words, "You should have died." Yes, she should have. She wasn't supposed to wake up, and yet...

***

Darkness surrounded her. Where was she? What was going on? She failed to remember. Pain... so much pain. What had happened? A fog clouded her mind. She should know, but her memory refused to work. She had to do something, but what? Her mouth—she had one, didn't she? A mouth served an important purpose, but what? Eat food! True, yet wrong. Hunger wasn't the issue.

What else, then? Speak. Yes, she could talk using her mouth! If she requested assistance, someone might help. Slowly she moved her lips. A searing ache coursed through her body. She persevered, but no words came, only weak, meaningless sounds. Still, she heard a voice. "Kriincesse! Whhoooa zat roozzy youg?"

Gibberish, but she wasn't alone. She dared hope whoever accompanied her would provide support and tried speaking again, but she uttered more rubbish. All that suffering for nothing; so unfair. She almost cried. Cried... yes, that's right, she possessed eyes! Eyes that produced tears when sad! But beyond that, eyes could see! If only she managed to open them. She focused. It hadn't been so hard before. Why was it so difficult now? She persisted and... a senseless blur served as her sole reward. A particular blur moved and approached her. What did it want? Her fear grew, and she sensed her body trembling.

"Princess! You're awake! Princess! Nurse! Come here quick! Nurse!"

Somehow, she understood this time. Though distorted, the voice seemed so familiar. She knew that person. Her father! No, no, he'd died during her childhood. The recollection broke her heart. Her dad had died. She'd never meet him again. Who, then? Who? Her adoptive... yes, she'd figured it out. The shape was Dominic Ricdeau, her new father. Or wait, perhaps Daniel? No matter. While she missed her biological father, she loved that man nonethe-less. Warmth filled her. It would be fine: he would take care of her.

At that moment, she remembered everything. She was Rose Branford, later renamed Rose Ricdeau. She was born with wings, cursed wings that doomed her into misery. Not long ago, she had caught a disease. Alcha... Alcharia. That wretched sickness had almost killed her. In fact, she'd believed her time had come. She'd lost consciousness, but against the odds had woken up again. Though feeble, she'd be fine. Once one opened their eyes, it signaled Alcharia's defeat. A little rest and she'd be back on her feet. Everything was all right.

Except... except, in reality, nothing was all right. There was something missing. No, not something, but rather a moving blur. A single one she counted. Impossible. There should be at least one more. That was an undeniable truth. Where was he? He had to be there. Rose forgot his name and his identity, but he'd be there no matter what. He'd never leave her alone...

Where was he? He must be near... But who? Who? Of course... her husband. Poor Miguel had remained with her during her whole stay at the hospital. Longing overcame Rose.

When Miguel had learned of her illness, it had devastated him. The idea that Rose might die had plunged him into depression. He had to be there; he wouldn't abandon her at the last moment. What if he hadn't noticed she'd regained consciousness? That seemed unlikely, but she lacked any other explanation. Perhaps if she called his name, he'd realize. He would be so happy. Oh, but her stupid mouth denied her speech.

How unfair. If only she could say his name. Rose had to try, even if it resulted in certain failure. Again, she moved her lips. Such agony to no avail. Another attempt, her torture intensified. "Mi... Mig... Miguel!"

Her father gasped. "I'm so sorry, princess. Miguel left. Don't worry, I'll find him. He'll be here soon."

No... no! No way he'd leave her like that. The poor soul slept on the floor so they wouldn't be apart He had to be there. But her father indulged in a cruel joke. "Miguel! Miguel! Miguel!" Though every fiber of her being begged her to stop, she pushed through. "Miguel!"

"Princess, please, I'll get him! Don't, please!" Daniel groaned. "Where is the damn doctor?"

No, he had to be there. When he saw her awake, he would be so happy. He had to be there. Then she felt a new sensation. Moisture... tears. She wept, or at least she thought so.

"Miguel!" After that final call, her mouth wouldn't open anymore. Exhaustion conquered her, and once again only darkness existed.

Chapter 16

From the rooftop she had accessed through careful climbing, Wrathchild studied the hospital with her binoculars. By pure luck, she'd overheard some BBR goons talking about Diabo's plan. The details left her breathless, and she thanked Ulgorack that they had decided not to involve her. The scheme sickened her. Blowing up a children's hospital should have that effect on anyone, but her past made it worse. Should she have taken part in this madness, Molly and Sebastian's disappointed stares would haunt her nightmares until her dying day.

Told Diabo bad idea, slapped me. Said didn't want me there, was none o' my business. Heh, after almost let him go alone. Almost. Had bad feeling. Fought all damn life, instinct warned shit would happen. Followed them in secret. Watched their back. Alcharia, met disease before.

—Thoughts of Wrathchild, Hocmar 28, 2134, on the Nirnivian calendar

***

Melissa kneeled beside Rose's bed, her head resting on the mattress. Tears ran down her cheeks as she sobbed. Why should such a gentle woman suffer this terrible fate? She didn't understand. Was this Ulgorack's will? Should she follow such a cruel God? No doubt Rose would say yes, and yet Melissa wasn't sure. Shame crept inside her heart as she recalled how, when they'd first met, she had spat in Rose's face. Their relationship had changed for the better since then.

Sensing Melissa's torment, Rose lifted her arms. Though her limb trembled, she managed to rest her fingers on Melissa's hand. "It's all right. Everything will be fine."

Between whimpers, Melissa said, "Please. Don't die. Must fight."

"I don't intend on giving up."

"Must live. Want to help. Can't... powerless. Hate being powerless." As a fury ignited inside her, Melissa clenched her fist and gritted her teeth. She gasped. "No... must control. Must control anger."

Rose moved from her hand to Melissa's head and caressed her short brown hair. "It's okay. You're not Wrathchild anymore: your rage can't rule over you."

***

Though it demanded an effort, Wrathchild forced herself out of her reverie. This wasn't the time to indulge in the past. That in mind, Melissa returned to the binoculars. The moment they rested over her eyes, she froze as a shiver ran down her spine. Ostarkiran soldiers approached the abandoned building BBR used as their base of operations. They threw unidentified objects at the windows, breaking them. More surprising, a metallic being accompanied the troops... Doctor Death. Why would he risk coming here? Wrathchild gasped, then swore. Her instincts had proved correct.

Before got ground, soldiers stormed into building. Fought since child. Assassin; vigilante. One against hundred, nothing to me. But didn't want endanger other. Might be killed during battle. Had other idea. Rushed for hospital.

—Thoughts of Wrathchild, Hocmar 28, 2134, on the Nirnivian calendar

Chapter 17

While not in the mood for a laugh, Diabo recognized the humor of his current situation. He had tried so hard to reach Doctor Death, and he'd accomplished his goal by getting captured. Too bad the Ostarkirans had wrapped chains around his weakened body, preventing him from tearing the president apart. In his normal state, he'd break the bonds in a snap, but the gas had left him so weak that standing posed a challenge.

Still, compared to Stalker, he'd suffered few consequences from the assault. The master of camouflage lay on the floor next to Diabo's leg, eyes closed and drooling. Without his chest rising and falling from respiration, he would have appeared dead. Who could tell how long he'd survive? Then again, given that a group of soldiers aiming machine guns surrounded both men, that proved true for Diabo as well.

As Diabo contemplated those thoughts, metallic footsteps echoed. Doctor Death approached, his arms crossed. The Ostarkirans encircling him and Stalker made way so the mechanical man could pass. They hadn't met since those experiments in that cursed laboratory. As he witnessed his tormentor walking toward him, an image from the past entered Diabo's brain—himself strapped to a table, screaming as several IV lines injected an unknown substance into his body.

Once the Doctor grew close enough, Diabo noticed the emoticon in his electronic eye animated in a manner suggesting a shake of the head. "Mr. Garland, I sincerely thank you for honoring me with your presence." The cyborg rubbed below his speaker. "Unfortunately, I must admit you have disappointed me. Did you believe such an amateur assassination attempt would succeed?" He shrugged. "Ah well, I suppose it is not surprising. On a physical level, you are a powerful opponent, but your mind runs on a single track. Predicting your actions is but child's play to me."

People said Doctor Death had developed incredible skills in psychology. They claimed he possessed an uncanny ability to determine how one's mental processes worked. From there, given a specific scenario, he deduced the potential choices an individual might make and assigned a probability to each of them. The method showed precision to the point that it resembled mind-reading. Diabo didn't believe a word of it. There were those in this world who eagerly overestimated the enemy. Though he wished to fire a sarcastic remark to this effect, the yellow haze had damaged his throat and nothing but incomprehensible growls escaped his lips.

"Your desire for revenge is well founded, Mr. Garland. Regrettably, you did not stand a chance. I am one of the leading characters in the story of this universe. I will not die so soon." The emoji's mouth straightened, and its raised eyebrows evoked a pensive expression. "Yet I must admit, I did not expect such a fate for you either. You do not exactly play a minor part. I assumed you would be around for longer. What can I say? Mr. Garland, none choose when their role is over."

Story of this universe? Was that some kind of joke? If so, it failed to amuse Diabo. That Doctor Death insisted on calling him Pierre Garland didn't improve his temper either. Furious, he gathered his strength and again attempted to speak. It demanded several coughs and gasps for air, but he managed a harsh, barely intelligible sentence.

"Pierre Garland's dead. I'm Diabo."

"So you still hide behind a silly code name. How childish." He tilted his head. "Then again, I understand the desire to forsake one's identity. Very well, I shall comply with this particular request, Diabo."

A minor victory, but Diabo would take it. In his position, every win counted.

***

An interesting dilemma presented itself to Wrathchild. She had little time, so she needed to move fast. In the movies, villains offered overwrought speeches explaining their plans and celebrating their victory. There was no reason to believe Doctor Death would adhere to that cliché. In fact, it might already be too late. Then again, rushing could lead to confrontations, slowing her down. At least, since she'd watched her colleagues' work, she knew the closest spot...

As a result, Wrathchild advanced at a brisk pace a notch below running speed. She focused on her environment as she progressed, scanning for any details clueing her in on the presence of people nearby. That was how she heard faint voices coming from the corridor she almost headed into. That cut off the optimal route to the closest spot. Stifling a curse, she backtracked and attempted another path. However, when she turned a corner, she came face-to-face with two armed Ostarkiran soldiers who pointed their guns at her. "What are you doing here? This place is in lockdown—"

With no trace of hesitation, nor fear, Wrathchild engaged what she called overdrive, thus unleashing her ridiculous speed. That done, she reached for her pistol and fired. Her aim proved true, resulting in a bloody hole in the first assailant's forehead. Still, he managed a shot before dying. Wrathchild rolled out of the way and, during the motion, pulled the trigger once more. Unfortunately, the second attacker mimicked her gesture. Given she was in the middle of her roll, evading was impossible. Instead, she grabbed her sword's handle, unsheathed it and struck the bullet with its edge. After the echoing clink, the remaining foe collapsed.

Normal blade can't stop bullets. Mine unique. Thanked Master Torkin again for giving it. Not good man, but... still was in his debt.

—Thoughts of Wrathchild, Hocmar 28, 2134, on the Nirnivian calendar

Chapter 18

Since her father had brought Rose the package, she had sat on her mattress, deep in thought. She didn't touch the bag in question. Instead, it remained next to her feet. With a sigh, Rose figured she had to get to it, so she rummaged through its contents and fished out a black robe. Rose suppressed a shiver. Despite understanding its origins and significance, the garment crept her out.

The mantle originated from Win-Kui-Noi, a religion from pre-old war Perz culture. Unlike other faiths, Win-Kui-Noi lacked a god. Instead, it held that the planet, solar system, galaxies, and even universes were sentient. Take a Gorumar body, for example. It was formed by cells, each living in their own right, and contained other life forms such as bacteria—some harmful, but many playing a necessary role. Win-Kui-Noi posited that the same was true for the planet. It was alive and the various plants, animals, and people were part of its anatomy. Meanwhile, galaxies were life forms composed of, among other things, numerous planets, each as individuals yet part of a greater whole. By the same logic, Gorumars also contributed to this system, though their exact role was debated. Nihilists even claimed they acted as a disease, killing their host.

Long ago, hard-core Win-Kui-Noi monks created what they called the Ulrata order. Since every Gorumar shared the same unknown purpose, they illustrated this by wearing black robes and leather masks. That attire gave each of them a similar appearance, symbolizing that despite skin-deep differences, they were the same.

Because of Win-Kui-Noi's peculiar nature, it proved compatible with other religions. After all, it didn't impose a god on its followers, and thus they were free to worship any deity they chose. This meant that Win-Kui-Noi possessed a far greater number of devotees when compared to other ancient faiths, such as Hynoism and Taidism. Because of this, the Ulrata order still existed, though in a less extreme form. The sect had evolved into a charitable organization, and the members only wore the robes when collecting donations.

As she reminisced about the garment's history, Rose stood up and wrapped it around her body to check if it fitted, and in appearance, it did. With the robe on, she peeked at her mirror. Lesions appeared over the face of the reflection staring back at her. After a shudder, the sight plunged Rose into her memories.

***

Thirsty... so thirsty. What an unpleasant sensation, but that meant Rose had returned to the world of the living. While groggy, her mind was much clearer than during her previous awakening. Rose opened her eyes, expecting blurriness, but her vision recovered. The hospital room appeared with a shocking sharpness. Rose surveyed the area and gasped. A weeping Miguel sat in a nearby chair, but she almost failed to recognize him. An untrimmed beard covered his usually clean-shaven chin. His usually well-combed hair formed a twisted mess. Dirt soiled his wrinkled shirt, and Rose even noticed a tear in his pants. What had happened?

"Miguel! You're here!" Rose's voice sounded hoarse, and speaking burned her throat, but overall, her condition had improved.

With a gulp, Miguel got to his feet in a rush, took a few steps, collapsed on the floor by her side and grabbed her hand. Though he squeezed too hard and hurt her, she didn't complain.

"Rose! You're awake at last!"

"Did I lose consciousness again?"

Miguel let out a forced chuckle as he dismissed the notion with a wave. "Oh no, my love, you fell asleep. You were all right, but I feared I'd somehow lose you. I'm so relieved. And so sorry... you woke up while I was gone. You poor thing, you strained yourself calling my name until you were exhausted. The doctors insist you shouldn't even have been able to talk. I'm so sorry, baby, I should've been here."

"Don't worry, it's okay. It's not your fault. I—"

"I'm so sorry," Miguel said again, interrupting her, thus Rose assumed he didn't hear. "In total, you had been unconscious for six days, so we were certain you would die. After four days passed, I had no choice but to accept reality, and I couldn't handle it. Looking at you in that bed, knowing you'd soon be gone, drove me crazy. Though I should've stayed by your side, I was weak. I failed to bear the torment, so after a while, I left and wandered through the city with no destination. Eventually, I came to my senses and returned, but I was too late, for you had already regained consciousness and then fallen back into slumber. I'm so sorry, will you ever forgive me?"

Confused by the incessant apologies, Rose giggled. "There's nothing to forgive, Miguel. If the situations had been reversed, I couldn't have stayed either. Don't feel bad, you were great." At that, Rose realized what her husband's words implied and swallowed hard. "Wait!" She blinked twice. "Six days? Did you say six days?"

"Yes, it's impossible, but it's the truth. Normally, I find such mysteries unsettling and need answers. However, this time, I'll simply be thankful for my blessings."

Six days... no one had survived Alcharia after being unconscious for so long. Rose was the first. No doubt her believers would claim Ulgorack had saved her. How could she blame them when she lacked any other explanation? A niggling worrying sensation warned that Rose's life would be even more complicated. But never mind; she lived and enjoyed the company of her spouse.

"Like a fool, I believed it was over and left in despair. I'm so sorry, Rose, so sorry—"

"Please, Miguel, it's okay. I'm not mad. Stop blaming yourself. We're together now."

Miguel lowered his head. "Nevertheless, I'm ashamed of what I did."

"You went on a long walk to calm your nerves. Maybe it wasn't good timing, but that's hardly a crime! Stop, you've done nothing wrong. I love you."

At last, Miguel ceased the futile apology and smiled. "I love you too. I have no idea why I'm so fortunate, for God knows I do not deserve you."

Surprised by the remark, Rose frowned. "Who are you, and where is my husband? The real Miguel would never use the word God like that."

"Oh, now, dear, I thought my world had come to an end. Can't you forgive a little slip of the tongue?"

Both laughed, and Miguel caressed her hair. Everything was so wonderful, and yet... "Miguel"—Rose bit her lip—

"I'm probably just being silly, but... do I look any different?"

"Your lovely visage still suffers from the ravages of Alcharia, but not to worry; that'll resolve itself soon. Besides, you're beautiful anyway."

"No, that's not what I meant. I... argh, I don't know." Rose patted her cheeks with her fingers as if confirming she possessed the same bone structure as always. "I feel different somehow. Like something important changed."

"Do not be concerned. I assume it's a side effect of your prolonged coma."

After a sigh, Rose nodded. "Yeah, I guess so. I still can't believe I'm alive."

Miguel crossed his arms. "After all these years, you have no faith in me. I promised you wouldn't die."

"Oh, you shouldn't talk. You lost faith too!"

Miguel didn't reply. Instead, he kissed her. His lips on hers drowned Rose in pain. Never before had she reveled in such sweet agony.

Chapter 19

Although the debilitating yellow haze was clearing from the room, Diabo wobbled on his feet. All his strength had vanished. A bit more and he'd collapse on the ground. In fact, he feared his health might continue to deteriorate, as now the cyborg in front of him appeared doubled.

While he observed Diabo having difficulty standing up, Doctor Death tilted his head sideways. "You are not feeling well, are you, Diabo?"

"I gotta admit"—a cough disrupted Diabo's response—"that gas packs a punch."

"For you, I am sure it does. It is quite an interesting toxin, and certainly effective." A shake of the head came from the mechanical man. "Alas, I cannot take all the credit. I developed my own weapons for use against you, but they were unsatisfactory. By hacking Nirnivian research facilities, I acquired data on prototypes. I assume NISDA produced them in case BBR became a bigger problem for them. It is true you are more of a threat for Ostark, and on the surface, it is to Nirnivia's advantage. However, BBR spilled Nirnivian blood occasionally."

He paused for dramatic effect. "In appearance, their weapons were even more pathetic than my attempts. Still, by combining some of their ideas with mine, I ended up with something far more potent. You know, the gas also penetrates the skin, so a mask is not sufficient."

A growl from Diabo interrupted him. "Charming... hey, we're havin' fun and all, but I gotta ask: why ain't I dead yet?"

"There are several reasons. First of all, dear Diabo, I wanted to apologize for the hardships I inflicted upon you."

"Cut the crap, won't ya?"

"Oh, but I assure you, I am most serious." Though he'd rather not admit it, when he stared into that one remaining biological eye, Diabo recognized a glimmer of sincerity.

***

Ran, ran, ran. Never stopped. Encountered WarBots. Didn't think were in service yet. Heh, no time worry 'bout that. Had get rid of 'em quick.
—Thoughts of Wrathchild, Hocmar 28, 2134, on the Nirnivian calendar

The instant Wrathchild spotted the two machines, they aimed their guns at her. While swallowing hard, she engaged overdrive. Speed would be of the essence. Torrents of bullets flew toward her. She bolted around, avoiding them. As a result, the pellets ravaged the wall and floor, causing dust clouds. In a display of intelligence, the War-Bots rolled along the corridor, positioning themselves so she'd be caught in a pincer. No matter how often she somersaulted, hopped or dashed to disrupt their strategy, the robots repositioned and regained their advantage.

Though their tactic put the WarBots in each other's firing trajectory, this caused no consequences. The projectiles failed to damage their hardened bodies. As such, Wrathchild realized her pistol proved useless in this conflict. She thus left it sheeted, seizing instead her sword. The dedudinanium alloy edge might be successful at piercing her foes' metallic frames. It remained to get close enough, and that posed a challenge. Yes, her incredible swiftness allowed her faster movement compared to her enemies, but whenever she attempted to approach one, the other cut off her path with their guns.

In appearance, they reached a stalemate, but in reality, Wrathchild was at a disadvantage. Maintaining such quickness demanded a considerable physical effort. Overdrive taxed her body. The longer she maintained the state, the greater the price. The encounter had lasted several minutes already, and her muscles were tearing themselves apart. Pain and aches spread all over. She grunted and whimpered as she evaded the machines' attacks. Thank Ulgorack they occasionally stopped moving for a moment. The clicking sound echoing at those points made her assume they reloaded their weapons. This gave her precious chances to pause overdrive for a fraction of a second and recuperate, but that only delayed the inevitable. Even worse, a loud cacophony erupted due to the battle. It'd only be a matter of time before Ostarkiran soldiers heard and intervened. In fact, Wrathchild was surprised no one had shown up yet.

Prey to desperation, the shadow of a plan formed in Wrathchild's mind. In truth, the word plan gave her idea far too much credit. Nevertheless, it was her only hope. She kept dodging until the WarBot on her left emitted the ticking noise that indicated a reload. Then she ran toward it. As expected, the other aimed at her, but, gathering her strength, she jumped and soared above the incapacitated foe. As part of her flight, she came into contact with the wall and pushed against it with her legs. This altered her trajectory, meaning she landed in a different location than the WarBot anticipated. Though she only intended to confuse it enough to get near and slash it with her sword, the maneuver brought about an astonishing effect. The robot spun in a circle and soon collapsed to the floor. Wrathchild figured she had confused its AI and it had shut down. Only one remained to dispose of.

Now facing a single foe, Wrathchild's odds increased to reasonable levels. She simply kept swerving around the bullets until the WarBot paused to reload. Then she rushed toward it and drove her sword through its torso. After a flurry of beeps and electric sparks, it expired. Victorious, Wrathchild took a few deep breaths and wiped beads of sweat off her brow.

Could've used rest. No luck. Voices getting closer. Kept going.

—Thoughts of Wrathchild, Hocmar 28, 2134, on the Nirnivian calendar

***

"Diabo, I do not blame you for hating me," Doctor Death said with his monotone voice. "You most definitively deserve revenge. I ruined your life."

"Sorry my ass, you're a freaking monster!" Though the yellow haze had left Diabo sick and weakened, his state improved with every breath of fresh air. Dizziness still weighted on him, but the nausea passed. He assumed he'd soon be able to stand straight but kept a slumped posture to hide his slow recovery. At this point, the chains proved too formidable a foe for his strength, but if the mechanical man continued babbling away, that might change.

"Yes, I am." The cyborg nodded as his emoticon adopted a sad face. "It was not always the case. Circumstances tarnished my sense of morality. I never wished it so. War is a dirty business, I am afraid. President Laforge forced us to perform experiments to create super soldiers. As test subjects, he chose Nirnivian prisoners. To refuse would have meant my end." A disappointed shake of the head came from the Doctor. "While choosing survival over morals shames me, I have one last mission to accomplish, and success is of the utmost importance."

Diabo growled, then spat on the floor. "Like I care 'bout your reasons anyway!"

"Fair enough. I realize the outcome is bleak from your point of view, but there is a silver lining. While the data you provided failed to create super soldiers, it allowed the development of several medicines. This probably will not be of any comfort, but your suffering saved countless lives."

"Yeah, lives o' my enemies."

"I suppose." Doctor Death crossed his arms and bent his neck. "I never wanted to be your enemy, Diabo. It happened that way, but it was not personal. You were simply an unfortunate soul who possessed a specific genetic sequence that served my purpose. Please do not judge Ostark for my failings. I am aware I hurt you, but you of all people should understand the necessities of war."

The cyborg paused. "Diabo, you fought us ruthlessly. You spared no one. In your quest to destroy Ostark, you killed more Nirnivians than I. That apartment building alone..." Inside his electronic eye, the emoticon's mouth morphed into a circle mimicking a shocked expression. "And many more innocents you murdered for your cause. In fact, today you condemned children to a horrible death. Worse, you were willing to blow them up along with everyone in this place. Have you even considered how many lives would have been lost by your hand?"

"Collateral damage. Yeah, it's messy, but it's worth it to stop a freaking monster like you." By now, Diabo's headache had vanished and the soreness in his muscles had diminished to a bearable level. Not quite there yet in terms of required power, but soon.

"Is that so? If this is the case, then we are in agreement, for I can use the very same argument. All I have done is to stop a monster of my own. One that is far more dangerous than I shall ever be."

"Gimme a break," an incredulous Diabo growled. "Rose is a wuss. She ain't the dangerous one here."

"Believe what you must, Diabo. The truth is, I would gladly let you kill me. You deserve vengeance, and I am tired of life." The president raised his metallic arm and rotated it. "I am tired of this body. Unfortunately, I cannot rest, for that would result in the victory of my nemesis. While I do not wish you harm, you are growing bothersome. I cannot risk dying before I've succeeded at my task, and so I must get rid of you. Though I would prefer it were not so, I do not expect you to believe nor forgive me. Still, this is the truth, and I needed to tell you before the end."

Diabo grunted before baring his teeth. "Hmmph, whatever."

***

Was lucky, got right behind him. Didn't saw me. Guess not so lucky fo' him.

—Thoughts of Wrathchild, Hocmar 28, 2134, on the Nirnivian calendar

How the soldier didn't notice her, Wrathchild would never know. She snuck up and grabbed him. Before he could shout for help, she covered his mouth with her palm. Though the Ostarkiran struggled, Wrathchild held strong and soon slit his throat with her sword. Blood splattered on her, and as she cut his flesh, the man emitted a sickening, disgusting gurgle.

Spattered blood, screams of terror, screams of death. Was used to it. As kid, those were my lullabies.

—Thoughts of Wrathchild, Hocmar 28, 2134, on the Nirnivian calendar

***

With his speech over, Doctor Death walked to a nearby soldier. The two of them exchanged inaudible words. The Ostarkiran presented a syringe to the mechanical man. No doubt this contained a lethal injection.

Though Diabo doubted he had recuperated enough to break his bonds, he realized it was now or never. Swallowing hard, he gathered his strength and waited for the right moment. The cyborg took one step closer, then another. Once he walked within range, Diabo intended to jump him and rip his head off. Of course, he'd join his enemy in death soon after. The remaining Ostarkiran troops possessed superior numbers, and his physical shape proved lacking still. Despite this, it was well worth it. Diabo deemed his sacrifice a meager price if it ensured the Doctor's demise.

"Let me assure you that, at the very least, you shall not suffer. This poison acts quickly and does not cause pain. If you will, consider this act of mercy a final apol—" Right on cue, Diabo roared. He stood up and pulled his arms apart, ripping the chains. The metal links flew across the room, and clinks echoed as they landed. All around, gasps erupted from the surprised soldiers. As fast as he could manage, Diabo reached for Doctor Death. Before his fingers seized the coveted neck, his target pointed his fist at him, and out of the wrist, a cloud of yellow gas spread. It must've been a concentrated form, for it ended up more potent than earlier.

The instant the haze touched his skin, Diabo itched all over, and aches coursed through his muscles. When he breathed the fog in, he erupted in a coughing bout. His lungs burned, his eyes watered. Overwhelmed, his legs buckled, and Diabo found himself rolling on the floor in pain.

"How predictable." The cyborg waggled a lecturing finger. "I am again disappointed. As long as you have such a one-track mind, you cannot win. Poor Diabo, I can read your every move. With you, it is always brute force. You cannot use strategy. It shall be your downfall. Though I suppose I did drop the syringe, so your pitiful attempt will prolong your life."

***

At last, Wrathchild reached her destination. As she'd hoped, the Ostarkirans had disarmed the explosives but hadn't removed them yet. Melissa grabbed a few. Time to prove she had completed her training in terrorism with flying colors.

***

The gas left Diabo lightheaded and disoriented. Again, his muscles ached and his stomach churned. No matter how hard he tried, his body refused to budge. Even breathing caused pain. Every inhale burned his lungs. While confused, he realized Doctor Death stood beside him with a new syringe.

One of the Ostarkirans tied a tourniquet on Diabo's arm to facilitate the injection. Meanwhile, the cyborg pushed on the plunger, removing the air within. That seemed pointless, though, given he meant to kill Diabo. Force of habit, he assumed.

Then the Doctor bent down so he'd be at his level and grabbed his limb. It was all over. At this point, Diabo didn't care much about losing his life. His only regret was that he had failed to complete his revenge. Perhaps NISDA would prove more successful, though he doubted it.

Still dizzy, Diabo imagined Wrathchild approaching the group of soldiers surrounding him. What a silly hallucination. Melissa wrapped a corset of explosives around her torso. A duo of red and yellow cables ran from the bombs to a metal bar she held in her left fist. In his mind, the fake Wrathchild said, "Doctor Death! Wanna die? Go ahead. Wanna live? Look here."

***

Were okay. So relieved. Well, Diabo was. Stalker not so hot. Wasn't over yet. Wasn't sure would work. Either all got outta there alive, or all died.

> —Thoughts of Wrathchild, Hocmar 28, 2134, on the Nirnivian calendar

Against the odds, Wrathchild entered through a broken window with no one noticing. Once inside, however, she yelled her warning, which revealed her presence. A fraction of a second later, the soldiers turned toward her and aimed. Melissa prepared to engage overdrive, but Doctor Death lifted his palm.

"Do not fire. I repeat, do not fire. She has a dead man's switch." So he'd noticed that quickly—impressive, and to her advantage. Wrathchild grinned. "If she drops that bar she is holding, her bomb corset will explode. At this range, the explosion would kill everyone present."

"Correct. Drop weapons. And syringe."

As requested, the cyborg disposed of his needle. Then he motioned for his men to disarm. As they obeyed, Diabo stared at her. "Wrathchild!" Diabo coughed. "Do it! Kill us all!"

She ignored him and said, "Want leave with friends." Wrathchild continued, ignoring her boss. "Could've come gun blazing, killed you. Ain't a fool. No way out then. Got demands. Follow precisely, or boom!"

The Doctor tilted his neck. "I have no quarrel with you, Melissa. If you stop this foolishness, you can leave here unscathed."

"Not good enough. Think quick. Got one minute. Plenty o' time for genius."

For several seconds, the cyborg stood still. His emoticon switched expressions at a rapid pace. Based on rumors, he had a reputation for predicting how people would act. Too bad he didn't know her well. Besides, she had shown erratic behavior in the past and hoped that would limit his capabilities. Soon, he crossed his arms.

"You are bluffing."

"'Fraid not!" She waved the detonator in a playful manner. "I'm terrorist now. Suicide bombing part o' the job. Don't believe? Try luck. Lobotomizer doubted me... decapitated." The Lobotomizer was an assassin that a notorious criminal organization had sent after Melissa when she was a vigilante. He'd tested her like no one ever had before. In the end, she had prevailed—at a price. The story was famous. The mechanical man had heard it. Everyone had heard it. "Got nothing to lose. Like fireworks anyway."

"According to my analysis, I determine there is a sixty percent chance you will not detonate. After all, your past history with explosives does not encourage using them. However, I suppose those are not great odds, and so I admit defeat."

Good for him. Wasn't bluffing. Ready to blow myself up. But feared bomb wouldn't work. Did it so quick.

—Thoughts of Wrathchild, Hocmar 28, 2134, on the Nirnivian calendar

"Wrathchild!" Diabo yelled while gritting his teeth. "Do it! Blow the son o' a bitch up! Doesn't matter if we die, freaking do it!"

The Doctor stared into her eyes. "What are your demands?"

"Dammit, Wrathchild! Kill us all!"

Felt hope, still wasn't over. Was risky, but had chance.

—Thoughts of Wrathchild, Hocmar 28, 2134, on the Nirnivian calendar

Chapter 20

Rose visited me radiating with happiness, a rare sight lately. Tessa, the girl sick with Alcharia, had fallen unconscious three days before, and in a couple hours, hope would be lost. I found it strange that she sounded so happy; it wasn't good news.

When I asked, she explained she was relieved because that meant she could execute her plan. Rose had decided from the beginning to go and pray with the family. Only Daniel knew. While he disapproved, he understood. Since everyone believed she wouldn't, Rose gambled that Doctor Death wouldn't realize she'd be vulnerable. She apologized for hiding it, but I didn't care. In fact, I mentioned that she should have waited until she'd returned to tell me. And Rose agreed, but she wanted me there. She didn't hide the risk and warned that safety wasn't guaranteed. I was reluctant. Not because of the danger; rather, my presence seemed inappropriate. Still, I accepted.

By then, I had forgotten about Doctor Death's riddle, but by agreeing, I got one step closer to the answer. Sometimes I wonder if I'd have figured it out otherwise...

Anyway, we dressed in black robes and leather masks, branding us as members of the Ulrata order. Those guys often went door to door collecting donations for the poor. Why in hell philanthropists wore borderline scary outfits that gave them a sinister look dumbfounded me. Rose tried explaining, but it was so boring I didn't pay attention. We stopped at a few houses and gathered contributions to maintain the illu-

sion. When I wondered aloud about what we would do with that stuff, Rose said we'd give them to the real order. Logic.

When we arrived at our destination and rang the doorbell, Tessa's mother opened and pointed out that this wasn't the best of times. Before she finished, Rose unmasked herself. The woman stopped speaking and examined her face. It was as if she recognized the Melkar but didn't dare trust her eyes. To remove all possible doubts, Rose dropped her cloak and spread her wings. The woman fell to her knees in tears and screamed "Your Holiness!" Several people then came. I guessed one was the father. The others must have been friends and relatives. They kneeled in awe, and that reminded me of what Rose represented to Nirnivians. I had gotten to the point where I saw her as a normal person. For crying out loud, we spent days talking, eating, sharing secrets, even trading dirty jokes. The sentiment of inadequacy I'd experienced when we'd met overcame me again. Who was I to deserve her company? She was a holy prophet. I was a complete loser.

—Thoughts of James Hunter, Hocmar 28, 2134, on the Nirnivian calendar

People bowed and showed no signs of getting up. If the attention had been directed at him, James would have blushed to death. Most stared at Rose as if a miracle stood before the group. For a few, her presence proved too intimating, and they instead gazed at the floor. Everyone displayed nervousness, from gaping mouths to fidgeting and even trembling.

Still masked, James leaned toward who he hoped was Brucie. "They, uh, look like they've seen a ghost or something."

"Hey, man, don't ya forget, Rose didn't get outta Valardir fo' years. Well, except when she saved ya, but nobody here knows 'bout that, ya know."

"Yo... Your Ho... Holiness." Tessa's mother's voice trembled. "What bu... business brings o... one of such grace to my family?"

With a smile drawing on her face, Rose approached the stranger and extended her arm. The woman gazed at the offered hand. It almost seemed as if she dreaded bursting into flames for touching the Melkar. After a moment of hesitation, she reached and grabbed Rose's fingers. Rose motioned for her to rise.

"I come to pray with you in this darkest hour. Please, do not kneel before me, for tonight we implore Ulgorack's mercy as equals."

The crowd obeyed, though several hesitated. A tall man with black hair and an incredulous expression said, "Your Holiness, how did you find out?"

As if to answer the question, a girl rushed into the room. She dashed straight to Rose. Numerous outreaching hands attempted seizing her, but she ran too fast and avoided them. Once near enough, she grasped Rose's leg and jumped around in excitement.

"You came!" the kid yelled in a high-pitched tone. "I knew you were a nice lady!"

"Anita!" The mother pointed a lecturing index finger. "What are you doing? Show proper respect to Her Holiness!"

While she caressed Anita's cheek, Rose giggled. "Such a beautiful child!" Then she picked Anita up and hugged her. "Don't worry about protocol. Children are always welcome with me."

"Please save her," Anita sobbed. "Save Tessa."

"If I had the power to cure your sister, I would without a second thought. I can only pray for her well-being, dear Anita. I hope that will be enough."

The tall black-haired man nodded as if he had figured out a crucial detail. James assumed him to be the father. "Anita! You sent that letter, didn't you? We told you not to!"

"Your Holiness"—the mother touched her husband's arm—"we're very grateful for your help, but you shouldn't be here! It's too dangerous, and you're too important. If something happened to you tonight, we would never forgive ourselves."

"Please, do not scold Anita. She did nothing wrong. Should the worst happen, it would be my fault. I came here of my free will and accept the risk." Rose paused. "However, my being here puts you in danger. If you prefer I leave, please say so. I won't take offense."

"Your Holiness, you've blessed us with your presence. I understand that prayer might not work, but we're desperate. I can't ask you to stay, but I can't ask you to leave either. The decision is yours."

"Let us pray, then." Rose put Anita on the floor and glanced toward her companions. "You guys should get out of those robes. It must be hot."

Now that she mentioned it, yeah...

—Thoughts of James Hunter, Hocmar 28, 2134, on the Nirnivian calendar

Rose's escorts consisted of bodyguards except for two people, James and Madeleine. When Madeleine removed her disguise, excited whispers spread through the crowd. The dad swallowed hard. "Oh, I must be dreaming! The holy prophet and the head priestess. We are beyond blessed tonight! Thank you for coming to our aid."

Madeleine offered a bow of the head. "It is an honor to be here with Her Holiness. I am merely performing my duties, there is no need for thanks."

Anita's father then introduced himself as Mark and his wife as Marie. Rose presented James only as Hunter; she followed her self-imposed rule of calling him only by his last name to the letter.

Mark scrutinized me and realized he had seen me somewhere before, but couldn't tell where. I gulped. I hadn't forgotten what had happened when I'd arrived in this universe. Of course, I didn't think they'd attack me with Rose there, but I chose not to test my theory.

—Thoughts of James Hunter, Hocmar 28, 2134, on the Nirnivian calendar

"You..." Mark scowled. "You were on TV. You're the human!" James cringed. "Well, I must admit I wasn't thrilled when I heard, but to have a visitor from another world taking the time to come here for my daughter... I'm touched."

James scratched behind his ear. "Um, it's the least I can do." The response shouldn't offend anyone, so he judged it safe.

It wasn't as bad as I feared. Sure, I can't say they welcomed me with open arms, but they weren't rude either. They had concerns about me, but they appreciated that I prayed with them for the sake of a stranger. After the pleasantries were done, we headed toward the girl's room. What a sad sight—an unconscious child covered in lesions. Despite this, Tessa was a cute kid and I hoped she'd be okay. People formed a circle around the bed and held hands.

—Thoughts of James Hunter, Hocmar 28, 2134, on the Nirnivian calendar

"Hunter!" Rose stared at James as he remained far from the group. "Don't be shy, join us."

His cheeks reddened. "Uh, but... I don't know the words..."

"Don't worry, you can't harm anything. Even if you say gibberish, it won't make the prayer any less effective. It won't help, but it won't hurt. Please, take place in the circle and listen. If the words become familiar, feel free to recite them."

"Rose speaks the truth, my child." Madeleine let go of the person on her left and presented her palm to James. "Do not worry. Take my hand and follow our lead."

And that's how I ended up sandwiched between Madeleine and a random guy. At first, I kept my mouth shut. Everybody closed their eyes, so I closed mine too. Eventually, I grew comfortable enough to join in. We prayed and prayed for hours. In the middle, I opened my eyes and saw Rose for a second or two. She was so beautiful. Her white wings, her enthralling voice... could she actually be an angel from heaven? For a moment, I believed so. No question, this was the most intense religious experience I'd ever had. I could have bathed in her splendor forever, but I remembered I wasn't supposed to look and I closed my eyes again. That took an effort, I'll admit that.

Don't ask me if we deserved any credit, but Tessa regained consciousness and squealed. The group rejoiced, thanking Ulgorack and Rose. Everyone claimed she had performed a miracle. While Rose denied it, I doubt she persuaded anyone. Tessa appeared disoriented and couldn't talk, so I wasn't convinced she'd be all right. The others promised that in a couple of days, she'd be running around and playing with Anita. The moment Tessa woke up, Rose prepared to leave. Marie and

Mark tried convincing her to stay and celebrate, but she refused to put them in danger for longer than necessary.
—Thoughts of James Hunter, Hocmar 28, 2134, on the Nirnivian calendar

Rose's escorts grabbed their black cloaks and masks, except for James. Overwhelmed by the events he had witnessed, he stood with his mouth gaping as everyone dressed. That image of Rose praying burned in his memory forever. Trading dirty jokes with her wouldn't be so easy in the immediate future. He'd never considered her to be a real prophet, and while he still didn't, the possibility seemed far more genuine than before.

Brucie noticed his dazed expression and patted his shoulder. "Hey, dude, now yer the one who looks like he's seen a freaking ghost."

"Um, that was..." He shook his head. "That was amazing. When Tessa opened her eyes..."

"Ah, gimme a break!" The bodyguard laughed. "Man, there was like fifty-two minutes left." A shrug came from Brucie. "Ain't even close, I tell ya. Way to kill the suspense."

"Always the critic, huh, Brucie?" Rose winked. "Can't you just enjoy the happy ending for once?"

"I'll try, I'll try."

After a scoff, Marie crossed her arms. "Perhaps it wasn't suspenseful for you, sir, but as Tessa's mother, it was more than enough for me."

"Oh yeah, don't ya mind me. I'm kidding around, ya know. That's the way God made me, and I ain't changing at my age."

Marie giggled. "My daughter's alive. Kid as much as you want, sir."

Concerned, Rose patted James's shoulder. "You sure you're okay, Hunter? You're so pale."

"Yes, don't worry. I'm, um... I've never been religious, but this is the closest thing to a proof of God's existence I've ever seen. I have to tell you, I didn't mean to, but I opened my eyes. When you were praying, you looked just like an angel."

Rose smiled at those words. Marie, however, frowned. "Angel? What is that?"

"Oh"—the alleged Melkar snapped her fingers—"angels are divine beings in his religion. They are like winged people."

And then I was no longer blind. I had solved the riddle. Nobody noticed, but I trembled out of shock. Goose bumps spread over my body. Rose had lied. She'd lied about the first human. Doctor Death was right. It was obvious, and I should have realized from the beginning.

When I met Rose, I asked if she was an angel. She smiled and said no. Somehow I failed to grasp it then, but thinking back, that didn't make sense. Rose should have reacted like Marie. She should have been confused and wondered what an angel was, since they don't exist in this universe. But she didn't, because she knew what they were all along. The only possible reason was that Rose had already met a human. Like me, he had called her an angel.

Terror filled me and I felt betrayed. Why make up that whole story? Maybe it was nothing to worry about, but I couldn't help but suspect my supposed friends' motive. Suddenly, I wasn't sure if there was anyone I could trust. I felt alone, desperate. The truth hurt so much, I didn't want to accept it and searched for another explanation. I recalled how the old security guard had mentioned they'd discovered books in the human's backpack. What if they'd mentioned angels? On the surface, that worked, but on closer inspection, it didn't fit with the facts. When I'd asked if she was an angel, Rose had not only understood what I meant—she'd seemed nostalgic. As if my question made her both happy and sad. Why would a random book have that effect?

—Thoughts of James Hunter, Hocmar 28, 2134, on the Nirnivian calendar

Chapter 21

Couldn't believe, we're back; alive. Was so happy. Saved 'em. So proud, then...

—Thoughts of Wrathchild, Hocmar 28, 2134, on the Nirnivian calendar

Now that they had returned to the hideout, Wrathchild's pent-up stress had left her body. Though she hadn't thought the plan would work, they'd survived. She turned toward Diabo with a grin, but as thanks for the daring rescue, he slapped her in the face. While Diabo didn't use his full strength, the impact still flung Melissa to the ground, and she tasted blood.

"You bitch!" Wrathchild struggled to rise. Blood dripped from her nose; it might be broken. Diabo stepped on her back, pinning her to the floor. "Who the freak do you think you are?" Pure rage tainted his voice. "You disobeyed my orders! I told you not to come."

"But... but saved you."

"Yeah, ya did good, but you didn't stop when you were ahead!" With those words, Diabo kicked Wrathchild in the chest, sending her rolling. Now she wept openly. Melissa hadn't cried like that since Sebastian and Molly.

"I ordered ya to blow the place up. You disobeyed again! Freaking bitch. You could've killed Doctor Death and didn't! Who do you think you are, Melissa? Who do you freaking think you are? You think you can disobey me without consequences? Lemme spell it out. You ain't special. You're just another thug. Never think you're more."

Melissa attempted to reply but ended up whimpering instead. Her whole body ached. She felt around her mouth with her tongue and discovered a gap in the upper row of teeth. The previous blow had broken a tooth. In addition, Diabo had cracked a rib at the least. He walked toward her, no doubt intending to strike again, but Stalker jumped in between, preventing the attack.

"Boss... please stop or you're gonna kill her. Yeah, she made a mistake, but I'm sure you can understand why. That couldn't have been easy—"

"There ain't nothing easy 'bout this business! We gotta do what we gotta do!" On that note, Diabo shoved Stalker aside. Then he lifted Melissa by the collar. "Don't ya dare disobey again, Melissa. Don't ya dare. My patience has limits." Furious, Diabo threw Wrathchild on the floor. She landed with a moan.

Was my turn in "clinic." Everything hurt. Worst part, didn't visit. Not once. Didn't care 'bout me. But, cared 'bout him.

—Thoughts of Wrathchild, Hocmar 28, 2134, on the Nirnivian calendar

***

With a yawn, Plague instructed his text-to-speech software to tell him the time. That act confirmed he worked well beyond midnight. No wonder he had grown tired; between his age and his ravaged body, such long hours were far too demanding, so he decided he'd go to bed. First, he stretched his arms, getting ready to move. Then he stood up and almost powered off his computer. That was when something blinked on the screen. Thanks to his poor vision, he failed to discern what had happened. No worries—

in a second, his TTS system's robotic voice informed Plague that Stalker was attempting to contact him.

While tempted to ignore the call and communicate with Stalker in the morning, Plague figured the fact that the master of camouflage called him this late implied an urgent matter. After an annoyed groan, he returned to his seat. Once comfortable, he entered the proper command, and the familiar blur representing Stalker appeared on the monitor.

Before Plague had the chance to utter a word, he yelled, "You bastard! You lied to me!"

"Uh, what are you talking about?"

The blur performed a motion suggesting Stalker struck his desk, and the resulting bang confirmed it. "That goddamn Alcharia virus! You said you faked the samples, but you gave us the real deal!"

"What?" Confused, Plague recoiled. "But... why would you think that?"

"Because if they were fake, why would Doctor Death show up?"

"Wait, hold on. How about you start from the beginning?" As instructed, Stalker recounted in detail the events of the mission. As he listened, a slight tremble assailed Plague. "It doesn't make any sense. That stuff was basically colored water. There's no way any kid got sick because of it."

Silence fell between the two as they contemplated the situation. Eventually, Stalker said, "Um, you sure you didn't mix up the vials or something?"

"Oh, please, I'm not that dumb. I destroyed the Alcharia samples before I created the new ones."

"So, you're telling me that Doctor Death went to the hospital for no reason?"

"Looks like it. I guess someone found out about our plans, and he used the opportunity to kill you and Diabo."

"Yeah, sure, but why risk coming in person?"

Plague swallowed hard. "I dunno, Stalker. I don't understand how that bastard's brain works."

"Well, whatever's going on here, I don't like it."

"Me neither. Doing something so pointless doesn't sound like Doctor Death. It's part of some kind of plan, I guarantee it." Plague paused. "At least he sort of did us a favor. Now Diabo won't ever suspect we double-crossed him."

"Yeah, but why would that freaking cyborg do that fer us?" To this question, both failed to provide an answer. Plague suspected he'd spend the night awake in bed trying to find one.

Chapter 22

I didn't say a word during the return trip. The others figured I was shocked by the miracle I had witnessed. That suited me. I wanted no one to know the real reason. I feared Rose's reaction. I was scared—terrified, even, for my life. Rose... Brucie... Janice... Mr. and Ms. Ricdeau... I'd been with them for months. I trusted them, considered them friends. Now everything was in question. If they found out I'd discovered their lie, what would they do? Imprison me? Kill me? Apologize and explain? Ignorance was torture, and part of me felt like confronting them to find out the answer. Still, a bigger part was too afraid to do that. Hey, I'm a coward, I admit it. As soon as we arrived in Valardir, I pretended I was tired and went to my room. There, I lay in bed awake.

—Thoughts of James Hunter, Hocmar 28, 2134, on the Nirnivian calendar

James suffered another night of tossing and turning without enjoying a single minute of sleep. Whenever he drifted toward slumber, his brain replayed the memory of his first encounter with Rose. Then the same questions overcame him one after the other. He glanced at his alarm clock often. The hours crawled by at a slow pace.

Eventually, when the display indicated six in the morning, James sat up with a groan and rubbed his brow. A headache assailed him as well as a soreness in his throat. Whenever he slept poorly, the symptoms of a cold showed themselves. Beyond that, he endured dry eyes as his vision blurred due to drowsiness. Exhausted, James debated remaining in bed but wondered if there'd be any point. No doubt he'd stay wide awake once more. Then a blue flash drew his attention.

The burst of light vanished as soon as it had appeared. Confused, James tilted his neck and scratched his head. A second later, the flash repeated, and adrenaline surged through his veins. Now far more energetic, James hopped to his feet. Curious, yet filled with apprehension, he advanced toward the source at a slow pace. That led him to his desk. Once close enough, he discovered a blinking light on his minicomp. Not quite thrilling in theory, but that had never happened before.

After a brief hesitation, James's trembling fingers grasped the device. Almost immediately, the screen turned on, revealing Doctor Death. For the first time in his life, witnessing the disfigured shape pleased James.

"Hello, I planned on giving you a hint, but based on your expression, I expect it might not be necessary." The emoticon in his electronic eye morphed from a generic happy face to a grinning one. "You deduced the proof by yourself, correct?"

James nodded. "Um, maybe this isn't what you meant, but when I met Rose, I called her an angel. She shouldn't have understood, but she did." He frowned and his lips twitched. "I'm almost certain someone called her an angel before, and only a human would."

The sound of two metal objects colliding echoed as the cyborg clapped. "Excellent, James. I trusted you would ultimately solve the mystery, and you exceeded my expectations. I assumed you would ask Rose if she was an angel because the first human did exactly that. Will you now heed my warning?"

With a sigh, James shrugged. "I admit I'm worried, but I still don't trust you. Rose and the others lied, but they could have valid reasons."

"Perhaps." The mechanical man's emoji saddened. "But, alas, I predict you will soon realize those people are not your friends."

"What I don't understand is, why hide the fact that Rose met a human?"

"Because that might lead you to discover what happened between them. As a bonus, hiding the truth serves as a precaution, ensuring that you never learn of Project Ekelon. He and that horrifying plan are connected to some degree. For the moment, ignorance is favorable to your health. Perhaps later, I will be able to share the details I am aware of without risking your life. Until then, I suggest patience. Do not investigate the matter. Do not mention Ekelon to anyone."

Project Ekelon. Somehow, that sounded ominous.

—Thoughts of James Hunter, Hocmar 28, 2134, on the Nirnivian calendar

"At any rate, be careful, James. NISDA is watching you. Valardir is a high-security military facility, after all. You might not have noticed, but your room is monitored by cameras."

James gasped as beads of sweat formed on his brow. "But then they know you've—"

"No reason to be anxious. I am not an amateur. I took care of the cameras. To them, you are playing with your minicomp. I believe you have received enough revelations for the day, but more are coming. Should you ever wish to relocate to Ostark for your safety, I can arrange it. However, I am sure it is too early for you to accept such an offer. I cannot stay with you any longer, they might find out if I linger. Farewell for now."

"Wait!" James leaned forward. "Um, how did you know he called Rose an angel?"

"That is a great question. We have run out of time, but I shall return later and provide the answer. As you wait, I suggest you think about it. It is always a good idea to use your head, lest you forget how. Goodbye, James."

***

Through the whole conversation with James, the Doctor sensed the weight of his presence. The laughing fool stood in the room, watching the exchange unfold. As usual, the cyborg ignored him, declining even a glance.

"So, it begins, huh?" the coarse voice said. "Things should get entertaining soon! Gwa ha ha ha. 'Bout time if you ask me."

While the mechanical man refused to answer, he had to admit the freak spoke the truth.

Deux Ex Redux

Chapter 1

Sometimes life is stupid. Like when I suddenly appeared in this world for no apparent reason. I guess it was foolish to think it wouldn't happen again. Except this time, well, we weren't talking about a human being.

—Thoughts of James Hunter, Hocmar 28, 2134, on the Nirnivian calendar

***

Kotar 1, 2134, on the Nirnivian calendar

After she put her final dot, Rose rested her pen upon the desk. Her muscle had grown stiff from sitting and writing for hours. With a moan, she got out of her chair and stretched her arms. The deed done, she then massaged her neck. Though Kristina cautioned she should take breaks during her task, Rose failed to heed her warning. Not that the assistant followed her own advice. Even now, the blond woman toiled on her minicomp, preparing for the upcoming event. She didn't indulge in a single pause either.

The first draft finished, Rose needed to review it. Under normal circumstances, she'd wait at least a day before editing. The delay helped distance herself from her text, making it easier to spot mistakes and inconsistencies. She lacked that luxury in this case; the date of her speech grew close and other duties awaited her attention. Ideally, she would've started writing sooner, but that whole business with Tessa and Alcharia had extended her usual procrastination period.

To think a centrist priest ascending to the next level of his profession had caused such a fuss. As was customary for the Melkar, Rose would speak at the ceremony to congratulate the achievement. That the one in question ended up being Christopher Parish made the occasion special: she'd have to bring her A game. Most had assumed Christopher would never attain this honor. Becoming a high priest twice sounded impossible.

Thrice, Rose reread her script. Filled with diligence, she crossed out words and added new ones in what space remained. The result suffered in terms of legibility, a problem she intended to resolve. "All right, once I type this up on the computer I'll be done."

Without lifting her eyes from her device, Kristina said, "You've been working hard. How about I do that and you take a break?"

"Oh, thank you, but I can't ask that of you. You're at least as busy as I am."

The assistant shrugged. "Go ahead, it'd be my pleasure."

"You're sure?" Kristina confirmed by acquiescing. "No, I appreciate the offer, but I better do it myself. This thing's a mess. You might have trouble understanding."

"Please, I'm used to that. With Madeleine giving you grief, you should relax while you can."

After a nod, Rose exhaled. "Yeah, fair point."

Though she loved her mother, the head priestess could be stubborn. Christopher's ascension had left a bad taste in Madeleine's mouth, and she'd protested vehemently. Given she led the progressive branch and not the centrist one, she lacked the power to intervene. However, that didn't stop her from complaining to Rose and anyone else who'd listen. She'd even attempted to convince Galan to change his mind on several occasions. Rose expected Madeleine's ire would only grow as the date approached, and from that perspective, the chance to put the whole situation out of her head sounded appealing. Besides, she hadn't checked on Hunter in a while.

"All right, I'll leave it to you, but you're getting a day off once things calm down, and you can't skip it this time."

With a rare smile forming on her lips, Kristina winked. "Fine. Things never calm down anyway."

"Now I feel bad again."

"Don't, it's how I like it."

***

Since I realized Doctor Death had told me the truth, I stayed in my room as much as possible. I didn't want to risk bumping into anyone, least of all Rose. The thought of engaging in small talk while pretending nothing had happened left me shivering.

—Thoughts of James Hunter, Hocmar 28, 2134, on the Nirnivian calendar

Skull resting on his pillow, the familiar inner debate raged within James's mind. Rose had lied about the first human. Why? Did that mean he should heed the Ostarkiran president's warning about her? After all she had done for him, he refused to believe she might be dangerous. And yet, he had no choice but to admit that his denial proved weak, given he remained stuck in a loop, alternating between doubts and trust.

Without progress, James's brain still engaged in this vicious debate when a strident beep made his heart skip. For a second, he almost jumped to his feet and opened the door, but he stopped himself. Perhaps if he stayed in bed, the visitor would assume he slept.

Dashing his hopes, a female voice echoed from the interphone. "Hunter? Is everything okay?" Rose's voice, no question about it.

"Oh, um." He swallowed hard, but then the shadow of a plan popped into his head. "Uh, yeah"—he faked a cough—"I'm not feeling too great. I'm so tired. I must've caught something."

That was pure bullshit. Physically I was fine; I simply didn't want to see Rose or anyone else. After my realization, I felt like staying in my room forever. I couldn't pretend like everything was normal. One day I'd have to get out there, but I decided I'd delay the inevitable.

—Thoughts of James Hunter, Hocmar 28, 2134, on the Nirnivian calendar

"Oh... I planned to propose a game of Kuhard, but I guess you're not in shape for that." After hesitating, she added, "You should see Dr. Greenberg as a precaution."

James winced but kept a normal tone. "No, I'm fine. It's probably a cold."

"All right, but promise me you'll go to the clinic if it becomes worse."

"Yeah, sure!"

"Is there anything I can do for you before I leave?"

"Thanks, but no."

"Okay, I'll let you rest."

With that, the communication ended and James exhaled. Though he expected Rose would return to check on him later, he'd avoided an unpleasant conversation for now.

Chapter 2

Ever since Diabo had attacked Wrathchild, everything hurt. That proved especially true for her two cracked ribs. The boss had shown little mercy. One of his punches had caused her to lose a tooth; another had broken her nose. Her arm rested in a sling because of a dislocated shoulder. Also, while a minimal injury compared to the rest, Melissa had twisted her ankle when a vicious blow had propelled her to the ground, and now she limped.

Most of her days Wrathchild passed lying on a stretcher, the only sort of bed BBR could provide thanks to a lack of resources. The slightest movement brought a burst of pain, and even when she remained immobile, her whole body ached. The painkillers helped somewhat, but not much. As that thought came to mind, Wrathchild realized she must be due for her next dose. With a moan, she sat up and reached for the two capsules waiting on a nearby table. As she stared at them, a nostalgic smile grew on her face. Though much smaller, they resembled the big blue pills she'd hated taking as a child. That memory reminded her of her mother and, filled with sorrow, she chased it away. Nothing good would come from reminiscing about the past. Instead, Melissa swallowed her medicine with a gulp of water.

The deed done, Wrathchild intended to attempt a nap when the sound of static echoed from her radio. Soon after, a gruff voice followed. "Hey, Wrath, you hear me?"

No question who attempted to contact her—she'd recognize his voice anywhere. "Plague. You doing well?"

The decrepit mutant chuckled. "Heh, I'm the one who should ask, but yeah, I'm fine. I wanted to check on you sooner, but things were busy. How are you feeling?"

"Okay."

"Kid, I want you to know both Stalker and me are pissed 'bout what he did to you. Diabo needs to calm the freak down. He crossed the line." Several coughs interrupted his words. "Ah, who am I kidding? He shat all over it."

Rang true. Believed him. Yet, sensed something in tone. Had to ask.

> —Thoughts of Wrathchild, Hocmar 28, 2134, on the Nirnivian calendar

"Think should've?" Then, realizing that might not be clear, she added, "Kill Doctor."

Plague sighed, and Wrathchild imagined him shaking his head. "Listen, Wrath, that bastard screwed us over. Stalker, Diabo, and me, we're all ready to die if it means bringing him down with us. Besides, my family's dead 'cause of him, so yeah, I kind of wish you blew him up."

Knew that. Maybe right; should've. Couldn't.

> —Thoughts of Wrathchild, Hocmar 28, 2134, on the Nirnivian calendar

Melissa whimpered. "Sorry."

"Don't be. I understand why you didn't, and I'm not mad about it. You still have a soul, we don't, and I can't blame you for that." He paused for a second. "In fact, I envy you."

Still failed Diabo's eyes. After attack, shouldn't care. But did.

> —Thoughts of Wrathchild, Hocmar 28, 2134, on the Nirnivian calendar

Chapter 3

Kotar 3, 2134, on the Nirnivian calendar

From her seat in the war room, Nicky noted the large number of empty desks and stations. Fewer people than usual manned this most important location. Based on the rumors going around concerning budget issues, the lack of staff might become the new normal. That didn't surprise Nicky. The failed security improvements had cost far too much, and that was only part of their money troubles. The war room served as the heart of Valardir. Everything in the complex could be monitored and micromanaged from here. As such, it played a crucial role in the military compound's operation. Should the reduced personnel prove permanent, she hoped it wouldn't negatively impact their—

A blaring alarm interrupted Nicky's reverie. The sudden sound startled her, and her heart jumped. She debated covering her ears but chose not to. Almost immediately, her accelerated pulse returned to normal as she focused. Panic never helped in critical situations, and her training had taught her how to resist its appeal. Around her, Nicky noticed a similar reaction from her colleagues. They exchanged worried glances, gasped, swallowed hard and so on, but soon reverted to a stone-faced facade, redoubling their concentration.

At the moment, Nicky was the highest-ranked officer present, so she asked, "What happened?"

"We're not sure," a soldier named Theresa answered. Other than somewhat faster-than-expected speech, she displayed no signs of nervousness. "The systems are reporting an intrusion in sector 5-06B."

Surprised, Nicky frowned. That was down on level five. How would an intruder get so far before triggering an alarm? Unease filled her as she wondered if Ostark had somehow mounted a stealth attack on them. That would be a major accomplishment on their part, and an immense falling for NISDA. One thing was for sure—they had to protect Her Holiness at any cost.

Clicking sounds echoed as Theresa typed at a frantic pace. "I'm pulling up camera footage now. Should be here in three... two... one..."

As promised, the image on the main screen changed. Nicky's eyes widened as she covered her mouth with her palm. "Dear Ulgorack!"

***

Daniel Ricdeau stretched his arms, and a yawn escaped his lips as he exited the corridor. The Koporal walked beside him, arms crossed. A familiar scowl adorned Ron's brow as he said, "Well, that was painful."

Daniel nodded in agreement. Both had spent over an hour discussing NISDA's finances with their treasurer and accountants. As expected, the strike and the revised contract they'd drafted had taken their toll money-wise. Of course, they'd studied the budget beforehand and prepared in consequence, but even their conservative estimates had proven too optimistic. The security enhancements had to go—that had been obvious from the start, and so they'd planned a scaled-down version. Even this ended up being beyond their means, however. Based on what the bean counters had just told them, it seemed they'd have to make do with their current measures. Many critics judged their proposed improvements unnecessary given Stalker had only accessed level one. Hopefully their detractors were right.

"We'll manage somehow." Daniel rubbed his chin. "Here's an idea—how about you donate next year's salary too?"

A humorless chuckle slipped out of Ron. "Heh, lead the way and I'll follow!"

"Oh yeah? I might take you up on that if—" A strange blurriness accompanied by multicolored flashes of lights appeared several feet ahead of them. The walls, floor and the air itself twisted and distorted. A piercing headache assailed Daniel, presumably a symptom of this unsettling phenomenon. To counter the discomfort, he shielded his eyes.

What was happening? Had old age caught up to him? Did he finally suffer a stroke because of the constant stress he endured? Or perhaps some other brain trauma? Those possibilities sounded genuine, but the fact that Ron also obscured his vision and shouted "What the freak!" reduced their credence. His Koporal's reaction made Daniel exhale in relief, but then he tensed up. Was this a ploy orchestrated by Doctor Death? At last, the view returned to normal. Great, except a large black animal occupied the void before them.

Paralyzed by shock, Daniel observed the creature with his mouth gaping. He had seen nothing like it. Larger than a morglar and covered in dark scales instead of fur, the beast aimed its round iris-filled golden eyes on the two men. For now, it remained immobile, studying its potential prey while tilting its head. Daniel stared at its sharp claws. No doubt the talons could slice both their skin and innards in one swipe, reducing them to shreds.

Sweat, as well as goose bumps, covered Daniel. The monster chose that moment to let out a furious roar that caused him to step backward. In addition, the growl exposed huge yellowish teeth stained by what Daniel assumed to be dried blood. Despite the distance, the stench of the beast's breath made him retch, though he somehow managed not to vomit. His only consolation was that this couldn't be part of an Ostarkiran attack. And that implied... a visitor?

"Oh crap!" Ron gulped. "We're screwed."

"Another human doesn't sound so bad right about now, does it?"

"Nah, I'd take about a thousand of 'em."

On that note, Daniel reached for his firearm. He lacked an automatic weapon, but a pistol hung on his belt. It served as a symbol rather than a true means of self-defense. His fighting days were long gone. Still, he possessed more than enough experience. Though he aimed, he never pulled the trigger. Two soldiers rushed to their side, firing their machine guns. More approached from the creature's flank, catching it in a pincer. A flurry of bullets struck the beast, yet it showed little reaction other than more roars. The scales remained intact, and not a trace of blood appeared. Then a man yelled, "Commander Ricdeau, get out of here! We'll handle it!"

For a fraction of a second, Daniel considered protesting. He was supposed to give the orders here! In the end, reason prevailed, and he fled, trailed by Koporal Tigh.

***

Nicky cringed at the image on the screen. The sounds of machine-gun fire resounded through the speakers, the target being an enormous black animal the likes of which Nirnivia had never witnessed. Despite the constant assault, its body remained unwounded. Not even a single drop of blood acknowledged the attack. The bullets' only effect turned out to be roars and growls, but Nicky sensed no pain from these howls, just anger. As if to confirm her suspicion, the beast pounced forward. While airborne, it slashed a soldier with its paw. A torrent of blood accompanied the sharp claws tearing through his flesh. The man screamed and collapsed. Nicky covered her mouth and gasped.

The others kept firing, hoping to distract the creature. Their colleague had suffered a grievous wound, but there might be a slight chance he'd survive if given immediate medical care. Alas, the onslaught didn't injure the monster, much less stop it. The beast continued hacking and slashing its victim without mercy. No one could sustain such evisceration and survive. A furious female voice yelled, "You bastard!"

Then a woman soldier positioned at the animal's flank grabbed her knife. Bullets caused no damage, so it seemed she'd settled on another approach. Fingers wrapped around the handle, she dashed toward the beast. Nicky clutched her fists. "No, don't!" But, of course, she couldn't hear. Once she got within range, the monster swung its tail. The appendage's tip comprised a ball of spikes. In one swipe, the biological flail decapitated the soldier. With a shudder, Nicky averted her gaze.

A goddamn visitor had appeared in Valardir. Worse, level five. Both the Commander and the Koporal were absent, as was anyone else who outranked her, like David. No time to wait for a superior to return. The whole room awaited Nicky's command. She had little choice but to lead to the best of her abilities. She lacked training for such a situation, so she'd have to improvise. The beginning of a plan formed in her mind.

Nicky cleared her throat. "Send a message on the interphone warning everyone on level five to evacuate ASAP to either area 5-13D or level four. Play it on a loop. We'll trap that thing in 5-06B with the blast shutters." Valardir had special partitions that sealed off different sections in case of an intrusion, though Nicky didn't remember using them during her service. Hopefully, they'd perform as intended. "Bullets are ineffective and explosives too damaging, so we'll try tranquilizer darts, see if we can put it to sleep. Also, have Her Holiness escorted to level four. In fact, get everyone out of there. I want that place emptied—it's a top priority."

"Why? They're safe there."

Nicky stared at the man who'd objected, and he bent his neck in apology. No point in disciplining him right now; she had other matters to attend to. Still, while asking had been a breach of protocol, she preferred keeping her subordinates informed so they knew she deserved their trust.

"Yes, but it's not about that. That monster is close to Her Holiness's quarters. If we're lucky, we can lure it in there and lock it up. It's not a critical area. We can leave that thing there for days if we have to."

"Good idea!" a familiar voice said. Nicky turned and saw the Commander standing there along with the Koporal. She exhaled in relief before saluting. Everyone else joined in on the gesture. "But we can do one better."

A smile appeared on Nicky's face as she realized what he meant. "Her Holiness's garden!"

Daniel pointed an impressed index at her and winked. "Exactly! We can let that beast starve for years if necessary. Poor Rose will miss her garden, but"—he shrugged—"she can have it back once that monster dies of hunger. Besides, better that than losing access to everything." On that note, he walked toward Nicky. Once near, he extended his hand. After an instant of hesitation, she shook it. "Excellent job, Nicky. I'm proud of you."

She felt her cheeks blush. "Thank you, sir!"

Chapter 4

In her office, Rose reread the piece of paper she held for the second time. Once done, she gave Kristina an impressed glance. Though the blond assistant sat right next to her, she failed to notice given her intense focus on her minicomp. As always, Kristina had performed an impeccable job when she'd typed Rose's upcoming speech. Frankly, it was perfect. No need for further revision.

The task finished, Rose stretched her arms. In doing so, she peeped at Brucie. The bodyguard leaned against the wall cross-armed. When in the presence of outsiders, he attempted to appear serious and intimidating, but otherwise the facade reverted to his normal nonchalant self. Not that Rose minded. Perhaps feeling her eyes on him, Brucie winked, and she replied with a nod.

At that moment, Kristina said, "Councillor Carlson sent me an email. She'd like to schedule a confession."

Jade's visage popped into Rose's brain. With a single look, one could sense the compassion in the old woman's smile, yet a hard edge remained visible. No possibility of doubting her indomitable resolve. When fighting for what she believed right, Jade never backed down. Despite this, she didn't hold grudges. Why, not long ago, Rose and she had suffered a bitter argument about assisted suicide, and now she requested a confession as if nothing had happened. Councillor Carlson's devotion to her religion played a role in this, but she displayed quick forgiveness with others. Everyone made mistakes, and while she refused to let those slide, she also accepted their inevitability and showed a willingness to move on.

"I'm afraid she must wait until after the ascension ceremony or see a confessor. Personally, I suggest the latter alternative." Kristina nodded as if she'd expected that answer, and she probably had. After all these years, she understood Rose lacked the credentials necessary for that rite. If only the general population shared her comprehension. Why did they view her role as a prophet as more than it entailed? Then Kristina's minicomp beeped, interrupting her reverie.

The blond woman picked up the device. "Oh, speaking of the ceremony, I received a message from Priest Munikh." Though it demanded an effort, Rose suppressed a groan. That Munikh contacted her incessantly, most of the time relating to matters that had nothing to do with her responsibilities. Kristina frowned as she read the text, but the scowl vanished the instant she finished. "He wants your opinion on some decorations."

"That's not exactly my department."

Kristina offered a sympathetic smile. "You know how it is with Priest Munikh, he's insecure. Your approval would mean a lot to him."

"Like everyone, he overvalues my opinions."

Of course, she appreciated the respect she received from her followers, but their reverence exceeded ridiculousness. After a sigh, Rose grabbed Kristina's minicomp and browsed through the images. She studied the multicolored ribbons, balloons and streamers congratulating Christopher for his accomplishment. Some might judge the effect somewhat tacky, but it seemed festive to her.

"Looks good! Tell him I'm impressed."

"Oh, you've just made Munikh's day!" Kristina giggled.

"Great, I—" Before she finished the sentence, the door opened by itself. Rose gasped along with Kristina. As for Brucie, however, he concealed his shock and sprang forward, gun in hand. To open the office door without their permission required a high-level security clearance. This meant the intruder was likely a NISDA officer, but a good bodyguard wouldn't take that chance and so Brucie acted. Soon, his large body shielded both Rose and Kristina.

As expected, Brucie's action proved futile. Two NISDA soldiers entered the chamber and Rose recognized them. Under normal circumstances, they lacked the rank to force open her door, so she assumed something serious had happened. The fear on their faces confirmed her suspicion.

Rose's heartbeat accelerated, and she touched her cheek with her fingers as one of them said, "Your Holiness, we have to take you to level four right now! Bring as little as possible, it's an emergency."

"What's going on?"

A female voice answered, "We'll explain along the way—we have to hurry."

***

It had been a while since I'd started pretending I was sick. Up to that point, Rose had bought it, but it wouldn't last. In fact, I was surprised she hadn't forced Dr. Greenberg on me yet. Whenever that happened, the jig would be up. No doubt Greenberg would see right through me. Ah well, just another worry to share with Nadia's picture.

—Thoughts of James Hunter, Hocmar 28, 2134, on the Nirnivian calendar

James lay on his bed wrapped in his blankets. Head resting on his pillow, he stared at the ceiling while he pondered his angelic realization. Nothing came of it, except the same questions circling in his mind. It was point-less; he realized that.

Though he only feigned sickness, James didn't feel so well. All the worries he endured affected his health. Beyond that, he lacked food. Given he avoided exiting his room, he had limited supplies. Since his appetite had vanished, he wouldn't eat more if offered the choice. The prospect of eating left him cold even when his stomach grumbled, which lately, it didn't anyway. Hunger gave way to that strange nausea one experienced when underfed for a while. What a counterintuitive symptom; humans were such peculiar beasts.

Between his anxiety and poor nutrition, James wondered how long it would be before his act morphed into a real disease. As he pondered that thought, the door slid open and two soldiers rushed inside. James sat up and recoiled. "What the hell?"

At first, I figured Rose had sent them to take me to Greenberg, but that seemed too extreme, so I reconsidered. Swallowing hard, I realize NISDA must've discovered I'd talked to Doctor Death, and those guys had come to arrest me. I almost confessed and begged for mercy. Good thing they spoke before me.

—Thoughts of James Hunter, Hocmar 28, 2134, on the Nirnivian calendar

"Sorry, Mr. Hunter, but we have to evacuate everyone out of Her Holiness's quarters. There's an emergency."

It sounded like he wasn't in trouble, and so James exhaled in relief. A second later, he grasped the implication and tensed up. What had happened? Was Rose safe? An uncomfortable sensation invaded James's throat. Even after discovering her lies, he cared about her. "Uh, is, ah, um..."

Though he lacked eloquence, the soldier understood and nodded. "Yes, Her Holiness is okay. In fact, everyone here is. It's the rest of level five that's"—he waved his own words away—"never mind, we'll explain later."

Chapter 5

The soldiers took me to the elevator, and we went to level four. They told me a new visitor had appeared in Valardir. That was insane. This time, it wasn't a human but rather a savage beast. They might've been exaggerating, but they said it had survived an assault with machine guns. That sounded downright impossible. Anyway, high command decided to trap that monster in Rose's garden so it couldn't damage any critical system. That seemed unnecessary since I figured they'd have it dead soon. How hard could killing an animal be?

—Thoughts of James Hunter, Hocmar 28, 2134, on the Nirnivian calendar

James arrived at the door where Rose, Brucie, and Kristina stood. The instant she noticed him, Rose gasped and then sprang forward. She reached for his wrists and seized them as if she wished to confirm his presence by touch. Meanwhile, Brucie offered a wave. As for Kristina, James admitted he might've imagined it, but her frown seemed to intensify the second she saw him.

"Hunter!" The prophet's voice trembled. "Thank God you're all right!"

"Um, I'm glad you're okay too."

It appeared she didn't notice his reply, for she kept going. "They said they'd keep that monster out of my quarters until everyone left, but you never know what can happen." Rose shivered. "Once, I heard of a visitor that teleported. It wasn't dangerous, and it died within five minutes. Oxygen was toxic to it. Too bad that doesn't seem to be the case for this creature, and if it has that ability, we're in terrible danger no matter where we hide."

"Yeah, that's scary."

Kristina scoffed, then shook her head. "There's no reason to panic. Nothing indicates it can do that. I'm sure it would've done so already. I mean, they've been shooting at the freak since it arrived."

"Yes, but bullets aren't hurting it, so maybe it just didn't bother. How can we tell?" Then Rose fixated on James and scowled. "Hunter, you look terrible." To put himself in her shoes, James recalled his appearance from when he'd last glimpsed a mirror. A paler-than-usual complexion along with bloodshot eyes and an untrimmed beard... yep, she had a point. "You should go to the clinic. I can have someone take you there right away."

He scratched behind his ear. "Oh, uh, no, I'm fine."

James's palms grew sweaty as he contemplated the possibility that Rose would force him to go, resulting in Greenberg discovering his deception. Luck turned out to be on his side as echoing footsteps distracted them. Commander Daniel Ricdeau walked toward the group, hands joined behind his back. Though his eyes were closed except for a slit, James sensed the man detected every subtle detail concerning everybody present, a quirk of his mutation.

"Hi, guys, I thought I'd check on you. Glad to see you're okay." He chuckled. "I hope the sudden evacuation didn't cause any trouble."

"Dad!" Rose leaned forward and swallowed hard. "Are the rumors true? Did three people die already?" No answer proved necessary. The manner in which Daniel furrowed his brow and dropped his shoulders served as confirmation. "Oh dear Ulgorack!" Rose gulped and rested her hands against her cheek. "What kind of animal can do this?"

Daniel shuddered. "It's a monster straight out of a nightmare. Well, I better return to the war room." The Commander pointed at the door behind them. "You should have everything you need for work in that office. Hopefully, this setback won't slow you down. I know you have to get ready for the ceremony."

I didn't like being trapped somewhere with Rose, not to mention Kristina, but they weren't giving me a choice. For a moment, I considered going to the clinic instead. But no, then Greenberg would tell her I wasn't sick.

—Thoughts of James Hunter, Hocmar 28, 2134, on the Nirnivian calendar

A roll of the eyes came from Rose. "Let me guess, you heard from Mom?"

"You bet!" Daniel burst into laughter and slapped his knee. "The way she's yelling about it, how could I not? She's furious."

"Yes, I'm aware." The annoyance in Rose's voice didn't escape James.

"Oh, she's making your life difficult. Don't be too hard on her. Your mother is stubborn, maybe even unreasonable, but you have to understand her point of view." Daniel patted her shoulder. "Christopher, he hurt her and her family."

Rose exhaled. "Of course I understand, but there's more at stake here than a distant feud. Especially when Christopher admitted his mistake decades ago."

"I suppose you're right, but forgiveness doesn't always come as easy as it should. Bah, everything will work out somehow. Oh, and, princess, I'm sorry about taking away your garden, but it's temporary."

After a snort, Rose dismissed the notion with a wave. "Please, that's the least of my concerns. Make sure that beast hurts no one else, that's what's important."

***

After Rose assured her father she didn't mind losing her garden given the circumstances, he began to leave. In all honesty, that sacrifice saddened her more than she wanted to admit. She loved her garden; it served as the lone sanctuary in her confined existence. There, she could pretend that she wasn't stuck in an underground prison. On good days, she even believed it for a second or two. Still, in the current situation, she admitted the selfishness of her feelings. No question dealing with the visitor while avoiding casualties was a far greater priority than her enjoying a fake sun.

As her dad advanced toward the elevator, a violent headache overcame Rose. She moaned in pain. The corridor spun around her. The people distorted. She stepped forward and stumbled, but somehow she didn't fall. Garbled sounds reached her ears—probably worried exclamations from her friends. Then everything turned black.

Soon, an unfamiliar candlelit room replaced the darkness. Numerous well-dressed individuals filled the chamber. So many tears... everyone cried. In the distance, a mass of people surrounded Daniel and Madeleine. The head priestess sat in a chair, hunched and concealing her face with her palms. Despite this, Rose heard her sobbing. Beside her stood a pale-as-snow Daniel. Streams of tears tumbled down his cheeks. Only once before had Rose witnessed him in such a devastated state. And behind them, that winged woman... herself, wearing black. Tradition dictated the Melkar always wore a white dress. That Madeleine had let her break the rule seemed impossible. Then a voice said: "No, not them..." She recognized her doppelganger, the one she spoke to in the mirror. "Look to the right."

Rose obeyed and discovered Brucie kneeling before a coffin. His head rested on his hands, which clutched the edge of the wooden box. Like the others, he mourned. Rose approached. "It ain't fair! Shoulda been there, ya know. If I had, ain't no way... ain't no way I'd let that thing..." The bodyguard whimpered, never finishing his sentence. With a sickening sensation filling her stomach, Rose took another step and recognized the deceased: Janice.

Suddenly the world returned to normal. Feminine hands grasped her, explaining how she remained on her feet. Soon, she realized they belonged to a worried Kristina. Meanwhile, James and Brucie kept asking if she was okay, and the blond man helped Kristina support Rose's weight. Daniel ran back toward them, screaming, "Princess!"

"I'm okay! Everything's fine!" She took a few deep breaths. "I'm just exhausted because of stress."

With a concern-filled expression, Daniel touched her shoulder. "Are you sure?"

"Yes."

Indeed, she felt like her good old self. No sign of weakness or fatigue, but those images still chilled her heart. For certain, they had to be a mere delusion brought on by her sudden faintness. Except, it was so real. Not just visually, but the sounds, the voices, the smells... what if she'd received a vision? No, that was ridiculous. She wasn't the Melkar; and yet...

"Dad, are you planning on having Janice help fight that thing?"

"Well, she's one of my best"—he performed finger quotes—"'men,' so yes."

That was logical. Besides, if he shielded Janice from danger, he'd receive accusations of favoritism. Should he disregard the criticism, Janice wouldn't cooperate. She'd refuse to stay behind while her comrades accomplished their duties. That wouldn't change even if Rose warned her of the potential vision she'd endured. As Commander, Daniel could order her to stand down, but she'd never forgive him. Rose refused to cause a rift between them over a hallucination. But what if...? Even if it was a single chance out of a billion, the price of ignoring the warning proved so high. Biting her lip, Rose came to a resolution.

"Dad, I can't explain why, but take Brucie with you. Whatever happens, make sure he's always with Janice."

Daniel scowled and his mouth opened, but a second passed before he answered. "Oh, um, Brucie would be a great asset, but he's not under my command. I can't order him to battle. But, if he's willing, I won't say no to another pair of hands! What about it, son?"

The bodyguard grinned and smashed his right fist in his left palm. "Ah, freak yeah!" Perhaps realizing his lack of decorum, Brucie adopted a serious expression and saluted. "Ain't no problem fo' me, sir! Been craving sum action."

"My boy, I appreciate your can-do attitude! I'll send soldiers to watch over Rose."

Rose exhaled in relief. Though unlikely, she might've saved her sister. Then an unsettling sensation pinched the back of her neck. No vision this time, only uneasiness. "Dad, please tell me you won't fight that monster too. With your leg—"

Daniel's laughter interrupted her. "Oh dear God, no. I'm way past that, princess. That kind of hunting is a young'un's game!"

That said, Brucie and her dad left. Once they entered the elevator, an unsettling thought confronted Rose. Had she traded Brucie's life for Janice's? If so, could she live with herself? She prayed she'd made the right call.

***

Daniel Ricdeau could've cut the tension inside the war room with a knife. Everyone sat a little too straight or fidgeted too much. Even the clicking of the keyboards sounded askew, contributing to the dread-filled atmosphere. Each officer present had survived war. They had grown familiar with death. This, however, was different. In the past, they'd battled Gorumars sharing their physiology. While a treacherous enemy, people could be reasoned with. Not so this time. There would be no rules of engagement nor chance for mercy. Against a wild beast, they'd have to rely on their intellect and pray it proved as superior as they believed.

"The shit never ends, eh, Dan?" a cross-armed Ron Tigh said.

"True as a freaking bell, old friend."

"Could be worse. At least it's just a dumb animal."

Daniel shrugged. "I guess we'll see if that's the case. Nicky, is Team B done preparing the garden?"

"Not quite, sir, but almost."

"Excellent! Once they're finished, give Team A the order to attack." He frowned. "We can't lock that monster in the garden without getting it in Rose's quarters first. Thank Ulgorack it's close."

Ron groaned. "Is this crap really necessary? It's a freaking animal, how hard can it be to kill?"

"Hard enough to survive several machine guns firing at it."

"Oh yeah, the bastard's got tough skin, I'll admit that, but we got better." Tigh chuckled. "Shove a grenade up its ass and enjoy the show."

Though his lips twitched, Daniel contained the coming laugh. One of them had to appear professional as an example to their underlings. "That's a delightful idea, old chum, and I'd love to try, but with our current budget problems, I'd rather not risk damaging the complex. Don't ask me how we'd pay for the repairs."

The Koporal answered with a reluctant nod. "Yeah, fair enough. That makes things harder." He joined his hands behind his head and slumped on his seat. "Ah well, it's a good exercise for the troops!"

Chapter 6

Like her colleagues, Janice grabbed a slab of raw meat from the cooler. She shivered as the cold sensation spread through her fingers. Though not frozen, the flesh proved well below room temperature. That way it shouldn't spoil before their prey arrived.

When Janice lifted the meat, drops of blood fell on the floor, staining it. With a sigh, she then walked toward the garden. A not-quite-putrid smell reached her nostrils. While not rotten, she assumed the product lacked freshness. That made sense—why waste fresh food on a savage animal? Despite the low quality, it should satisfy that beast's needs.

Once Janice stepped inside the garden, the soft wind produced by the special fans tickled her cheeks. She even had to shield her eyes from the fake sun. A smile grew on her face. While it was far from a perfect simulation, whoever had designed this place had done a fantastic job. Had she been the one trapped within Valardir, Janice would have been driven insane. No doubt this interior paradise helped her sister avoid that fate.

After a second of observation, Janice noticed the stack of flesh her colleagues had built. It seemed silly to her to offer so much food to an animal they meant to starve. Based on what she had heard, a zoologist had been consulted and had suggested that, based on the beast's size, a significant amount of meat would be required to ensure it fell for the lure. Fair enough, except this opinion was based on the behavior of Nirnivian animals and might not correspond to a creature from another universe. Either way, Janice had no say in the final decision, so she approached the mount and dropped her own piece. The deed done, she stared at the crimson stains on her hands. "This stuff is disgusting."

A chuckle echoed. "Heh, steer clear of the cafeteria, then."

Janice fired a glimpse at the source and recognized George. She shrugged. "Hey, at least it's cooked before we eat it."

"True enough."

And that ended that pointless exchange. Really, she shouldn't complain. Team B handled the easy part. Sure, they dealt with animal blood, but Team A risked bathing in their own. If only they could use the same strategy to lure the creature into Rose's quarters. The higher-ups judged that having soldiers carrying meat where that monster lurked would only result in them being attacked anyway. They might as well mount a direct assault and pray it succeeded. Shame crept inside Janice as she considered her assignment. Not that it was her fault. They'd formed the teams at random, and she would've accepted the fight without hesitation had she been chosen. And so she chased those thoughts from her mind with an exhale.

As she headed for the exit, Brucie's large body blocked the open door. Why in the world had her dad sent him along? He wasn't a soldier. Not that she minded—he had considerable skills, and despite his less-than-charming traits, she deemed him a friend. On most occasions, anyway.

While smirking at her, Brucie tilted his neck. "Ya sure look good today babe." He whispered so the others wouldn't hear.

"You got a bloodstain fetish or something, big fellow?"

"Nah." He winked. "But I like a dirty girl."

Janice sneered, then crossed her arms. "Hope you also like harassment complaints."

"Ah, come on, gal, that ain't your style and you know it."

"You're right." With a smile, Janice formed a fist and waved it. "I'm more into using this baby."

Brucie laughed the threat away. "Ain't 'fraid o' ya. Got this sweet body armor on me."

"True, your crotch is safe for now, but you'll have to remove your protection one of these days, bud."

"Okay, fine, I'll leave ya alone, ya spoilsport."

As promised, Brucie left, freeing up the path. Janice sighed. Though she'd made her feelings clear years ago, he still tried. A harassment complaint might indeed be the sensible course of action. Except he was right: that wasn't her style. She preferred handling those types of problems on her own terms. Not that she looked down on any man or woman using the bureaucratic option—few enjoyed muscular assets comparable to hers. Besides, she actually liked having Brucie around, so she didn't want him fired.

***

While gritting his teeth, Charlie jammed the black rod he brandished into the creature's neck. Upon contact, the dark baton emitted a faint blue light, and as hoped, the beast wailed and staggered backward. Ostarkiran pain sticks—maybe not a clever name, but accurate. Nirnivian soldiers had learned of their existence during the war and confiscated a few through raids. They served as a most effective instrument of torture. Though they were unassuming in appearance, a scrape against the skin plunged the toughest Gorumar into agony. How it worked went over Charlie's head, but he'd heard they somehow activated pain receptors with a low electrical current. Because of Nirnivia's strict laws against torture, pain stick usage was illegal and so they proved mostly useless to NISDA. When facing a visitor, however, the rules didn't apply.

Right after he jabbed the animal, Charlie raised the riot shield he wielded. After his successful attack, he expected retaliation. The enemy didn't disappoint and clawed at him, leaving a scratch on the industrial-grade plastic forming his shield. Impressive that it left a mark, considering the material's strength.

Two other soldiers flanked Charlie—Daemon and Lauretta. The three of them blocked the corridor, preventing the creature from escaping. Each armed with pain sticks, they pushed it back inch by inch, their destination being Her Holiness's quarters. The doors had been kept open, and the moment that monster crossed the threshold, they'd close them from the war room. The process demanded time, but little by little they grew closer to victory. Things proceeded well considering how dangerous this plan was. Unfortunately, they'd had to fall back on this last resort. First, they had tried tranquilizer darts, but the needles had broken against the animal's armorlike skin. Other weapons, such as gas grenades, had also failed.

When Charlie or one of his teammates connected with the pain stick, the beast growled and countered. Then they lunged forward with their shields, striking the animal, thus propelling it backward. This helped speed up the process beyond what the pain sticks alone could achieve.

Through perseverance, they eventually found themselves within about fifteen feet of their goal. Sweat covered Charlie's body as he took deep breaths. The intense physical exertion explained the perspiration, but it wasn't the only reason. Stress served as a secondary cause. The fact that he put his life on the line justified his nervousness. That'd be true for anyone. Of course, thanks to the war, he had plenty of experience with that sensation and so he'd learned to manage it, but fear of death never went away. It wasn't just that, however. Something didn't feel right. Yes, the pain stick hurt the visitor. Upon contact, it wailed, moaned and retreated ever so slightly. Still, the animal recovered in an instant and showed no sign of significant damage.

All of a sudden, the beast lowered its head to the ground. Charlie scowled and opened his mouth, about to yell a warning. He couldn't tell why, but his intuition warned him of something bad coming. Then it flung its tail forward. The improvised whip smashed into Loretta's shield, shattering it. Plastic shards rained down. Charlie blocked one that headed for his face by raising his arm.

A spike scraped Loretta's throat, cutting it open. Torrents of blood poured out, and she collapsed to her knees while producing gargling noises as she attempted in vain to breathe. Nausea invaded Charlie upon the sight, but he forced himself to recuperate. As for Daemon, his pale Zarg skin reddened from anger and he yelled, "You freaking bastard!" Then he raised his pain stick and hopped toward the monster, jabbing the weapon at his target's ribs. The animal copied his strategy and also leaped. It opened its massive jaws and crushed Daemon's shield, severing his hand at the wrist. Poor Daemon screamed as the beast slammed him down with its paw before proceeding to maim and gnaw him on the floor.

With a shudder, Charlie swallowed hard. Both his colleagues were dead, no point attempting to help. His instincts had been right. The animal could've taken them down from the start, but since they posed no risk, it had played around with them instead. At least until it had become bored.

Now that he was alone, the shadow of a plan formed in Charlie's mind. With the beast occupied by Daemon, a slight gap in the corridor presented itself. Without thinking, he ran. After a few steps, something inside begged him to duck. Thanks to this impulse, the spiked tail swung into the space above his skull. He kept sprinting and soon reached the door. Then he turned around and stared at the monster.

The creature now disregarded Daemon and Loretta, instead focusing on Charlie. It let out a terrifying growl. Not fleeing demanded every remaining ounce of his courage. He had an idea—well, half of one anyway—but it posed a major risk. No question, he doubted his chances of survival. At least he'd met Her Holiness before the end. That crossed off the top item on his incomplete bucket list. He owed that James fellow for the favor, but it seemed he'd never repay it.

Gathering his resolve, Charlie seized the gun strapped to his back. Bullets failed to pierce his enemy's skin, so he wouldn't bother firing. Instead, he relied on a hunch. Those big yellowish eyes with pupils shaped like vertical slits... it might be nocturnal, and if so...

The rifle had a small light mounted on it. Charlie flicked it on and aimed the beam right into those giant eyes. As hoped, the beast averted its gaze and shook its head in every direction as it roared. Charlie kept blinding it. Its anger increased with each second until it dashed toward the source of its discomfort.

Every fiber of his being itched for Charlie to escape, but he stayed firm. He waited and waited until the beast's putrid breath stung his nostrils. That was when he rolled onto his side. Against the odds, he avoided the storming animal. Fooled, the creature kept charging right into Her Holiness's quarters, and the officers in the war room closed the gate. A loud bang echoed, accompanied by growls. Charlie imagined the source was that animal slamming into the door.

He succeeded. Charlie sat on the floor and took several deep breaths. Once he recuperated enough, he caressed his brow with his fingers as if to confirm he was intact. A giggle escaped his lips, fueled by the thrill of having survived. Then he remembered Lauretta and Daemon, and the laughs turned to tears.

Chapter 7

The reaction Charlie displayed on the screen matched the war room's mood to perfection. A dark weight lifted as the panic brought by the beast's carnage vanished. The mission had succeeded, the creature trapped in an empty sector where it couldn't harm anyone. A few people let out victorious exclamations or smiled in celebration. Yet the dread lingering in the air subdued the overall effect. Two soldiers had died. The third one made it, but barely. Though they'd attained their goal, failure loomed over them. They expected such efficiency from the Ostarkirans, but not a dumb animal.

"All right, everyone"—Daniel clapped to draw their attention—"it's not over yet."

Ron Tigh crossed his arms. "Maybe it should be! What the freak is that thing? Its skin is like tank armor!" He grimaced. "Team B is hiding in the elevator. Let's have them escape to level four."

That was accurate. In other to protect the members, they couldn't let them hang around Rose's quarters. Also, they might need to intervene to lock the creature in the garden should the plan fail. As such, Daniel had ordered the soldiers to hide inside the elevator. In there, they'd be able to either confront the visitor or flee in an instant.

Daniel rubbed his chin as he considered the Koporal's suggestion. Ron had a point—that monster had proven dangerous. And yet... "No. We can't tell how long that beast can survive, especially not since we've given the bastard a large supply of food. It might be days or weeks before it starves. I'd rather have Rose back on level five ASAP for her safety. When she moved here, NISDA gave her and Nirnivia the solemn promise that we'd guarantee her protection. We can't put the holy prophet at risk, even if it's minimal."

"Fine, but it doesn't have water. No way it'll last a week!"

A shrug came from Daniel. "And if it doesn't need to drink?"

Tigh's lips quivered as he intended to respond. In the end, he stilled his tongue, scratched his head and averted his gaze. "Son of a gun, I didn't think about that." He stopped and thought for a second before standing up and clutching his fists. "Are you ready to put Janice in danger just to keep Rose down here?"

Daniel sighed. "No, but they're safe in the elevator. That beast can't get to them. If we're lucky, it'll follow the meat trail and enter the garden by its own choice. There's no danger in keeping Team B close by in case we need their help."

After a grunt, Ron said. "Fine, I guess you're right."

That matter dealt with, Daniel returned his focus to the monitor, where he saw the visitor explore Rose's quarters. Everything they'd witnessed suggested invulnerability and yet... somehow he doubted that possibility. No animal he'd encountered enjoyed immortality. Besides, whenever he looked at the creature, his enhanced senses warned he'd missed a crucial detail he failed to decipher. With a smirk, he joined his fingers in a dome and concentrated twice as hard.

Chapter 8

Rose and Kristina worked frantically and didn't pay atten-tion to me. That was fine. I didn't want to speak with either of them; I wasn't ready yet. After a while, they took a break. Rose approached me with her mesmerizing smile. Ready or not, I had to flex my acting muscles. Damn, now I felt like Brucie...

—Thoughts of James Hunter, Hocmar 28, 2134, on the Nirnivian calendar

"Hey, Hunter, sorry for ignoring you. I have matters to handle."

"That's okay," James mumbled, head bowed down. He preferred not looking in her eyes as he feared she'd sense his uneasiness.

"Isn't it weird how that monster appeared out of no-where? We've received plenty of 'visitors' over the years, but not inside Valardir. And they say it's very dangerous. I hope everyone will be all right." Rose paused as if expect-ing a response, but James didn't reply. "Hunter, are you okay? You're so silent today." James shrugged and an-swered with a noncommittal grunt. With a frown, Rose tilted her head. "Did I do something wrong? Are you mad at me?"

I almost let it all out. How Doctor Death had revealed the truth about the first human. How she'd met him and he'd called her an angel. I intended to lay it out in the open and see her reaction. Then it'd be dealt with. I stopped myself at the last second. As much as I wanted to, I was far too terrified. I could have talked about the first human without mentioning the mechanical freak; bring up how she'd responded strangely when I'd called her an angel. That option didn't occur to me. Anyway, the point is, I've never been one to act quickly. Instead, I worry and worry until it becomes too intense and I explode.

—Thoughts of James Hunter, Hocmar 28, 2134, on the Nirnivian calendar

"No, um, it's not you... I'm not feeling well..."

To James's surprise, Kristina turned toward him and beamed. "Are you having a headache? I get tons, so I have pills. I guess they weren't made for humans, but the doctor said our physiology is almost the same, so it shouldn't hurt."

In hindsight, based on their lies, they shouldn't know much about the human body. Dr. Greenberg ran tests, but not many. They must have learned a few things from my predecessor. They weren't even doing a good job of hiding their deceptions. It was insulting, actually. "Yeah, that James fellow is dumb: he won't put the pieces together." That's true, but still...

—Thoughts of James Hunter, Hocmar 28, 2134, on the Nirnivian calendar

"Thanks, but it's not a headache. I'm, uh, tired lately, doesn't matter how much I sleep. I've been homesick too."

Rose adopted a mischievous grin. "Let's get you out of that slump." She winked at Kristina. "Two fun hot ladies can do wonders!"

The blond woman gasped, then stepped backward. "Leave me out of this! I'm not fun—or hot."

"Oh, but you are hot," Rose assured her with a giggle. Poor Kristina blushed until her cheeks attained a tint of red James had never witnessed. The prophet covered her mouth with her palm. "Oh, I'm sorry, Kristina. I've been hanging out with Brucie for too long."

"That's fine... forget it."

"Though that cute fellow Mark would agree. He has a crush on you. And he's nice. I don't understand why you won't give him a chance."

"He's..." Kristina hesitated. "Not my type."

"That's funny. When I met Miguel I thought the same, and yet..." She lifted her hand, showcasing the ring on her finger. A sudden touch of sadness tainted her voice. "Sometimes we're wrong about those things."

With a groan, Kristina crossed her arms. "Aren't we supposed to be cheering up James? Why are we talking about my love life?"

"Okay, I get the message. Again, I'm sorry. I want you to be happy, Kristina, but it's not my business." She turned toward James. "Hunter, how about going to the clinic?"

"Um, no, that's unnecessary. Listen, if you guys don't mind, I'll sleep for a bit. I'm tired. Besides, you're busy and I don't want you to waste your time on me."

Rose exhaled and rested her hand on his shoulder. "It wouldn't be a waste, I assure you, but I can tell you're not in the mood for a conversation." She frowned. "Then again, sleeping in a chair? Wouldn't you be more comfortable in the clinic? You'd have a bed."

"Um..." Searching for an excuse, James scratched behind his skull. "Hospitals kind of freak me out, so I'd rather not..."

"That's fair, I'm the same way."

Chapter 9

Inside the elevator, Janice and the others waited while watching a camera feed tracking the beast on a minicomp. The creature noticed the first meat slab, not surprising given they'd put it in plain view next to the entrance. Though the monster sniffed the raw flesh, it declined to eat, instead showing more interest in playing with the meal by hitting it with its paws. Once bored, the animal walked along the trail of blood to the following mountain of food, which was also ignored.

At least the visitor headed toward the garden, even if it showed no interest in the bait they'd laid. The major question being, would it enter the room? That remained to be seen. Janice tensed up with every step from the creature. She wasn't alone; her companions displayed similar signs of nervousness. George fidgeted with his fingers. Carla chewed on her nails. And Brucie, well, he attempted to maintain a strong facade, but she caught him biting his lip on a few occasions.

While it seemed to take an eternity, the monster soon arrived at the garden's open gate. It approached the opening and, once close, sniffed the air, then growled. Something bothered it. Based on the report from Charlie, the beast might be nocturnal given it disliked light; Janice guessed the problem was the fake sun. She grabbed her radio and sent a message demanding the war room shut off the UV lamp. Though Nicky listened, it ended up in vain. The animal kept going past the intended trap.

As Janice watched their plan fail, she cursed aloud. The others reacted in a similar manner. She heard a slap that was probably someone face-palming, and Brucie fired off a series of expletives that put her own swear to shame. Frustrated, she glimpsed the pain stick leaning against the wall. Those somewhat worked against their target, according to Charlie, and Rose needed these quarters to do her work as the Melkar and a councillor effectively. Not to mention she'd be safer here. Determination filled Janice as she reached for the torture baton, then she gazed upon her colleagues.

"Stay here, I'll take care of that freak!"

Before anyone could react, she pressed the button and rushed out. She had seen footage of her opponent in action and understood its formidable strength and speed. Confronting that thing might be insane. Several soldiers had suffered defeat, leading to a painful, pointless death. Still, her mutation granted her a special advantage compared to those who had fallen earlier. Janice deemed she had a chance, though she admitted the possibility of foolish optimism on her part.

When Janice reached the monster, it sat down and rested near the garden. It presented its back, unaware of her presence. With a smile, she tiptoed toward it, careful not to make any noise. Once within reach, Janice jabbed the animal's rear. A terrible wail echoed as her target jumped onto all fours. Then it flung its deadly tail at Janice, but she hopped out of the way. The appendage crashed into the floor, resulting in a metallic clunk.

Madness in its eyes, the beast clawed at Janice. She dodged and ran. It engaged pursuit, but its spikes penetrated the ground, slowing it down. In a mere second, it set itself free at the price of a face-first tumble. After a mocking snort, Janice exploited the short incapacitation to climb on the monster's back, riding it while standing up.

Filled with rage at the unwanted passenger, the creature roared and dashed forward, but not in a straightforward path. Instead, it twisted and turned to throw Janice off. Through the rough ride, she almost stumbled repeatedly. By extending her arms and adjusting her position according to the beast's thrusts and lunges, she somehow held on. Thank Ulgorack for the mutation she'd inherited from Daniel.

Eventually, the animal grew tired and slowed down. Though grateful for a sign of weakness, Janice kept focused on her task. She had an idea and reached for her pistol. Then she aimed for one of the large yellowish eyes and fired a single bullet. The projectile ricocheted against the glasslike surface with no damage.

"What the freak?" Could this thing be injured? Still, Janice maintained hope, for the beast's mad race brought it back to the garden.

With a laugh, Janice jumped off her mount, landed and rolled inside the chamber. The real soil forming the floor smeared her uniform, but whatever. Once on her feet, she waved the monster forward and yelled, "Come and get me!"

Eager to obey, it rushed at her. As it entered the garden, Janice sprang out, scraping the black body. When she passed by the creature, she took the opportunity to poke its spine with pain stick she still held. Another agonizing wail, which filled her with satisfaction. Too bad that ended up being her fatal mistake. The motion caused her to botch her landing. Her elbow collided with the ground and she moaned.

The beast pounced, taking advantage of Janice's injury, but at last, the officers in the war room closed the door. Too late—the gate crashed into the animal's side. While the metal structure slammed into the creature, it bent under the pressure. The door was broken. The plan had failed. At least the delay had given Janice a chance to recuperate. She attempted to stand but twisted her ankle and collapsed again as the spiked tail dropped on her. Unable to evade, Janice closed her eyes and sighed. Ah well, she'd had fun while it had lasted.

***

Praise be to Ulgorack that Brucie had followed Janice despite her command not to. Not interested in starting an argument, he'd waited in the elevator before leaving so she wouldn't notice. When he caught up, she'd already mounted the beast. Brucie let out a whistle. She had skills and guts, maybe too much of them.

Before he could do anything, Janice jumped into the garden and taunted the animal into charging her. With perfect grace, she sprang out of the chamber as it stepped inside. It remained to close the door, but the creature proved too fast. The gate slammed into its side and bent with a flurry of sparks. Worse, Janice stumbled and collapsed, unable to move. The monster flung its tail, aiming for Janice.

Fueled by a surge of adrenaline, Brucie rushed toward Janice while the appendage moved as if in slow motion. With a mighty growl and a mighty pull, he tossed her away. The attack failed, but their enemy wasn't done. Less than a second later, it lobbed its improvised whip once more. Though Brucie attempted to dodge, a spike sliced his flesh. He collapsed on his knees as pain-filled screams escaped his throat. Tears rolled down his cheeks. Then he tumbled forward face-first.

Brucie guessed he shouldn't, but a sense of morbid curiosity made him touch his injury. So warm and gooey. He grimaced in disgust. People claimed when you were dying, your life flashed before your eyes. It was a cliché he'd heard in several stories, be they fiction or the tales of Gorumars who'd survived balancing on the edge of death. For him, though, a single scene materialized in his mind, from when he had been around eight or nine, perhaps ten.

***

After a day of school, Brucie arrived home with a bloody nose, his face covered in scratches. His big brother Pierre took him to the bathroom, wiped off the blood and cleaned the gashes. At least their mom wasn't there. The poor woman suffered constant stress, a fact exacerbated by being a single mother. As such, witnessing her youngest son so battered might've sent her in a panic attack.

The truth was, Pierre had grown used to tending Brucie's wounds. Since the start of the school year, a group of bullies had targeted Brucie. In general, the mistreatment consisted of verbal abuse and the odd swirly, but occasionally, they resorted to their fists. That day, their leader had accused Brucie of taking his new toy car. The vehicle might've been stolen, but not by him. Despite his pleas, they'd struck him again and again, showing no mercy.

"Well, ya ain't too bad looking now, li'l bro," Pierre said as he admired his handiwork. "But these guys ain't leaving ya alone. I'll call the director again 'morrow."

Frustrated, Bruce crossed his arms. "What's the point?" Even at his young age, Brucie noticed he sounded whiny despite his best efforts not to. "They ain't gonna do anything." He whimpered and bent his neck. "They never do anything."

After patting his shoulder, Pierre nodded twice. "Yeah... sum things never change. The cowards did nothing back in my day either."

"So, what am I supposed to do?" Brucie sniffled, then rubbed his chin. "How 'bout ya beat 'em up? Not too hard, ya know, just 'nough so they leave me alone."

"No, Brucie."

"But why? You're big and strong! One punch and they'll never touch me again!"

"Adults can't go 'round clobbering kids. Not even if they're little a-holes like 'em guys. Ya wanna have the coppers throw me in jail?" After another sob, Brucie shook his head. "Good! Was 'fraid ya wanted to get rid o' me there." Pierre winked, confirming he jested.

"So, ya ain't gonna help me?"

Pierre scowled for a second before his mouth opened again. "Nah, I ain't said that. Come with me, won't ya?"

On that note, Pierre led Brucie to the basement. The dust lingering in the air irritated Brucie's throat, and he coughed. That place could've used a deep cleaning. Once they went down the stairs, Brucie noted the dirt-stained punching bag hanging from the ceiling. Hitting that thing was Pierre's favorite form of exercise. That said a lot, given that Pierre enjoyed all kinds of training and it served as his main hobby, or rather passion.

As he surveyed the area, Brucie glimpsed several rusted weights lying around. Tucked in a corner, he spotted a ragged bench press that gave the impression it might break should one dare lie on it. The family lacked money, and Pierre had built this makeshift gym from lucky finds at the dump and dirt-cheap second-hand equipment that barely functioned.

Pierre stepped toward the punching bag, formed a fist and struck it. A soft *plock* echoed and the sand-filled sack swayed. "Was thinking o' teaching ya how to box when ya got older, ya know? How 'bout we, uh, start now instead? Get you in shape to take care o' those bullies."

Brucie gasped and recoiled. "But, Mr. Arbuckle said violence is bad."

"Yeah, and he's right." With that, Pierre kneeled and rested his hand on Brucie's shoulder. "Ain't ever good to start a fight, Brucie. That ain't fo' good people like you or me. But, sometimes, some jerk will bring the fight to ya, like those guys at school. And when that happun, well, ya ain't got much choice but finish it or they'll trample you."

As he contemplated Pierre's words, Brucie recalled his beating and nodded. Then he frowned. "But ain't I gonna get in trouble? Ya know, like expelled or sumthing?"

"These days, schools are so messed up, I could see 'em punishing ya just 'cause you defended yourself when they wouldn't do it fo' ya like they s'posed to." He smiled. "But at least you ain't gonna be bloody no more. Can't let those thugs ruin that pretty face o' yours. Would be a shame fo' the future ladies!"

As promised, Brucie's boxing lessons started that day. It took a while, but Pierre taught him how to punch, block, dodge, and every nuance of the sport. When the bullies used violence on him again, Brucie was ready. He didn't hit them more than necessary. He didn't cause any serious injury. He did enough—the bare minimum so they'd realize he wasn't an easy target anymore.

While they had trained, Pierre had assured Brucie that most bullies were cowards. At first, Brucie had doubted this, but Pierre had explained that they usually chose the weakest prey and avoided those that presented any resistance. In his case, that turned out to be true. Those kids never bothered him again. Compared to the peace he earned, that he was expelled for three days had seemed like nothing. Too bad boxing was ineffective against this goddamn monster he now faced.

***

Janice blinked twice. She'd *survived*? Something had saved her. Once she regained some of her senses, she realized it wasn't something but rather someone. Brucie had rescued her. That douchebag was a pain in the ass, but you could always count on him to stand beside you when needed. She took a deep breath and then spotted the tail swinging back. She yelled Brucie's name, but too late. The spike struck his side, and he collapsed. Enraged, Janice screamed and shouted as she reached for her gun. Bullets had proven ineffective before, but whatever. She refused to let her friend suffer such a fate without retaliating.

The beast faced her and roared, showcasing its sharp teeth. Janice used the opportunity to aim inside its mouth. Before the mission, high command had shown both Team A and Team B footage from the first fight against the visitor. A deceased soldier had tried that strategy back then, to no effect, but she lacked a better idea.

Right before she pulled the trigger, a female voice reached her ears. "Janice, don't." In the distance, she spotted Carla and George. They both fired at the monster. Distracted, it dashed toward the new arrivals. They ran.

Without delay, Janice grabbed Brucie in a firefighter lift. The instant she touched him, he moaned and said, "Hey, babe, I know ya can't resist a hot stud like me, but be gentle, won't ya?" Janice giggled. He was alive! And still a total douche! She wished to escape by the elevator, but Carla and George had fled in that direction, so she instead carried Brucie to Rose's office. The people in the war room understood her plan, and they opened the door.

Chapter 10

Inside the control room, a pale Daniel Ricdeau stared at the main monitor, mouth gaping. The Koporal shared a similar expression as he shook his head at the horror they witnessed. Carla and George ran like death pursued them. Though they reached the door, the creature caught up to them. It immediately sliced and gnawed the two soldiers. The claws and teeth tore through the flesh; blood and guts soiled the walls and floor. They were long dead, yet the beast kept shredding their remains into smaller and smaller chunks. Daniel winced. Through decades of military service, he'd experienced more than his share of violence, but nothing this visceral.

The scariest part was that Janice had almost suffered their fate. As Commander, Daniel should remain impartial, but she was his daughter, and a sense of duty couldn't change that. He refused to grant her special treatment, and she'd resent it had he tried, but if she died today...

After a hard swallow, Daniel chased that thought away. No reason to imagine such a dire scenario. Then he recalled a detail he'd forgotten and scowled. Rose had asked for Brucie to accompany Janice. A strange request that broke protocol, but given her status as the Melkar, he'd decided he should listen even if he didn't understand. Thank Ulgorack he had. Brucie had saved Janice's life. Without him, Carla and George wouldn't have completed their rescue attempt. Had Rose had a vision? If so, she'd deny it and make excuses. For a prophet, she was blind to her own gift.

"What a freaking mess," Tigh said, interrupting Daniel's reverie.

"I couldn't agree more. Carla and George are heroes. I want them to receive the courage medal posthumously." The highest honor in NISDA, and they'd earned it. Afterward, he continued for the other officers. "Please contact Private Ricdeau on the radio."

"Right away, sir. The connection is ready."

"Private Ricdeau, do you hear me?"

Janice's voice echoed through the chamber, and that lifted a weight off his shoulders. Daniel had known she'd survived, but talking to her made it concrete. "Are you all right?" He'd almost added a "Sweetie" to the beginning of that sentence and bit his tongue not to. That would've been unprofessional. "Is Brucie alive?"

"I'm fine, sir, and yes, Brucie is alive. There should be an emergency medical kit somewhere in here. I'll use that to keep him that way, but I'm not sure how serious his injury is."

"Understood. I'll let you get to it."

The communication ended. With a groan, Daniel rubbed his chin. Then he hopped to his feet and paced. "The good news is, Brucie's alive. The bad news is that means we must deal with that monster fast or he might not make it. Killing it is a priority. We can't wait until it starves." He groaned and clutched his fist. "We were close, but with the door busted—" Daniel threw his hands upward. "We'll need another plan." He paused before proceeding. "It's weird. It ate none of the meat, nor the body of its victim. Why?"

Ron shrugged and flashed a smile. "I dunno. Maybe the freak's an herbivore."

"Sure doesn't look like one. Anyway, I digress when we don't have time."

"I'm gonna tell you what I told you before." The Koporal enumerated on his fingers. "Grenade. Ass." He brought his arms apart from his body in a grand fashion. "Boom!"

Daniel sighed. "I wouldn't ask anyone to risk the ass part, but other than that I agree. Damage be damned— we've lost six people to that creature and I don't want another victim. Hopefully Rose likes our improvised redecorations because we might not be able to afford to fix it for a while."

Chapter 11

Once inside the office, Janice laid Brucie on his side so the gash faced upward. Then she studied the room and spotted a small cabinet on the wall containing a first aid kit. Without delay, she grabbed the white box and rested it near Brucie. A click echoed as she opened it.

Janice reached for the latex gloves within and put them on. Then she seized a surgical mask along with the black flashlight. "I better look at that wound." She pointed the light toward Brucie's torso.

"Don't worry, it's just a scratch."

"Yeah, but it's a freaking big scratch. I don't think the spikes hit any major organs." However, the bodyguard bled profusely, staining his uniform red. No doubt Janice's clothes had suffered the same fate when she'd carried him. Since Janice preferred not to alarm Brucie, she kept her observation about the hemorrhaging silent. "But I need to get a better look to be sure. Sorry, Brucie, but your body armor is in the way."

He grimaced. "I ain't removing that. Gonna make things worse, ya know?"

"No, buddy, I'll take it off, trust me." On that note, she reached for the special safety latch on the sides of the armor and pulled them. The front part detached from the back, allowing her to lift it off the bodyguard. For the shirt underneath, she returned to the first aid kit and fished out a pair of trauma shears, a type of scissor designed to cut clothes. With a few well-placed snips, Janice got rid of the offending fabric.

"Ah, gal, can't stop yourself from undressing me, can ya?"

Even in this state, he remained the same jackass. Janice almost fired off a mean-spirited rebuttal but swallowed the words and instead said, "You saved my life back there, Brucie." The view now clear, she confirmed her previous diagnosis. The bodyguard had suffered a serious blow, but it could've been far worse, and with proper care, survival shouldn't pose a problem. While not a doctor by any stretch of the imagination, Janice had learned about medical treatment during military training. She'd be able to do a decent job at treating Brucie, at least good enough to allow him to wait for assistance.

"Right back at ya." He hesitated for a moment as he gazed at his lesion. "Janice, ya know... well, I... I dunno, but... wanna give it another shot?"

Startled by the sudden change of subject, Janice almost dropped the flashlight. She frowned. "It's not a good time to joke about that." Indeed, she had plenty on her hands. First, she had to assess the wound. She patted around the area and Brucie grimaced.

"I ain't joking, babe."

Janice shook her head in disbelief. She realized he was still interested in her, or more precisely her body. He always complimented her appearance and flirted in his own obnoxious way, but this was far more direct than usual. How did he even dare ask such a question after their history?

Years ago, they had dated for a short period. Nobody knew: it was their little secret. Just as well—she could imagine her father's lecture. He'd explain she should avoid intimacy with a guy like Brucie. Lie down with dogs, wake up with tentacle slime covering your face, as the maxim goes.

Their relationship had ended on a sour note. Somehow, she had forgiven him. The fact remained that Janice had learned what to expect from him. All you could hope for with Brucie Garland was a night of fun. She admitted, on a few occasions after their breakup, she had accepted that offer, but that was the past, not the present.

"Brucie," she began in a sweet yet firm tone, "I'm done being your booty call. You'll have to find someone else." Was that a sob she heard? That surprised Janice. Men like him detested showing potential signs of emotional weakness. Whatever, she had more pressing matters to attend to. With a sigh, she rummaged through the first aid kit in search of saline. She needed to clean the gash.

"Janice, I love you."

Janice burst into laughter as she grabbed the syringe and the accompanying catheter. "You've learned some new words! Very impressive!"

"I'm serious."

"Brucie... it's the wound talking." As she uttered that, Janice fixed the catheter on the syringe. "You had a near-death experience—it shook you up. Tomorrow you'll be back to your good old self." Then she opened the saline bottle, plunged the syringe inside and filled it up.

"That ain't true!" As Brucie denied her allegation, Janice remembered she required protection from splatter. She located the goggles and apron from the kit. "Babe, I got ya on my mind for freaking years. Listen, I treated you like shit. I dunno why. Was young; stupid... I changed. Would be different now, ya know."

Janice stopped tying the apron and glared at him. "No, it would be exactly the same!" Though she didn't wish to hurt him, a touch of bitterness stained her voice. "Yeah, you treated me bad, Brucie, but it wasn't because you were young or even stupid. It's because you're enslaved by your small friend down there in your pants. You care more about 'him' than me, or anyone really."

"Hey, he ain't that small! Uh, I mean, babe, gimme one last chance, I'll show ya you're wrong."

Janice slid the goggles over her eyes. "Nah, you had your chance. Now shut up so I can finish before you bleed to death."

Thank God he closed his mouth. Janice approached him and irrigated the wound with the disinfecting liquid. Reddish water rolled down Brucie and soiled the ground.

Chapter 12

Kristina poked on her minicomp, Rose talked to her mother on a videophone and I moped in the corner. I wasn't sure what Rose's conversation was about, but it involved some kind of ceremony Madeleine disliked. I watched them with semi-attention as a distraction from the dark thoughts that had haunted me for the last three days. Whatever was going on, Madeleine proved difficult. Rose smiled, but I sensed her frustration. I'll admit, given her lies, seeing her so tormented gave me a certain satisfaction and I'm not proud of that. She had her flaws, and she committed many sins, but that doesn't make enjoying her misery right.

—Thoughts of James Hunter, Hocmar 28, 2134, on the Nirnivian calendar

Despite the monitor's small size and the distance, James recognized the head priestess. That cylindrical purple hat alone confirmed her identity. No other Nirnivian he'd encountered wore anything similar. In fact, James assumed it served as a symbol of her position. While the elder adopted a benevolent smile, the steel in her voice contrasted her benign appearance. No question who wielded the power in this relationship. Rose might've been the holy prophet, but Madeleine was her mother.

"I understand you disagree with the centrists' decision, but it's theirs to make," Rose said in a diplomatic tone.

"That is correct. Galan is in charge of the centrist branch and I am powerless to stop him. However, I can choose whether to attend this travesty he calls an ascension, and I refuse."

"But, Mom, if you decline his invitation, it'll be a slap in the face to Galan. Isn't there enough hatred between your two branches and the orthodox? You taught me that despite each branch having different beliefs, unity is key for everyone to follow Ulgorack. Your not attending will cause a rift between the progressives and the centrists. The church will be more divided than ever."

"Perhaps so, but Galan is responsible. He brought this schism by ascending Christopher. That man..." The senior's cheeks reddened in what James assumed to be anger. "He is undeserving, for he acted in a most despicable way by dishonoring my mother."

"Mom, I've heard the story before on several—"

Madeleine ignored Rose's objection. "My mother was once a high priestess of the centrists. By studying scripture, she concluded that the holy Melkar would soon return through reincarnation. Christopher was the centrists' head priest. He refuted her claim and publicly mocked her." She paused for a second. When she continued, the venom in her voice doubled. "If he had stopped there, I could let it go, but he did not. Christopher accused her of incompetence and demoted her to a mere priestess. Then he isolated her, removed her from any important functions, making sure she'd never rise again. Out of a sense of loyalty, my mother stayed with the centrists despite threats of excommunication. I, however, could not abide by what Christopher had done. Years after her death, your birth confirmed she was right. Was her fall from grace fair?"

"Of course not, but—"

"Of course not indeed. With this ascension, Galan is spitting on my mother's grave. Yet it is me you accuse of stirring trouble."

"What happened to Grandma Sophia was horrible, I don't deny that. Christopher made a terrible mistake and he regrets it. When I was born, he resigned as the head priest in shame and demoted himself. After that, he sought redemption through charity and helped many." Rose sighed. "Now he's a dying man. Galan ascended him to recognize his effort at penance. Can't you forgive a dying man who blames himself for his sin?"

Madeleine grimaced. "It appears I cannot."

"Though I never met Grandma Sophia, somehow I doubt she would be so unforgiving."

"Correct, but I am not her."

Madeleine usually had a sense of dignity, but now she acted like a kid. I guess even when we're old and wise, we can be childish sometimes. I felt bad: I spied on them. Yet it was my only distraction. When I stopped listening, my thoughts returned to what I'd recently learned. I wondered again and again if Rose was a friend. When I grew tired of that question, I focused on Rose's animated debate with her mom again, despite my remorse.

—Thoughts of James Hunter, Hocmar 28, 2134, on the Nirnivian calendar

Chapter 13

With Brucie's wound cleaned, Janice returned to the first aid kit and grabbed the dressing gauze along with bandages. She pressed the dressing directly on the gash as it should be. The bodyguard winced and moaned at her touch. No doubt she hurt him, but she had little choice.

Now applied, the gauze should help stop the bleeding. Janice hoped it was the type that also contained painkillers, since the kit lacked them. Though it was self-adhesive, she secured it with bandages. Better safe than sorry.

The task completed, Janice took a step back and sat down on the floor. She exhaled. With the gash covered, she studied Brucie's impressive pecs and realized she hadn't seen him half-naked for years. Janice hated to admit it because of his ego, but he had a great body. He stayed in shape, kept a strict training schedule, and it showed. Perhaps because he sensed her stare, a slight smile formed on Brucie's face. "Babe, don't ya dare say we didn't have fun."

Not that again...

Janice groaned. "Yeah, we did. Too bad you're such an asshole, or we would've had more." Brucie's lip twitched, and she regretted her words a bit, but just a bit. He deserved them, but he'd suffered enough today. No point bruising his ego when he already endured a physical injury. Once it healed, however, that'd be another story.

"Will ya ever forgive me?" his voice broke as he asked.

"Oh, Brucie, I've forgiven you a long time ago. That doesn't mean I have to make the same mistake again." That said, Janice found her mind wandering to the past, revisiting when that error had happened.

***

Not a cloud in the sky, and Janice liked it this way. Then again, given she lay in a lawn chair, enjoying the sun, that shouldn't surprise anyone. She spent hours swimming in her parents' pool, the main reason she visited so often. Her own house lacked this luxury, but she dreamed of rectifying that omission. Until then, Mommy and Daddy would relish their eldest child's company.

Thanks to the warm weather, the water droplets lingering on Janice's skin dried up in no time. When she'd arrived, the strong chlorine odor had assailed her nose, but she'd since grown used to it and instead basked in the smell of fresh-cut grass. Between that, the excellent view, the birds singing and the sun rays, four of her senses found themselves in paradise. Only taste remained, but the druikinaka cocktail she indulged in took care of that. That reminded her, she hadn't sampled her drink in a while, so she reached for the glass filled with the bright blue liquid and took a sip.

Once done, Janice rested it next to her. As she did, she heard footsteps. She noticed Rose approaching while waving. Two large men followed her. On her right stood Yves, the bald bodyguard who'd protected Rose for years. He offered Janice a greeting in the form of a nod. As for the new guy, well, he smirked and winked at her. Janice resisted a sigh and wondered why her sister had hired such a buffoon. Sure, he'd saved her life, but that didn't mean she had to give him a job. Perhaps she should ask Rose if she would mind not having him along to their parents' home anymore. She had plenty of other bodyguards available. Yes, that was a good idea, but she'd wait until later. Bringing it up in his presence would be rude and awkward.

Soon, Rose stood beside Janice and beamed. "Hey, Janice, how's the sun?"

"Pretty great, sis, you should join me!"

The adopted sibling waved the suggestion away. "That sounds fun, but I'm afraid I'm here on Melkar business. Mom's waiting for me. I only came around to the backyard because I thought you'd be here and wanted to say hi."

"Fair enough."

They chitchatted for a moment, but Rose proved true to her word and had to leave not long after. Without requiring any instruction, Yves trailed her. The new guy, however, lingered behind as Janice had expected. Her jaw tightened. The young bodyguard walked to the pool and crouched. Then he dipped his fingers in the water.

"Yeah, it's freaking nice, ain't it? And the water's perfect—makes me wanna go fo' a swim."

Gritting her teeth, Janice pulled her beach towel over herself. Hardly a required gesture considering the warmth, not to mention that she didn't need to dry off. Instead, she meant to block his view. She knew at least part of the reason he loitered around her whenever he had the chance was to peep at her wearing her bikini. She didn't mind people seeing her in such attire but preferred not to give him that kind of pleasure.

"You're not exactly dressed for the occasion, big boy."

With a grunt, he rose and, spreading his arms, scanned the black suit accompanied by a white shirt and tie. "Yeah, ain't that right." He chuckled. "Ah well, can always strip to my underwear." A wink came from him. "I'd be okay showing 'em to ya!"

Janice bit her tongue while cursing herself in silence. What was she thinking? She'd walked into that one, and it had been so obvious. To add insult to injury, she failed to find a reply to rebuff him. All the leisure had dulled her quipping instincts; she'd have to rectify that.

"Hey, uh, is that a blue paradise?" He pointed at her beverage.

"Good eyes."

The bodyguard shrugged. "Oh, it's easy, had plenty o' those so…" In a quick motion, he removed his shades. "Ya know, there's this cool place that makes a killer blue paradise. Wanna give 'em a try this weekend?"

It demanded all Janice's self-control not to burst into laughter. Even so, she only lessened the hilarity rather than suppressing it. Had the jerk asked her on a date? She'd never imagined… yes, he hung around and admired her looks, but this was unexpected. For crying out loud, he was a child. Ten years younger if not more.

"Listen, kid—"

"Brucie."

"Yeah, Brucie, no offense, but I'd eat you alive. Go date someone your own age."

"Hey, babe, just 'cause I'm young, that ain't mean—"

"Enough. You're on the job right now. How about doing it for once?"

Brucie opened his mouth, then closed it and nodded twice. "Yeah, I guess I should. Sorry to bother ya."

He started to leave but hadn't progressed far when a new figure appeared. The red T-shirt and shorts contrasted with the usual uniform, but Janice would recognize that gray haircut and wrinkled face anywhere. Same for the charming smile she hated so much.

"Sweetie! What a surprise!"

She forced a giggle. "Stop lying. I'm here whenever I'm off and the weather's nice."

"All right, you caught me in the act!"

"And no need for fancy heightened senses either!"

"Yes, you're a natural."

"If you're here, everything must be going great with NISDA."

"Seems like it. First vacation day in ages where I haven't been called in for an emergency." An awkward silence then followed that statement. Despite being parent and child and working together, they had little to say to each other. Though that was far from a revelation, Janice's chest tightened. The way Daniel fidgeted suggested he endured a similar sensation. "It's so nice out here, I think I'll take the dog for a walk. I haven't done it for so long he might not recognize me."

"Have fun!"

"Will do!"

Brucie stuck around for the entire conversation, though he made himself small. Once Daniel left, he returned to Janice at a timid pace.

"So, uh." He scratched behind his head. "Things are kinda rough with your dad?"

Janice lifted her irises to peep at him from above the sunglasses. "Not really. How is it your business, anyway?"

"It ain't, it's just, um." Brucie winced. "I can tell 'cause I'm in the same boat, ya know. My old man bailed on us when I was a kid. Messed me up bad. Freak, messed up the whole family. Mom kinda gave up after that. My bro had to stop school to take care o' us." Brucie's voice broke and he even sobbed, shocking from a man like him. "Was so shitty o' him. If I see Dad again, I dunno if I'll hug him or punch him." He paused for a second. "Sorry 'bout that. You're right, ain't my business. It's just, because o' what happened, when I see a family that ain't getting along it gets to me."

To her own shock, Janice said, "I feel the same way about my dad."

"At least he stuck 'round. Didn't he?"

"Oh yeah, he was always there for us." Tears formed in Janice's eyes, but she kept them at bay. "I have a brother and... long story short, he and Dad had a fight, and he ran away. I haven't seen him for years."

Brucie winced. "Oh, that sucks, babe. Without my bro, I'd go crazy."

"I've been pushing Dad away ever since. Sometimes I tell myself that I'm being stupid. That I should be happy I have one of them left instead of avoiding him."

"Maybe, but it's hard, ain't it?"

"Yeah."

***

After that fateful conversation, Janice had accepted his invitation to share a blue paradise cocktail. Things had progressed from there. Despite his macho facade, Brucie could be surprisingly sweet and they had a lot in common. Soon, she wondered if perhaps the age difference wasn't the obstacle she'd imagined it to be. Sure, he was young, but still an adult. She had put her new hope to the test and embraced their relationship.

To stop the images from the past from filling her mind, Janice rummaged through the first aid kit. She didn't expect to find anything useful but then stumbled on a transparent box containing syringes prefilled with a pink liquid. The label claimed them to be antivenoms and antidote cocktails that counteracted common poisons. Though that creature showed no signs of being venomous, it might be. Janice's gaze alternated from the container to Brucie. Even if that monster had poisoned him, it'd be with a foreign substance, making the injection pointless. Still, no harm in trying.

"Hey, Brucie, I found antivenoms here. I'm thinking maybe I should give them to you, just in case."

"Yeah, sure."

Permission obtained, Janice located a vein in his arm and cleaned the spot with an alcohol swab. Thirty seconds later, the skin dried and Janice plunged the needle into his flesh. Brucie remained stoic.

"Babe, ya got my blood all over ya." He pointed at the remaining medicine with his chin. "How 'bout ya…"

"Point taken."

Once she finished, Brucie said. "I was a freaking jerk, babe. But I swear, I wanna be with ya—only ya."

Janice sighed and closed her eyes.

***

With an angry pull, Janice opened the door. It swung with great force, causing a metallic bang, but she ignored the sound and stormed inside the fast-food restaurant. With balled fists and gritted teeth, she scanned the place. While cheap in terms of price, the yellow-and-orange dining room was clean and appealing, not that it appeased her. Neither did the tempting smell of fried cytelicus and mishusq. Normally, her stomach would grumble at their aroma, but not under these circumstances.

Her rage being clear, the people inside stopped eating and fell silent. Awkwardness overcame the place, but she didn't care. Some stared at her, their eyes filled with questions. Others averted their gaze as if embarrassed. One little girl ogled Janice, mouth open in shock. The poor soul dropped her cup in dread. Red juice stained the floor. That sight thawed Janice's heart, and a wave of regret crashed into her. She hadn't meant to scare that child. For a moment, her anger cooled, and she considered apologizing and buying her another drink. That was when Janice spotted her target and her fury returned.

At a table in the back sat Brucie. A half-eaten burger and a few mishusq chips rested on his plate. That he'd lied about never eating such junk, Janice could forgive. The petite redhead on his lap, giggling between kisses, she could not. A friend worked here, and he told her he had seen Brucie in there with another, younger woman. At first, she dared believe he'd made a mistake, so he proposed he'd call her if it happened again. Thanks to that, she confirmed the unfaithfulness with her own eyes.

At a determined pace, Janice advanced toward her so-called boyfriend. "Brucie!"

"Hmm?" He turned his neck and smiled as he recognized her. "Hey, babe! What's up?" Perhaps finally noticing her posture, his expression sobered.

"What's up?" Janice forced a derisive laugh, then shook her head. "I catch you here with some bimbo and that's all you have to say?"

A flash of comprehension shone in Brucie's eyes. "Babe, I'm so sorry. I thought ya knew. Yeah, I wanna be with you and get married and all that stuff, but in an open relationship." He chuckled and pointed at himself with his two thumbs. "Can't deprive the ladies of this stud! There'd be riots and shit! Hey, ya can have fun on the side too, ya know. Ain't fair otherwise."

An open relationship. A freaking open relationship. Her parents had that kind of arrangement and she remembered the pain it had brought. Remembered how she'd cried whenever one of them had left on a date with someone else. Remembered the fear that they would abandon their family for this other partner. Janice wanted children, and while Brucie proved reticent toward the idea, she sensed a seed of desire for that dream. She expected he'd change his tune as he grew older. But she'd never raise a child in a goddamn open relationship. Not after what she'd endured.

The worst part was the betrayal. Why hadn't he told her from the start? Then she would've broken things off with no hard feelings. Janice searched through her brain for words that might sting him like his stung her. In the end, she decided Brucie didn't deserve the effort and showed him her middle finger before turning around and leaving.

"Babe, wait!"

A few gasps, along with a high-pitched scream, echoed as he sprang to his feet and his mistress fell on the floor. By that time, Janice had reached the door. She didn't look at Brucie. Instead, she presented her full palm, showing she wouldn't hear any of his bullshit. Then she stepped outside.

***

As Brucie's last sentence replayed in her brain, Janice scoffed. "Only me... had a sudden change of heart, uh?"

"Ain't so sudden. Let me tell ya, when I saw ya with other guys after the breakup... made my blood boil, ya know. When you got married to that jerk, I thought I'd die. Almost ran to ya and... was too young back then, too proud. Just wasn't ready, Janice. But I am now. I wanna marry you and have kids."

Janice closed her eyes. Despite everything, she still cared for him. A part of her yearned to hug and kiss him, but he was her past: she had to focus on the future. She assumed he was sincere, that he believed his own crap. However, Janice knew him better than he knew himself. After a few months, he'd grow weary, and he'd wander off. Such was his nature.

"It's too late."

Brucie grasped her hand; she reluctantly let him. "Janice... I don't deserve it, but please, gimme a chance, won't ya?"

Janice scowled. "No. Long ago, I..." A ball formed in her throat and she whimpered. But no tears. Those she refused. "I cried over a man."

In her mind, flashes from the past appeared. Her dad, teaching Rose Kuhard as they laughed together. Herself crying as Daniel called her adopted sister princess and Janice yelled, "Daddy! I wanna play too! Daddy! I wanna be a princess too! Why can't I? Why can she? Daddy!" But she was stuck as a sweetie, forever.

"Let me tell you, I hated it, and when I got older, I promised I'd never cry for a man again. But you, you made me break that promise... and that's on me, but if I let you make me break it again, I'd... I'd never forgive myself."

***

At last, Brucie understood it was truly over. Nothing he could say or do would change his fate. So, he accepted it and fell silent. Janice promised herself never to cry over a man. As far as he knew, she'd kept that vow even through her divorce from that jerk. A jerk who'd cheated on her. A jerk who'd resembled Brucie far too much for his taste. A jerk he intended never to be again, a resolution that came too late.

Unlike Janice, Brucie hadn't made such a vow, and so he cried in the office. He proved so discreet she didn't notice. Or, she chose not to acknowledge his tears. He had to admit, crying over a woman, he hated it too.

Chapter 14

Armed with a grenade launcher, Patricia stood before the gate leading to the Melkar's quarters. The door slid open a third of the way, blocking the animal yet providing sufficient space for her to pass. The previous confrontations had shown the beast's imperviousness to bullets and tranquilizer darts. With Janice and Brucie pinned in the office, getting rid of it had become urgent, so high command had approved the use of explosives. About time. While Patricia understood the desire to minimize damage, that monster had to be stopped.

Given the ridiculous death toll imposed by the black creature, the Commander vowed not to endanger another Gorumar. Patricia appreciated that, especially since they'd selected her for the next assault. That was why she waited near the door. She could fire at the animal and escape if the attack proved unsuccessful. Not that she expected failure.

To lure the visitor, the speaker system broadcast voices. That way, it should approach from the optimal path, providing plenty of distance between it and Patricia. At least, that was what they hoped. For what felt like hours, Patricia waited for her target's arrival. She focused on the direction they planned for it to arrive from. In truth, she expected mere minutes passed. Still, the beast took its sweet time. Apprehension gripped her. What if it declined to follow their audio trail? In a quick motion, she turned her head. Nothing. A nervous laugh escaping her throat, Patricia looked where she was supposed to again and... a dark shape popped around the corner.

For a fraction of a second, relief spread through Patricia's body. Their strategy had worked. Then the reality of the situation came back to her, and her heartbeat, as well as her breathing, accelerated. Without delay, she aimed and fired. A grenade flew and landed a foot away from the monster with a metallic clink. It twisted its neck sideways, giving the impression it contemplated what had happened. A low-volume roar accompanied the motion. Perhaps out of curiosity, the creature stepped forward and smelled the foreign object, and boom! A ball of flame engulfed the visitor. Patricia laughed and pumped her fist. She got it!

***

The main screen displayed the explosion swallowing the beast, and the control room erupted in celebration. People cheered, clapped, threw their hands upward and so on. Daniel himself couldn't resist laughing, and his Koporal adopted the largest smile he'd witnessed from the grumpy man.

Then the flames and smoke cleared. The chamber gasped in unison before falling into a deep silence. Everyone stared at the monitor, mouths gaping. Once the initial shock had passed, everybody started talking simultaneously. In particular, Ron yelled, "What the freak?"

Daniel ignored the commotion, hopped to his feet and advanced toward the screen, frowning. The animal stood in one piece without a trace of an injury. All this carnage and not a single drop of blood shed. What was more, it seemed unshaken by the attack. Sweat covered Daniel's brow.

Patricia didn't hesitate for a second, and three more grenades landed near their enemy. It didn't bother reacting, as if it had learned not to fear the green orbs. After a roaring explosion that made Daniel cover his ears, a sea of fire engulfed the creature, scorching the wall and floor. The smoke cleared... against logic, the beast remained in one piece. With an annoyed groan, Daniel noticed that the attack had caused damage to Valardir, but not their target.

"That's impossible!" Ron shouted in disbelief. "Is that thing immortal?"

Rubbing his chin, Daniel considered the possibility. That was a scary prospect, but unlikely. Several strange beings from other universes had visited them, and while some were tougher than others, they'd all succumbed to death in the end. Besides, the way it walked... he hadn't figured out what his heightened senses were trying to tell him, but he felt certain the animal didn't move like an invulnerable creature. Its movements betrayed fear. Something about the left front paw.

"Maybe, but I doubt it."

Another grenade flew. The beast hopped forward and interrupted the projectile's trajectory by catching it in its mouth. Then it swallowed. Tigh jumped in joy and pumped his fist. "Ah, freak yeah! It's screwed now!"

After a loud blast, the creature staggered and collapsed. Everyone sat on the edge of their seat, too afraid to express any sign of victory, except for Ron. In his mind, Daniel noted that even if Patricia had killed the visitor, its body remained intact, suggesting incredible toughness. Of course, they knew that already, but to this point?

Against the odds, a roar escaped the animal. It stood up again, shaking its head. Once it regained its bearings, its jaw opened and emitted a sound reminiscent of laughter.

"Ah, son of a bitch!" The Koporal slammed his right fist into his left palm. "Does that mean even its insides are indestructible?"

Daniel shrugged. "I don't know, but I get the impression the bastard enjoyed it!" He sighed. "This is useless. Abort."

***

The door now closed, Patricia sat against it while holding her head. The monster had eaten a grenade with no visible consequences. How could that be possible? How were they supposed to hurt it?

Patricia had survived the war and witnessed countless horrors. Dead bodies by the hundreds; mutilated comrades lying in hospital beds. Once, Ostark had captured her, and she'd endured torture via pain sticks, a brutal ordeal. The memories brought a shiver. Still, nothing she'd experienced had come close to causing the same dread as that creature. Gorumars showed cruelty beyond measure, but when you shot them, they bled. That animal defied all the rules she thought she knew.

Chapter 15

"All right, buddy, let me take that out." With those words, Janice pulled the thermometer from under Brucie's tongue. Despite her care, the bodyguard had taken a turn for the worse. Shivers assailed him, and covering him with an emergency blanket she'd found in the first aid kit failed to alleviate them. Janice frowned and looked at the red liquid within the plastic tube. "Yeah, you have a fever, but nothing big."

Though true, the observation did little to calm Janice's worries. Brucie's health kept degrading. She checked his wound, but it seemed decent all things considered. The blood loss had stopped, or close enough at least. A nagging feeling that the creature had poisoned Brucie popped into Janice's brain. If that was the case, they were in trouble. Yes, she'd injected him with an antidote cocktail, but his symptoms had progressed anyway. Not surprising, given the toxin would be foreign.

Brucie needed proper medical attention. Even then, nothing guaranteed he'd make it, but he'd have a chance. Too bad a quick rescue seemed improbable. Based on the last communication, the beast had survived several grenades unscathed. It had swallowed one, and still the explosion had caused no visible damage. Janice quivered. What kind of monster could survive such an impact? At this point, her father and his underlings lacked a plan. They might be stuck here for hours, or days. She'd be all right, but Brucie...

As if reading her mind, the pale-skinned bodyguard stared at her with bloodshot eyes. Instead of the fatalist comment concerning his fate Janice expected, he said, "I know why ya don't wanna get back together. There's someone else."

"Oh, come on, as if that's any of your business. Not that I have to tell you, but, no, I don't have a boyfriend."

"Yeah, ya ain't got a boyfriend." Brucie coughed. "But there's a dude you like, ya know." After a scoff, she dismissed the notion with a wave. No point dignifying that with an answer. "It's James, ain't it?"

That took the breath out of Janice's lungs. Once she recuperated, she laughed and rubbed her brow. "What? That's... you're insane, Brucie."

"Ain't no use denying it, I saw how ya look at him. Always playing Rubarg with him and shit, pretty damn obvious." He paused for a second as if he expected her to reply.

"Ooh la la, you sure have a lot of imagination. Yeah, I play Rubarg with him. Poor guy had some really shitty luck, I'm just trying to make his stay here more hospitable. And, hey, I like Rubarg, so why the freak not?"

"Bullshit! Ya scared o' admitting it 'cause I might kick his ass or sumthing. Don't worry, I won't. Damn it, babe, I wanna break him in two, but I won't. James's a good guy, ya know. I ain't gonna beat up a pal 'cause I've been stupid enough to drive the woman I love into his arms. My freaking fault."

"How surprisingly mature of you." Janice giggled. "But that doesn't mean you're right, bud."

"Dunno 'bout that, babe... ya kinda stick to him when he's 'round."

After a groan, Janice rolled her eyes. "Fine, he's kind of cute." She blushed. "Those sad puppy eyes... it's like the guy feels the whole weight of the world on his shoulders. Sometimes, I want to give him a hug and tell him everything will be okay."

Brucie snickered. "Got no freaking idea 'bout what makes a guy cute, but if ya say so."

"I guess I do! But, whatever, I'm surprised you'd think I'd be hot for James. He's not really my type."

He shrugged. "Ah, ya mean guys like me and your ex-husband? Figured you got sick o' the macho men and were lookin' fo' something different."

"Fair enough, dating my type never ended well." Janice furrowed her brow. "Still, James's the other extreme. He's too... hmm... not enough... whatever, we're not even the same species."

"Close 'nough fo' it not to be that weird. Didn't sum doc on TV say a human and a Gorumar could have kids?"

Janice chuckled and shook her head. "That's just his theory, buddy, and trust me, I'm not the one who'll put it into practice."

"So I'm full o' shit, huh?"

"Yep!"

"Good fo' ya. James's cool and all but he's hung up on some other chick, ya know?"

"Psst, how couldn't I? He's always bringing up his girlfriend. Nadine? No, Nadia." She sighed. "Poor bastard... he must realize someday that he'll never return home and has to make a new life for himself without her. Sure as freak I'm not the one who'll tell him, though."

"Yeah, me neither. Let 'im dream fo' a while, right? Thing is, I ain't talkin' 'bout her."

A sudden spike of interest filled Janice, and she leaned forward. "Oh?"

"I'm talkin' 'bout Rose."

An impressed whistle escaped Janice's lips. "Whoa, James sets his sights high. I pegged him for an underachiever, but I must reevaluate that." After a moment of silence, Janice scowled. "He told you that?"

Brucie dismissed the notion with a wave. "Nah, denies it like his life depends on it, but I can tell, ya know? Spending so much time together, Even wakes up 'fore sunrise to"— he performed finger quotes—"'train with her.' Freak, he's learning Kuhard fo' her. Babe, that has to be love."

The mere mention of the overly complex game prompted Janice to gag. The rules made no sense, no matter how hard her father, sister and brother protested the claim. "You have a point there... poor James is shit out of luck. Rose's stuck in the past. She never got over you-know-who, and she won't. Too bad, they'd make a cute couple."

"Yeah, I think so too." A smirk appeared on Brucie's face. "So, I ain't started a fight 'tween ya and Rose, right? Ya know, 'cause o' jealousy and crap."

Janice face-palmed. "Ooh la la, Brucie, you don't give up easy." Despite her words, something deep within Janice warned she protested too much. She did enjoy James's company, and he was cute in an unconventional way. Besides, considering her exes had cheated on her, it might not be a terrible idea to try someone different. But, no, she wanted a man with a backbone, and no offense to James, but he lacked one. "Buddy, I swear, it's not like that with James."

"Oh yeah? Ain't so sure I believe ya." He pointed at the opposite corner of the room with his chin. "My pal over there, the blue dancing treeneling, he's on my side, ya know."

Janice understood there couldn't be such a creature present, but she turned around. Something in his voice sounded so... real. However, reality prevailed, and she found only open space. Janice glared at Brucie, intending to chide him for the lame joke, but when she did, she witnessed him grinning and offering his imaginary friend a thumbs-up. After a gasp, Janice's mouth gaped and then she covered it with her palm. With a hard swallow, she reached for her communicator and activated it.

"Commander Ricdeau, sir, I'm afraid our rescue might be more urgent than we thought."

Chapter 16

Daniel Ricdeau sat in his chair while his fingers formed a pyramid. The position improved his concentration, and he needed it as he stared at the monitor. Footage from the past battles with the visitor played. The first contact, where Tigh and Daniel had fled as their men sacrificed themselves. Charlie's valiant effort, which allowed for imprisoning the beast in Rose's quarters. The failed yet stupidly brave attempt by Janice at sealing it within the garden. The grenade bombardment. He watched them in a loop, scanning every pixel for a detail he'd missed. There was something there, but what?

"How long are you gonna watch them being killed again and again?" a cross-armed Ron asked. "It's making me sick."

"Trust me, I don't like it any more than you do. We need a new plan, and I'm relying on my special gift to find one. Got any other ideas? I'm all ears."

The Koporal grunted and shrugged, confirming he had nothing. Daniel returned his gaze to the screen when Nicky's voice echoed. "Commander, we're receiving a communication from Private Ricdeau."

"Patch it through."

"Commander Ricdeau, sir, I'm afraid our rescue might be more urgent than we thought."

The apprehension in her tone made Daniel's muscles tense. While not on Tigh's level, Janice had nerves of steel. Her being worried implied troubles ahead.

"Brucie is deteriorating. He has a fever and is hallucinating. I'm no medic, but I'd say we must get him to a hospital ASAP."

A few almost inaudible whispers spread across the room, and the already dark mood grew somber. Daniel felt its weight on his shoulders. As he slumped in his seat, he rubbed his brow while Ron instead opted for a few choice swears.

"Copy that, Private Ricdeau. Hang in there, we're coming." The transmission ended, and a headache assailed Daniel. What a nightmare. "This just went from bad to worse."

Tigh groaned. "Yeah, I'd say."

Nicky turned toward them. "Sir, should we mount a rescue team?"

"What's the freaking point?" the Koporal asked after slamming his armrest with his fist. The resulting bang caused everyone to recoil. "That thing's unkillable. Why send a bunch of soldiers to die for one guy? The math just doesn't work. Brucie's screwed."

Each person in the room including Daniel glared at Ron. Instead of backing down and apologizing, he stood and pulled his chin up. "Are you offended? Come on, people, you know I'm telling the truth. Don't blame the messenger."

Daniel cleared his throat. "You're half right. Yes, the math doesn't work, but that monster's not immortal. There are signs of vulnerabilities in its body language, but I can't—" As he spoke, he stared at the monitor. The scene showed the soldier who'd distracted the creature, allowing Daniel's previous escape.

"Wait... there..." Daniel's eyes widened and his lips twitched. Then he snapped his fingers and laughed. How could he have been so blind? Old age must've caught up to him. "Rewind, slowly. There, pause!" He pointed at the display.

The Koporal scowled. "And what the freak are we looking at?"

"Its left paw. It moved the moment they fired."

"So?"

"So that might be a clue. Continue playing the footage in slow motion." They obeyed and, as predicted, whenever bullets flew, the animal performed a similar movement. "It's protecting itself."

"Bah, you're grasping at straws."

"Maybe. Let's check the part with the pain sticks. Stop!" Daniel smiled. "When Charlie jabbed the bastard, it twisted its body so he couldn't touch its belly."

Ron scratched the back of his head. "So, you're saying its weakness is a soft belly like a fairy-tale Dargan?"

Daniel shook his head. "No, we're not that lucky. There's a spot behind its left paw it's keeping out of reach. I'd guess about two square inches. I'm willing to bet that's where we can do massive damage."

"Not sure I am. No offense intended, but I freaking don't want to risk several lives on a hunch."

"Neither am I. That's why I'll do it."

At first, nobody reacted, but as the words sank in, Ron blinked twice and the rest stared at each other in disbelief. "Have you lost your goddamn mind? That monster will eat you alive!"

"Don't be ridiculous, it hasn't eaten any flesh so far."

"Damn it, you know what I mean! You're too old for this shit!"

"He's right, sir!" Nicky said. Once she realized what she'd implied, she blushed. "Oh, not about your age. Um, you're the Commander, you're too important to risk your life like that."

Daniel laughed. "No worries, I'm well aware I'm an old geezer. Normally, I'd agree with you two, but the situation is desperate." He gestured at the screen. "That spot is so small and the creature so fast, hitting the mark would take a miracle for even our best shooters. If only we had some kind of mutant with super vision and reflexes. Oh, we do! I'm the only one here who has a chance of success. It has to be me."

"Don't spew that bullshit at me, Dan." Tigh pointed a menacing index finger toward Daniel's sternum. "Sacrificing the Commander to save a bodyguard is dumb as shit. Why the freak would you care so much about Brucie?" Then his face lit up in comprehension. "Oh, wait. Of course you don't—it's Janice. With all the crap going on, I forgot she's trapped there too."

Daniel nodded. "Yes, I can't abandon her when there's a chance I can save her. I"—he grimaced—"haven't always been the best father. Since Laurence left, our relationship has been strained. I messed up then, but I won't mess up now."

"But, Dan, Janice is fine. There are emergency water bottles and military rations in there, like everywhere in Valardir. She can survive for weeks. That gives us plenty of time."

Daniel sighed. "Janice is fine, yes, but Brucie isn't. He's a dick, but he's still her friend. I don't want her to blame herself over his death." He shuddered. "God knows I've been there."

Ron lowered his gaze as he considered Daniel's argument. Then he nodded. "Okay, I get you." He rested his palm on Daniel's shoulder. "But I won't let you go alone."

The Koporal jabbed his thumb toward himself. "Sorry, pal, but you're stuck with this asshole!"

Both burst into laughter and clenched their hands in a secret handshake they'd shared back in their fighting days. "Wouldn't have it any other way! First, I'll need a gun. I'm thinking a PA-506 would do the job."

Chapter 17

They argued for over an hour. Rose wasn't smiling any-more. She looked tired and annoyed, but to her credit, she never raised her voice. Not so for Ms. Ricdeau. The dispute somewhat amused me at first, but I grew frustrated with Madeleine's constant bitching about Christopher. Don't ask me how Rose endured that crap without screaming. It was so petty I wondered how the head priestess would deal with a life-threatening situation. Based on how Madeleine behaved, I guessed by whining like a baby until she died.

—Thoughts of James Hunter, Hocmar 28, 2134, on the Nirnivian calendar

Rose massaged her temples. "Mom, I understand why you're angry, but please be reasonable. This goes beyond your feelings or mine. It's about the future of the progres-sive and centrist branches. You may be the head priestess, but you're not unstoppable. If your feud with Christopher damages the goodwill between both branches, the board might demote you. Is a grudge worth that much?"

Despite the distance, James sensed the pure rage in Madeleine's glare and he shivered. "Has anyone dared ut-ter such a threat?"

"Oh, no!" Rose covered her mouth. "No one's suggested that. I'm only speculating, I swear."

"Good! My position is justified, and if the board uses it as an excuse to attack me, they will rue the day they dou-ble-crossed Madeleine Ricdeau. I shall sue should that prove necessary."

Rose sighed. "For someone who preaches forgiveness, you sure hold a grudge. Maybe you should remember passage thirty-four of the Builto scrolls."

"Forgiveness does not imply erasing one's sins, nor does it preclude a fair punishment. I've forgiven Christopher, but that does not mean he deserves to be a high priest. Failure to accept the consequences of our actions is a step toward nothingness. I argue that my disapproval of his ascension is motivated not only by outrage at how Christopher treated my mother but also by the desire to protect his soul from past transgressions. This is backed by the same verse you quoted, plus passage seven from the Yuul scroll and others." The old woman smirked. "Do not attempt to out-scripture me, child. You may be the Melkar, but I have been memorizing sacred texts since before your birth."

"Yes, I can't deny that. Luckily, I don't have to. Intentions matter. Even if you can justify your actions religiously speaking, it doesn't change a thing if the reason for your refusal is selfish. Sorry, Mom, but I have difficulty believing Christopher's soul is the cause of your objections."

"Can you read people's hearts now, child? I think not, for otherwise you would concede that I am sincere. Regardless, that others doubt my motives has no impact on the gods' judgment. No matter if the doubter in question is the holy prophet."

"All right, this is going nowhere. It's clear you won't attend for protocol's sake. Instead, would you consider attending for me? As the Melkar, I'm supposed to promote unity between the branches. If you refuse the invitation, I must take a stand and denounce you publicly. I don't care if you hate Christopher and mumble insults under your breath through the whole ceremony, but please come and perform your duties. For me—not the Melkar, but your daughter. Please help me out. You're putting me in a difficult situation."

"Parents claim they would do anything for their children, and I always believed that was the case for me," Madeleine said after a moment of silence. "Today I am proven wrong. I am sorry, Rose. I love you, but you demand the impossible. Please understand, this is beyond us. Promoting Christopher to high priesthood is immoral, and not because I resent him. As I explained before, going to the ceremony would imply I approve of his ascension, and I cannot do that in good conscience, not even for you."

Finally, Rose reached her limit. She broke down in tears. That didn't soften Ms. Ricdeau, who warned Rose that such weeping was unbecoming of the Melkar and it wouldn't change her mind. That was cold.

After I discovered her lies, I questioned Rose's friendship. Part of me wanted to hate her. Still, her crying awakened something in me. I recalled the experiences we'd shared. How she'd come looking for me when Stalker had kidnapped me. How she'd saved my life when I'd tried to hang myself. How she'd taught me to play Kuhard. How she had become kind of crazy over euthanasia. I wished we could go back to those simpler times and I could trust her with no doubts or fears.

I felt bad for Rose; she only asked for a small favor. Plus, Madeleine irritated me. I didn't fall for her "beyond us" crap. She hated Christopher's guts, and that was it. Anyone who knows me can tell I don't make waves. I stay in the shadows and observe, afraid to act, taking the frustration without a word, and when I'm pushed too hard, I explode. In my sleep-

deprived state, I was pushed and then some, so I got to my feet and did something out of character.

—Thoughts of James Hunter, Hocmar 28, 2134, on the Nirnivian calendar

After a groan, James slammed his hand against the desk where he sat. A thundering boom echoed. Kristina almost dropped her precious minicomp and then recoiled as she stared at him. As for Rose, she turned toward James, mouth gaping. "*Hunter?*"

James ignored the winged woman and approached the videophone at a quick pace while glaring at Madeleine. Once close enough, he pointed at the old lady. "What the hell is wrong with you?"

"I beg your pardon?" Ms. Ricdeau replied in a tone indicating she didn't appreciate his manners.

A hint of menace tainted Madeleine's response, but rage coursed through James, so it failed to intimidate him. Instead, his already high volume grew a notch louder. "I said: what the hell is wrong with you?"

Madeleine's face whitened and she didn't answer. Rose gasped out of shock. She had never seen me like that before. She couldn't believe her eyes. Thinking back, I can't believe it either...

—Thoughts of James Hunter, Hocmar 28, 2134, on the Nirnivian calendar

"You're the high priestess and have responsibilities, but you blow them off because you don't like them. I know nothing about the branches, or Christopher, but seeing the effort Rose is putting into convincing you, it seems important."

"As I have said, this is not about my opinion, but rather—"

"Bullshit!" Thanks to the strength of James's interruption, Madeleine became paler. "Pure bullshit. You don't like Christopher, so you sulk. Worse"—he gestured toward Rose—"you're wasting her time because now she has to babysit you until you do what you're supposed to. Everyone here's always babbling about how busy Rose is. You don't give a rat's ass! You're making your daughter's life miserable and you don't care. And why are you complaining, anyway? It's nothing! What do they want you to do? Go to a ceremony for Christopher? Say nice things? Do some rituals? Nothing at all. You're acting like a freaking kid. A woman your age—you should be ashamed!" A ball formed in James's throat.

"There are people fighting for their lives out there"—while he meant those battling the beast, James couldn't help but include himself in that statement—"and you're whining about a party? Why not shut up and go? Or get a note from your doctor or whatever! Or, quit and follow my example: find a dead-end job. Yeah, I wonder how much you'd enjoy dealing with angry customers who treat you like shit and clean the toilets soiled with—well, literal shit! I bet after less than a week, you'd kiss Christopher's feet to be the head priestess again."

The tirade left Madeleine frozen on the monitor. Meanwhile, Kristina appeared to focus on her minicomp but occasionally fired a glance in James's direction. As for Rose, her fingers covered her lips, and she muttered, "Hunter..."

Though she seemed appalled, James expected that, in reality, she approved of his message but couldn't admit it in front of her mom. If she had wanted to silence him, she could have done so while he'd ranted. Then Rose rested her hands on her hips and scowled.

"Hunter, what's wrong with you? That's our head priestess and my mother—"

On the screen, Madeleine presented her open palm in a sign for Rose to stop. "That is quite all right, dear." She regained most of her color and even her smile. "Mr. Hunter, that was uncharacteristically rude. You have shown a great lack of respect to an elder, and after such language, I should wash your mouth out with soap, young man." A smirk formed on the elder's face. "And for the record, I cleaned plenty of toilets during my training for priestesshood, as learning humility is a large part of the process. I will, however, concede that I would prefer not to return to those days." The senior sighed.

"But I digress. This poor old fool must confess that you spoke the truth. My stubbornness is due to a personal grudge. While I dislike Christopher, he did everything in his power to attain redemption. Under this light, I suppose I understand why Galan wishes to recognize his efforts, though admitting it causes me pain. My conduct is unworthy of my position. Thank you, Mr. Hunter, for making me realize how childish I was. And, Rose, you deserve an apology for the trouble I caused."

Rose blinked twice in what James assumed to be disbelief. "So, you will attend?"

The head priestess bent her neck. "I am afraid not. Oh, I should, but my ego is fragile. To be frank, if I go, I cannot guarantee I would be on my best behavior, and that might cause a greater rift than a simple refusal."

With a moan, Rose rubbed her forehead as if prey to a headache. "Just when I thought it was over."

"Ah, but it is." Madeleine nudged her chin toward James. "This brave young man offered us the solution, though I suspect he is not aware."

I wasn't.

—Thoughts of James Hunter, Hocmar 28, 2134, on the Nirnivian calendar

"I will accept the invitation, but when the date comes, I shall suffer a minor but inconvenient illness. I am confident my doctor will supply a note to that effect. A small delegation will attend as a show of support while I will be apologetic for my absence and will approve of the ascension in public. Galan will not be fooled, but he will pretend to be to preserve the peace between our branches."

"Well, that should work, but somehow I'm not happy about it."

"Nor am I. To denounce this travesty would have brought such satisfaction. But, that is fine. Many claim the best compromises make neither side too happy."

That didn't end as badly as I'd feared. Sometimes, being a total asshole gets results. Not that I recommend that course of action in general. Rose and Madeleine finished their talk, but I didn't pay attention. Once she was done, Rose gazed at me with a grin.

—Thoughts of James Hunter, Hocmar 28, 2134, on the Nirnivian calendar

"You surprised me! I had no idea you had it in you; you're so shy. That was harsh but helpful. I'll admit I wished to scream at her too toward the end, but I could never speak to my mom like that."

James shrugged. "I, uh, don't know what came over me. I haven't been feeling well lately, and I was tired of her constant bickering. Uh, I guess she pushed me over the edge. Sorry."

"Ah, you returned to normal! That's okay, Hunter, no harm done. I should thank you. Without that unexpected outburst, we'd still be arguing." Rose giggled. "I'll have to be careful now that I'm aware of your temper."

James scratched the back of his head. "Yeah, I guess." On that note, he joined in her laughter.

For the first time in three days, I remembered how much I appreciated Rose's company. She was a great friend. Beyond that, she had given me a home and protection. I'd met her only a few months before—still, we were so close, as if we understood each other intuitively. At least that's how it was before Doctor Death messed everything up. I hated my distrust. I hated my suspicion. Yeah, she'd lied, but I didn't know why. I decided I'd assume she had good reasons until proven otherwise. She deserved the benefit of the doubt. I mean, without her I'd be rotting in jail, or starving, or dead already. Of course, I wasn't stupid enough to ignore the potential threat. I figured I'd discover the truth about the first human, but subtly. Only problem was, how the hell was I supposed to do that, anyway?

—Thoughts of James Hunter, Hocmar 28, 2134, on the Nirnivian calendar

Chapter 18

Daniel and Ron stood before the door leading to Rose's quarters. By pure bad luck, the officers inside the war room warned him the beast lurked right behind the gate. To enter the area now would ensure a swift end, and so they delayed until they received confirmation their target had moved to a suitable position. From there, they'd sneak up on it and attempt a surprise attack.

As he waited, Daniel studied the pistol he held in his hand. Model PA-506... he'd used one often during his youth. It had been years since he'd last wielded such a fire-arm in actual combat. At least he visited the practice range, though for pleasure rather than training. An automatic gun sprayed a fatal cloud of bullets that'd tear apart a Gorumar but lacked the precision required for the current task. This gun, however, went in the opposite direction. It fired a single shot at a time but allowed excellent accuracy at close range.

In an ideal world, they'd have a professional sniper hunt down the animal. With the proper rifle, they'd kill it from a more-than-safe distance. Alas, the corridor-based layout of Rose's quarters didn't provide that kind of real estate, rendering a sniper useless. The good old PA-506 would have to do. These thoughts in mind, Daniel caressed the barrel of his gun.

"You don't have to go through with this madness," Ron said with his perpetual scowl.

"I know." Images popped into Daniel's brain. The soldiers who had fallen to the creature. Brucie pushing his daughter out of harm's way at the price of receiving the blow meant for her. And of course Janice, trapped in the office along with the injured bodyguard. Daniel tightened his grip on the pistol's handle. "The thing is, I kind of want to." He forced a smile. "If only I was sure I could do it."

Before the Koporal answered, Nicky's voice echoed through their radio.

"Sir, the beast finally left the entrance area."

"Roger that."

The okay being received, they entered Rose's quarters. Trails of blood stained the floor. No doubt the monster had stepped on its victims' carcasses and spread the life-bearing fluid. In a corner, Daniel spotted mutilated cadavers. The brave souls who'd distracted the visitor while Janice had escaped. A sickening sensation invaded his stomach, but he endured it without complaint. He'd witnessed carnage before and learned how to handle it.

By following Nicky's instructions, they tracked down the animal. It loitered near a corner, allowing them to approach while avoiding entering its vision. Pressed against the wall, Daniel was assailed by a putrid odor. Ron confirmed he also smelled it by pinching his nose, but Daniel lacked that option. A proper aim required two hands.

The beast presented its backside to them. Impossible to make the shot from this angle even with Daniel's mutation. No choice but to wait and hope it'd face them. Several minutes passed before it did. The instant the animal turned, Daniel raised his weapon and aimed, but the beast's left paw blocked the weak spot. Worse, it growled and looked around, sensing a trap but failing to see them. Or so Daniel assumed. Otherwise, why would they still be breathing?

After scanning the area for a few seconds, the creature walked away. Tigh whispered a curse, then said, "This is impossible. Let's get out of here before we're both dead."

Without replying, Daniel rested his index finger against his lips and advanced toward the visitor. The Koporal tapped his shoulder. "Dan, no! Let's circle around!"

Perhaps a wise suggestion, but Daniel's instinct warned him to ignore it. Instead, he continued his approach. He proceeded at a slow pace, making sure not to produce a sound. Pearls of sweat rolled down his whole body. A single noise and it'd be over. Despite his fear, he kept progressing. Then he stopped. What was he thinking? He was too old for this. His eyes were still sharp, but even he lacked the skills. Even if his target exposed its weakness, he'd miss and the beast would tear them to pieces. Daniel took a deep breath. Self-doubts only lessened his chances.

To calm himself, Daniel recited a prayer in his mind. Praying helped him focus; it brought solace in his darkest moments. Right in the middle, the monster spun around, facing him while emitting a chilling roar. Out of pure instinct, Daniel pulled the trigger. The projectile found its mark. A blue liquid sprayed out. The beast collapsed on the floor. He gave a victory shout. It bled after all.

Without delay, the creature attempted to get up. Not that Daniel intended to let it. Again, he fired. Again, it fell as a torrent of azure goo soiled the ground. A shrill, high-pitched shriek of pain escaped the animal. It tore through Daniel's ears, but he smiled. Success had never sounded so awful, yet satisfying. "That's for all the people you killed, you freaking monster."

It learned from its mistake and rose slowly, taking great care to conceal its soft spot. Undeterred, Daniel recoiled, giving himself more space. Once up, the creature hopped toward him. Dodge or shoot. His reflex only allowed one. With a gulp, he squeezed the trigger. "And this is for Janice." Then he closed his eyes and exhaled.

Something grabbed him and pulled. Tigh... of course, due to the intense action, he had forgotten his Koporal accompanied him. The beast's claws scratched Daniel's arm, and he winced. Still, Ron's intervention saved his life. The creature landed in a perfect position to conceal its vulnerability. Daniel stifled a curse—that complicated matters. Then a beam of light shone, striking the animal's pupils. A turn of the neck showed Ron brandished a flashlight. He must've searched for it while Daniel had fought, and thank God he had. The brightness caused the animal to yelp and contort. Again, Daniel aimed and fired another bullet. And another... and another... and another... and another... and another...

"Dan, stop, it's dead!"

And another... and another. Then Daniel stopped as requested, but he kept the pistol up. He took several deep breaths. The monster didn't move. Daniel dropped his gun, burst out laughing and hugged his Koporal while patting his back. "It's over!"

"You did it! You bastard, you did it!" Unable to contain their excitement, the two men giggled like children. "Come, Dan, let's go see Janice."

Daniel nodded. "Yeah, let's."

They started walking, but then Daniel's leg stiffened. An excruciating pain spread in the muscle. Gritting his teeth, he stumbled and dropped to the floor. His leg had cramped, as it often did. Ron sat beside him, shaking his head. "You're a lucky son of a gun!"

"You'd be dead too, you know."

"Nah, I'd have run like crazy while that thing slashed you." They both laughed at the morbid joke. Daniel massaged his leg and Nicky's voice echoed through his headset once more.

"Sir, are you all right?"

"Yes, just an old injury acting up."

"Good. We're sending a team to get Brucie to a hospital. They'll pick you up along the way."

"Perfect, thanks, Nicky."

"So," Ron said with a smirk. "Does this crack the top ten?"

"Hmm, yes, it has to be at least above the Tiberna Desert."

Tigh's mouth gaped in shock. "Are you freaking kidding me?"

"Well, you didn't fight the thing, so I understand why you're skeptical, but trust me, it was worse."

"Age is screwing around with your memory, you old coot. We had to drink piss out there!"

"Hey!" Daniel waggled a warning finger. "We're not supposed to talk about that." Then he winked, and they continued recounting their glory days.

***

We finished a cabinet meeting and everyone prepared to leave. That included the Good Doctor. When he headed for the exit, his minicomp beeped and he checked it.

—Thoughts of Evelyn Losier, Hocmar 28, 2134, on the Nirnivian calendar

"I received a most interesting message," the cyborg said as he studied the device he held. His electronic eye displayed an O-shaped mouth emoticon. "According to my source in NISDA, an aggressive visitor appeared on level five of Valardir. It caused quite a commotion."

"Enough so we might get to Rose?"

"Alas, the crisis is already over. My source informs me with an apology that it could not contact me before now. How unfortunate, it is a lost opportunity."

Evelyn sighed. "I wish you'd tell us who your mysterious source is."

How he extracted classified information out of Valardir, he refused to reveal. He even used gender-neutral pronouns to hide whether the spy was a woman or a man. In fact, he relied on "it" instead of "them," implying an object rather than a person. Perhaps that was the case. Or not... regardless, the source had its limits and had failed to provide game-changing revelations so far.

"The fewer people know its identity, the lower the chances it gets discovered. At the moment, I am the only one aware of its true nature and that makes it quite safe. I assure you that my secrecy in this matter is in no way due to a lack of trust."

Despite this being a logical explanation, being kept in the dark still stung.

—Thoughts of Evelyn Losier, Hocmar 28, 2134, on the Nirnivian calendar

Chapter 19

Fifteen minutes after Madeleine and Rose reached a compromise, soldiers showed up. They told us the beast had been dealt with. Daniel Ricdeau accompanied them. At first, I assumed the Commander was injured because he limped, but it turned out his leg cramped up every so often. Later on, I heard he killed that monster, but he didn't mention it. I guess he preferred not risking an argument with Rose. Oh, speaking of Rose, she asked about Janice the second Daniel arrived. Her dad assured her she was fine but said that Brucie had suffered an injury. Medics prepared him for transport to a hospital and Janice stayed with them. Poor Brucie—he was an asshole, but still a friend. Anyway, Rose insisted she wanted to see them, so we returned to her quarters.

—Thoughts of James Hunter, Hocmar 28, 2134, on the Nirnivian calendar

The instant the elevator door opened, Rose rushed out. While James followed suit, his speed proved slow compared to hers and he lagged behind. Still, a short distance separated them from their destination, so he soon arrived anyway. Though a brief run, the effort left James huffing and puffing, a fact that discouraged him more than he'd like to admit, even if he was well aware of his lacking physical prowess.

Medics carried Brucie out of Rose's office on a stretcher. The bodyguard just lay there, staring at the ceiling. For now, however, Rose ignored him. Instead the redheaded prophet sprang toward her sister, yelled, "Janice, thank Ulgorack you're all right!" and trapped the gigantic woman in a hug. The force of the impact ended up so great that Janice stepped backward and wavered. An impressive display of strength given Janice's size, but not quite enough to cause a fall. Right after she regained her balance, Janice stiffened and broke free of the embrace.

Maybe Rose hugged too hard for comfort. I could see that, given her enthusiasm. Then again, Janice tended to be cold toward Rose, so who knows? Either way, I could sense Rose was hurt by her sister's rebuke even if she chose not to show it.
—Thoughts of James Hunter, Hocmar 28, 2134, on the Nirnivian calendar

Having greeted her sister, Rose then turned toward her bodyguard and gasped. "Brucie!" She stepped toward the stretcher and James joined her. The big fellow gazed at them and smiled but remained silent. James assumed Brucie would eventually fire off one of his sarcastic remarks, but no. His lips remained sealed. Perhaps he was too tired to talk.

A silent Brucie... what a strange sight.
—Thoughts of James Hunter, Hocmar 28, 2134, on the Nirnivian calendar

"Don't worry, Your Holiness," one of the medics said in Brucie's stead. "The spike on the beast's tail was venomous, but he should be fine with proper care. This soldier"—he bobbed his head toward Janice—"patched up his wounds and injected him with an antivenom cocktail, and it looks like it slowed the venom. That was a genius move. It probably saved his life."

A light blush reddened Janice's cheeks as she shrugged the compliment away. "Heh, I just figured it couldn't hurt. Any idiot would've done the same."

The medic chuckled. "I doubt that. Either way, great job! We're lucky the shot worked this well. With a visitor, there was no guaran—"

A familiar voice then interrupted the sentence. "Ah, there you are!" A pleasant laugh followed. "To think you'd leave your poor old father behind. For shame! I can't run like I used to, you know?"

James faced the source of those words and spotted Daniel approaching them, still encumbered by a slight limp. Rose covered her mouth with her fingers. "Oh, Dad, I'm sorry for rushing out like that."

He giggled. "No problem, I understand." With that, Daniel glanced at Brucie. "Will he be all right?"

The other medic nodded. "Yes, he should be, Commander Ricdeau." She licked her lips. "But we better get going. He needs proper medical attention."

"Don't let me hold you up."

"Uh..." Janice scowled slightly and gestured toward the stretcher. "I'll go along and keep an eye on Brucie."

"Sounds good to me." Before she left, Daniel approached her and patted her shoulder. "Sweetie, you were amazing! I'm proud of you."

"Thank you, Dad."

On that note, the medics left, accompanied by Brucie. Almost as soon as they were out of view, Daniel smiled at Rose. "And you were amazing too. You're the one who asked me to send Brucie along. If you hadn't, Janice might..." Daniel grimaced and waved his own observation away. "No, I'd rather not think about it. Ulgorack must've sent you a vision."

After a brief shudder, Rose shook her head. "No, nothing like that." She lowered her gaze, and her lips twisted for a second. "I simply thought Brucie would be more useful as an extra fighter than a guardian in these circumstances. If anything, my feminine instinct spoke to me, not Ulgorack."

"Well, whoever it was, we're lucky you listened." Daniel sighed. "Ron went back to the command room and I better join him. The monster's dead, but something tells me we'll be dealing with the repercussions for a while." He winked. "Call it my Commander's instinct."

***

After Daniel left, Rose rushed for her garden. Again, I had trouble keeping up. Maybe I should've trained with her after all. Then I might not have been so out of shape.

—Thoughts of James Hunter, Hocmar 28, 2134, on the Nirnivian calendar

As James approached the garden, he reached instinctively for his key card. He wrapped his fingers around the plastic slab but let go once he realized how needless the gesture was. The beast's attack had bent the door, creating a large enough opening for him to step through. Through that hole, he spotted Rose standing in the grass, her back to him.

Without a trace of hesitation, James joined Rose. Soon, he stood right beside her, but she showed no reaction to his arrival. Instead, she remained frozen in place, staring at a bunch of trampled flowers. Also, the sun chair she often used had been flipped over, but other than that, the damage appeared minimal. James opened his mouth, about to comment on the garden's state, but before he did, Rose spoke, still not looking at him. "Considering everything that happened, it feels selfish, but I'm glad I haven't lost this place, even if only for a short while."

James forced a chuckle. "Well, it's the only"—he performed finger quotes—"'sun' you get."

"I suppose so."

James glanced at her and Rose averted her gaze further, as if meaning to escape his eyes. "Um, are you okay?"

"Yes, of course." She sighed. "I'm just a little shaken."

"That's not surprising. You should rest for a while."

"That sounds tempting, but I have a lot of details to finalize for Priest Christopher's ceremony and I better get to it. I'll see you later."

Given the circumstances, I thought that could wait until tomorrow, but something told me I shouldn't object. Rose went to her office and I returned to my room.

—Thoughts of James Hunter, Hocmar 28, 2134, on the Nirnivian calendar

***

Exhausted, James sat on the bed, taking deep breaths. His stress relented, but not as fast as he wished. Being trapped with Rose while wrestling with his inner dilemma demanded more energy than anticipated. Not to mention the "debate" with Madeleine. Verbally assaulting a person in a position of authority was a far cry from James's normal behavior. During the argument, adrenaline had overshadowed his cowardice, but now that the situation had calmed down, the significance of his words crashed into him. He hoped for a tranquil evening alone to recuperate. A ringing doorbell shattered that dream.

James considered not answering but decided it might be important. With a sigh, he opened the door. Rose waited there, eyes red and swollen. She must've been crying. Without a word, she entered James's chamber before he invited her in. Rose went straight for the mattress and sat, holding her head.

"Rose, is everything okay? Uh, is your mother causing trouble again?"

"No, worse," Rose whispered after a sob. "I was so distracted by Mom, it slipped my mind. I need to talk to someone. There's no one else I can turn to. You're the only one I can trust." She then stared at James with quivering lips. "Promise you won't mention this to anyone."

I sensed how important it was, so I agreed.

—Thoughts of James Hunter, Hocmar 28, 2134, on the Nirnivian calendar

"Thanks." Rose shuddered. "When the soldiers transferred us to that office for safety, pictures popped into my head. We were mourning Janice. Brucie said he would have saved her. To me, it seemed like a warning. Thank Ulgorack everything worked out. Janice is fine and Brucie will be. But, he saved her like he said he would in the 'vision.' Since my birth, people have claimed I was the Melkar, the holy prophet. I came to believe they were wrong, but now this... I still think I'm just a random mutant, but I can't deny the possibility that Ulgorack sent me a message, and that's terrifying."

James frowned. "Why? Um, if that was a vision from God, it saved your sister. As far as premonitions go, it's a good one."

In hindsight, maybe not for Brucie. Then again, he'd put himself in danger to save Janice, so I figured he would have agreed with Rose's decision.

—Thoughts of James Hunter, Hocmar 28, 2134, on the Nirnivian calendar

"Yes, and I'm glad, but... Ulgorack never communicates with anyone except the Melkar. If he talked to me, I am a prophet." A tremor coursed through Rose's body. "I don't want that. Oh God, please let it be a coincidence."

James's scowl intensified. "I don't understand. Um, I mean, you're already acting as the Melkar. In your place, I think I'd be reassured to learn I'm qualified."

"That's a fair point, but"—she exhaled—"I've made so many mistakes, Hunter." Tears dropped onto her cheeks. "I tried my best, but sometimes it feels like I've made everything worse. If I'm not the Voice of God, then at least it's not completely my fault. I've been misguidedly put on a pedestal and given an impossible task. There's no way I can fulfill what's expected of me. But what if I am the Melkar? In that case, Ulgorack has guided me all along and I've still failed. What kind of pathetic loser would I be? If I'm a holy prophet, then I am a terrible one and I'd never forgive myself for it."

"I don't know what your wings are, or if you're a mutant or a prophet. I don't know who put those images in your head. What I do know is you're not a loser."

"How can you be so sure?"

He winked. "I'm the all-time loser: I'd recognize my kind."

Rose hugged me then. It was a warm, comforting embrace. After a while, I wrapped my arms around her. As I held her, I realized I had been ridiculous. Rose was so sensitive, so caring... she couldn't be the monster Doctor Death claimed. Or so I hoped. Through her lies, the mechanical freak had planted a seed of suspicion in my heart. I could slow its growth but not stop it—no matter how hard I tried. Whatever was going on in this crazy world, I had to discover the truth before it swallowed me whole.

—Thoughts of James Hunter, Hocmar 28, 2134, on the Nirnivian calendar

Investigating Her Hollowness

Chapter 1

Kotar 7, 2134, on the Nirnivian calendar

With a sigh, James closed the book resting before him. The deed done, he caressed the cover depicting a folder with the word "classified" written on it in red text. A slight cold sensation permeated the touch. Like the others similar tomes he'd consulted, the contents had ended up being nonsense. Around him, a few people walked around in search of a volume tickling their fancy, but they remained silent. Not that surprising for a library, he supposed.

In the distance, James spotted the soldier accompanying him. He stood nearby, pretending to study a shelf with great interest. Nobody questioned his presence. That he'd traded his uniform for normal clothes helped. No point risking a commotion. Besides, having him dressed in formal NISDA attire might lead the library's patrons to take a closer look at James, defeating the purpose.

When James had explained to Rose how bored he was and asked if there'd be the possibility of visiting a library to borrow reading material, she'd shown enthusiasm. In appearance, at least, she'd seemed thrilled to see him interested in going outside. However, she'd remarked that he'd need an escort to ensure his safety. Months had passed since his arrival, but people might still be on edge about having a human among them. That assumed anyone would recognize him, but why risk it? A few days later, Rose had arranged for a soldier to accompany James.

The moment they'd stepped inside the building, James had run into a hurdle. He had forgotten about library cards, although they used the same system back home. Since he lacked the proper identification, he couldn't apply for one. His guardian proposed to borrow a book or two for James. The problem was, he preferred to keep the literature he meant to consult a secret. Then again, now that he reconsidered the matter, James figured he couldn't have smuggled the tomes into Valardir without being discovered. He'd have to study on the premises regardless.

Perhaps sensing James's gaze, the soldier turned toward him and tapped his watch. A signal that they needed to leave. Fine by him—this trip was useless anyway, so James responded with a slight nod. Then he stood and grabbed the two novels he'd picked up as a decoy. If he returned empty-handed, it might raise Rose's suspicions. As for the volume he read from, he concealed it in his jacket. Thank God his chaperone didn't notice.

That was a total bust, but at least I tried. To begin with, I searched for information about the first human but didn't find any books on him. Even the newspapers didn't mention him, but that was because they only went a few years back—long after he popped up in Nirnivia. I didn't give up and looked up Rose. Not much there either. Some news articles about her confinement in Valardir and fluff pieces. I also discovered records of several biographies supposed to be in stock, but they were all checked out. Just my luck! That only left me with one option: Ekelon, the secret project Doctor Death had warned me about. No way I could ask Rose, but the library might have something that talked about it.

Through my research, I learned that Ekelon was a classified project headed by NISDA. Even the Council was unaware. The details are vague, but imagine an AI-based system manipulating and censoring information on the GlobalNet in real time to influence the public. Large-scale social control, in short. That sounded bad, but it was hard to take seriously coming from the sources offering those gems: the cloud people, obedience drugs in the water, Doctor Death is an alien from outer space, false flag attacks engineered by NISDA, Rose died during the war and was replaced by a double, which is why she's hiding in Valardir, and chemtrails. Always freaking chemtrails. So, yeah, Ekelon was a goddamn conspiracy theory. What a waste of an afternoon. Ah well, I would've wasted it anyway!

—Thoughts of James Hunter, Hocmar 28, 2134, on the Nirnivian calendar

As they walked toward the counter, James noticed a woman typing at a computer. Envy filled him. The machines required a library card. You slid the plastic slab into a mounted slot and it turned on. Without one, they proved useless. That kept the GlobalNet out of his reach. Who knew what he'd have dug up using it? Beyond that, the computer would've simplified locating books. Instead, James had to browse through the card catalogs for keywords, and that demanded a major effort. He had overcome his natural shyness and asked his escort if he would unlock a computer for him. The soldier had refused, claiming that could get him banned if caught. Though James considered attempting to cajole him into changing his mind, his nerves stopped him.

Soon, they arrived at the main desk, and James's guard entered the checkout line. Meanwhile, James approached the return slot and reached for the tome he'd hidden in his jacket. Before he could drop it inside, a voice echoed, causing James to hop in shock.

"Sorry to tell you, but that thing is bullshit."

With a gasp, James turned around. A thin black-haired man in a trench coat and sporting a ponytail pointed at the volume. A young boy accompanied him, hiding behind what must've been his dad, though he extended his neck to peep at James.

That almost gave me a heart attack. Once I recovered, I realized he was Jonathan Rivers, the guy from the strike. We'd only met once, so I was surprised he recognized me.

—Thoughts of James Hunter, Hocmar 28, 2134, on the Nirnivian calendar

"Oh, um, yeah, I know. I"—James scratched his neck—"I find, um, stupid conspiracy theories entertaining."

"Sure, but be careful or you'll start believing them and then it's too late. So, how have you been doing, James?"

"Oh, same as usual. How about you?"

Jonathan adjusted his glasses. "Pretty well, actually. Ever since I left NISDA, it's like a weight has been lifted off my shoulders. I needed a break and I'm lucky enough to have a lawyer as my wife, so I could afford to quit. Spending the day with my boy is a blessing." He snapped his fingers and gazed at his son. "Oh, hey, Paul, say hi to James!" Instead of complying, Paul recoiled and whimpered. "Sorry about that, he's shy."

"That's fine. I was the same way."

"So, which one is your favorite?"

James frowned. "Uh, what?"

With a laugh, Jonathan tapped the book, causing a soft sound. "The conspiracy theories."

"Oh, I don't know."

That's when I had an idea. Since it involved computer science, maybe Jonathan had heard of Ekelon before. I could gauge his reaction if I mentioned it. Hey, he gave me the opportunity, so...

—Thoughts of James Hunter, Hocmar 28, 2134, on the Nirnivian calendar

"But the one I find the most creepy is Ekelon. It's, uh, far-fetched, but can't you see the government trying something like that?"

Jonathan acquiesced. "Yeah, but don't worry: it's technically impossible."

"Um, really?"

"Trust me, that kind of AI is decades away. Nah, Ekelon's a load of crap." With a smile, he waggled a warning index finger. "It's the cloud people you should be afraid of."

"What if they're running Ekelon?"

Jonathan chuckled, then winked. "Now you're getting it."

A whining voice rose through the air. "Dad, I wanna read *The Adventure of Lala*!"

"Oh, yes, of course. Nice to see you, James, but we have to go. I promised Paul I'd bring him here before his dentist appointment, and we have to hurry."

"All right, um, it was nice to see you too!"

***

The return to Valardir presented some annoyance. While the trip back went fine, once they arrived, draconian security procedures awaited James. That included interviews, scans, pat-downs and more. The fact that he lived in level five only increased the scrutiny. It took at least half an hour before James entered his room. Once there, he lay on the mattress, hands joined behind his head, and stared at the ceiling as he recapped what he had learned.

My first reaction was that visiting the library had been pointless. I'd found nothing interesting about Rose and the previous human. As for Ekelon, it was just a ridiculous con-spiracy theory. When I considered it more, though, I realized that was an important detail. Ekelon had sounded suspicious from the start, and what Jonathan told me confirmed my be-lief: Doctor Death had invented a story and pulled the name Ekelon out of a conspiracy book, figuring I'd never check— meaning he couldn't be trusted. That relieved me, but I couldn't trust Rose either. She'd still lied. Maybe I was para-noid, but it felt like both sides had tried to manipulate me.

At any rate, I needed to plan my next step. The first human and Ekelon were dead ends. Nobody would answer any ques-tions about them, and asking would raise suspicions. The only option that remained was finding out more about Rose and her past. I doubted anyone would tell me anything significant, but you never knew—I might find clues in whatever gossip I overheard.

—Thoughts of James Hunter, Hocmar 28, 2134, on the Nirnivian calendar

Chapter 2

Kotar 8, 2134, on the Nirnivian calendar

A familiar scene presented itself before Diabo. BBR had mounted similar attacks on countless occasions. Dead soldiers littered the ground while his goons looted the derailed truck's contents. Allison leaned against a tree, whimpering and weakened by the telepathy she had unleashed. The acrid smell of gunfire lingered in the air. Ah yes, most familiar.

Despite the similarities to previous assaults, there was a major difference: their victims wore not the green Ostarkiran military uniforms but rather the dark blue NISDA ones. No matter Plague's and Stalker's protests, it had finally come to this. Losing some of their contributors had taken its toll and their supplies had run low, in terms of both food and weapons. They lacked options and now had started raids on Nirnivia to compensate. It remained to be seen how NISDA would react. Not well, Diabo expected. Unlike his colleagues, he wasn't afraid of their response. Those Nirnivian pencil pushers had no guts, as their failure to stop Doctor Death showed. Their response would be weak. And if he was wrong, it wasn't like they had much of a choice. One thing was for certain: BBR would survive, he intended to make sure of that at any cost.

***

Since Brucie was on medical leave, Rose's dad assigned her one of his soldiers as a temporary bodyguard. For the most part, he kept to himself. Even when asked a question, he mumbled a short answer at most. Beyond that, he didn't help with her exercise routine. Brucie prepared programs and cheered, but the new guy stayed out of it. Still, Rose managed fine. Usually, she trained in the morning, but that day she overslept, so she moved the session to the evening. She wanted me to tag along, and I figured why not? I might learn something for my "investigation." Whenever we went to the gym before, it was empty, but this time someone else was present.

—Thoughts of James Hunter, Hocmar 28, 2134, on the Nirnivian calendar

The moment James entered the room, a female groan reached his ears. A quick turn of the head revealed Janice lying on a weight bench. The number of weights the gigantic woman lifted proved so impressive James decided not to count them. He expected that determining the exact amount would result in him feeling inadequate. In fact, he already did and preferred not to diminish his lacking sense of self-worth further.

"Janice!" Rose said with a joyful tone. "You're here late."

"Yeah." Between words, she pushed the metal bar she gripped upward again. Then she rested the dumbbell on the holder and exhaled in relief. "Don't have that kind of equipment at my house!" Janice sat up, and James noticed perspiration stains on her T-shirt as well as her glimmering skin caused by the light reflecting on her sweat. "Okay, I'm done now. I'm gonna hit the showers and go home."

"Oh." Rose bent her neck. "That's too bad, I was hoping you'd stick around and coach me. That would've given us a chance to talk. We haven't had a good chat in ages."

"Sorry, sis. Wish I could, but I have stuff to do."

Somehow Janice would've seemed more sincere if she'd bothered looking at Rose when she spoke.

—Thoughts of James Hunter, Hocmar 28, 2134, on the Nirnivian calendar

On that note, Janice walked away. Rose waited until she disappeared, then sighed. "What did I expect? She's been avoiding me for years, why would that change today?"

From the start, I'd realized that Janice kept her distance from Rose. That confirmed it. It was probably some sister fight that didn't concern me, but deep down I wondered if it could have anything to do with the bad stuff Doctor Death had warned me about. Doubtful... but probing a little couldn't hurt.

—Thoughts of James Hunter, Hocmar 28, 2134, on the Nirnivian calendar

After scratching the back of his head, James asked: "Um, she's not always nice with you, is she?"

"You think?" A touch of sarcasm tainted the alleged prophet's voice. "I don't know what her problem is." She moaned. "Janice avoids me like the plague, Hunter. I wish she would at least tell me why."

A scowl formed on James's brow. "I thought you had a fight."

Rose shook her head. "No. It happened overnight. One day she was her usual charming self, the next she wanted nothing to do with me. I'd prefer if we'd had a fight. Then I'd understand! And maybe I could fix it."

"So, Janice wasn't like this before?"

"Dear God, no! We used to be close, Hunter. We'd shop, hang out, watch girly movies. Janice was so supportive, and always there for me. How I miss those days." Rose whimpered again. "Now we barely speak. Sometimes I wonder if I did something wrong. I can't remember anything. I mean, sure, we bickered, like any siblings, but nothing warranting this cold shoulder treatment. If I offended her somehow, I'm willing to apologize. I asked, but she acted as if everything was great and brushed me off. Why can't we work it out?"

While that was sad, I felt a tad amused because what Rose described reminded me of Nadia. She'd become angry, yet deny there was a problem, or worse, say something like "If you don't know what you did wrong, I won't tell you!" I considered making a joke about it but decided Rose wasn't in the mood for that.

—Thoughts of James Hunter, Hocmar 28, 2134, on the Nirnivian calendar

"It's hard for me," Rose continued. "We've been close since we were kids. Well, since that incident anyway..." The winged woman chose that moment for an extended pause. Something in James's body language must've betrayed his curiosity, for she giggled. "Oh, what a nosy boy you are, Hunter. You should be ashamed of yourself. You want to pry in my personal business, don't you?"

"Um, no, no"—he presented his palm as a shield—"you're the one who brought it up."

Rose laughed again. "What a poor liar you are! Fine, I'll tell you what happened."

***

With a clank, the door closed. Surprised, Rose spun around and confirmed what her ears implied. The impact caused clouds of dust to rise, and she coughed as her eyes itched. Once Rose recovered, she pushed on the door, but it refused to budge. High-pitched chortles suggested her siblings blocked it with their weight.

For a second, Rose scanned the closet. Such a tight space... long ago, it must've contained clothes, but now it stood empty except for a metal bar where a lone coat hanger dangled. Rose gulped as she imagined the walls closing in. Then she clenched her hands into fists and slammed on the door. A thundering bang echoed with each strike.

"Let me out! Please!"

More laughter served as a response. They'd tricked her. How could she have been duped so easily?

The whole year since the Ricdeaus had adopted Rose, Laurence and Janice had tormented her. At first, they didn't dare cause serious harm, but they still made their displeasure clear. Both refused to talk to her, play with her or share their toys. As time passed, her brother and sister took greater and greater risks. They teased and insulted her, broke her dolls. When caught, Daniel and Madeleine punished them for disrespecting the Melkar, whatever that might be. Rose understood it referred to her and con- cerned religion, but trying to comprehend the concept hurt her brain. In any case, her wings mesmerized people, she realized that.

No matter how harsh the punishments grew, Janice and Laurence refused to stop. Their meanness increased with every reprimand. That was why Rose felt so stupid. That morning, both claimed they'd discovered a hidden cache of candies in the basement. Their parents had hidden the treats in a closet, perhaps as preparation for an upcoming party. From lollipops and gums to gummies, an abundance of sugar-filled delicacies awaited. Foolishly, Rose had fol- lowed and was trapped.

Again and again, Rose struck the door. Her fists hurt and their skin reddened because of the repeated impact. Still, she kept pounding the wooden surface. "Let me out! Janice! Laurence! I'm scared!"

Her brother said, "Sorry, Rose! That is your new home! Better get used to it, you will never escape!"

That had to be a joke. Nobody could be so cruel. They'd let her leave, even if only because they'd grow tired of blocking the door. But... but what if they decided to push a piece of furniture against it? With that realization, Rose's mouth gaped and then she whimpered. Defeated, she sat down and cried while her palms covered her eyes.

She remained in that position until a buzzing drew her attention. Its volume kept increasing. Curious, Rose lifted her neck and spotted a winged bug descending toward her. The long worm-like body and huge red eyes disgusted her, and it approached at a rapid pace. In a rush, Rose hopped on her feet and banged on the door once more. Kicks joined her punches, as well as loud screeches. Soon, her throat ached, but she continued screaming.

"Laurence, we have to let her out. Mom and Dad will kill us if they hear her!"

"No matter, she will nark on us anyway!"

At last, the door opened, but Rose didn't expect that development and she fell face-first. Gleeful giggles escaped Janice and Laurence as they high-fived. Still terrified, Rose ignored her siblings and ran upstairs bawling.

***

Once her new mommy and daddy saw Rose running and crying, they attempted to console her and asked what had happened. Still in tears, she said she'd explored the basement and an ugly bug had attacked her. Daniel explained the bug was probably attracted by the salt in her sweat.

Spying from the corner, Laurence and Janice followed the whole scene. Their parents didn't notice, but Rose sensed their presence. New Mommy and Daddy had matters to handle, so when Rose felt better, they left. Rose wanted to return to her room, but that entailed passing her siblings. She'd rather avoid them, but she gathered her courage and started walking.

A frowning Janice asked, "Why didn't you tell on us?"

Rose ignored her, so Laurence answered in her stead. "Because Melkar means dumb!"

On that note, he laughed and raised his hand, expecting a high five that never came. In silence, Rose kept going.

***

In her room, Rose lay facedown on the mattress and cried. Why were they so mean? What had she ever done to them? Soon, she heard footsteps and turned her head. Janice stood at the open door. As she gritted her teeth, Rose averted her gaze and yelled, "Leave me alone!"

"Rose, I'm sorry. It was a joke!"

"Shut up! You're a big meanie! I hate you! I hate both of you!"

"Then why not tell on us?"

"Because"—a sob escaped Rose—"because you'd be angry and hurt me more! You're so mean!"

Janice frowned and crossed her arms. "That's because we don't want you here! We don't want another sister! We were happy without you! Mommy and Daddy are always talking about you! Melkar this, Melkar that! They always play with you, buy you toys! You don't get punished! It's not fair. They're not your mommy and daddy, they're ours! Why won't you leave, you thief?"

An intense fury invaded Rose, and she sat up before hopping onto her feet. Tears still rolled down her cheeks, but from rage rather than sadness. "Because I can't! Mommy died and Daddy's gone! I don't wanna be here! I miss my daddy! I want him back, but he's gone! And they sent me here! And you hate me!" Rose's sobs doubled. "I want my daddy!"

Janice lowered her gaze for a second and then she walked toward her. Dreading the worst, Rose twitched. She feared a slap, but instead Janice wrapped her arms around her in a hug, caressing her red hair.

***

With a smile, Rose said, "Then Janice carried me to a rocking chair and rocked me for an hour."

"I, uh, wish I could've seen that. It must've been so cute."

"I guess so, huh?" a blushing Rose admitted. "Since that day, Janice and I were like perfect sisters. Until about two years ago, when we drifted apart."

The story was so sweet yet sad that I didn't realize Rose had revealed something new. Soon, I noticed the oversight, however.

—Thoughts of James Hunter, Hocmar 28, 2134, on the Nirnivian calendar

"Wait"—James scowled—"you have an adoptive brother? You never mentioned that before."

As James uttered those sentences, Rose closed her eyes and frowned. "But I did."

As she said that, I remembered her mentioning a brother. I couldn't recall when. Maybe during a Kuhard match.

—Thoughts of James Hunter, Hocmar 28, 2134, on the Nirnivian calendar

"I don't know where he is or if he's alive. His name is Laurence Ricdeau. He despised me. To him, I was an intruder who usurped his family." Rose shivered. "He clashed with Dad too; they always argued. The last time I saw him, Laurence screamed at Dad that he hated him, then left. He hasn't been seen since."

Well, that became awkward quick. Rose just sat there in silence for a minute. That gave me a chance to think, and I realized that, sure, Rose claimed she didn't understand why Janice acted coldly, but she might've lied. Hell, she had before. It was a long shot, but what if Rose feigned ignorance because it was connected to the first human? Far-fetched, but I kept the possibility in mind. Eventually, Rose forced a smile and looked at me.

—Thoughts of James Hunter, Hocmar 28, 2134, on the Nirnivian calendar

"How about you? Any brothers and sisters?"

James dismissed Rose's interest with a wave. "But... but, I'm so boring!"

Rose chuckled. "Oh please, it's only fair!"

Truth is I never enjoyed talking about myself. I believed my existence was pointless and best left ignored. But, she'd answered my questions; I owed her the same.

—Thoughts of James Hunter, Hocmar 28, 2134, on the Nirnivian calendar

"Um, no, I was an only child. There was no one but me and my parents."

"That must've been lonely." Rose's voice barely reached the volume of a whisper.

"Yeah, sometimes." James sighed. "But I had a few friends, so it wasn't that bad. Sometimes I think I missed out. Sometimes I think I was better off alone. Um, I guess there's positives and negatives either way."

Rose nodded. "Probably."

"My parents are the unlucky ones." He forced a laugh. "A single kid and it's a total loser."

"Don't say that, Hunter!" The alleged prophet patted his shoulder. "You're not a loser. I'm sure your parents love you very much. Why, your disappearance must be driving them crazy."

"That doesn't make me feel better."

After wincing at her faux pas, Rose said, "I guess not. How stupid of me. I'm so sorry. You've been around for months, Hunter, but there's a lot we don't know about each other. Let's play this game again later."

"What game?"

A giggle escaped Rose's lips. "The one where we both reveal details about ourselves. Kinda like we just did."

"Why not? Sounds fun."

With that, Rose began exercising. We kept chatting, but nothing important. That suited me fine, I wasn't in the mood for a serious discussion. I reflected on my parents, my friends and Nadia. Rose was right, they must've been worried sick and feared I was dead or worse. Nadia had witnessed my disappearance, which could've landed her in a mental hospital. Because I knew they worried about me, I worried about them. The worst part was, there wasn't a freaking thing I could do about it. It was out of my control.

—Thoughts of James Hunter, Hocmar 28, 2134, on the Nirnivian calendar

Chapter 3

Talking about Laurence with James brought back bad memories. It was after midnight, and Rose still twisted and turned in bed as she recalled past events. Her brother had always resented her. She had done nothing to warrant such animosity, but that didn't change the facts. Laurence had tried everything he could to make her miserable, and he'd often succeeded.

So many pranks and dirty tricks he'd pulled, each meaner than the previous. One had scarred Rose the most. In appearance, it was a minor incident: Laurence had done far worse, yet nothing had hurt her as deeply. Back then, she had been around eight.

***

Janice helped her built a magnificent block castle. They toiled for hours; Rose never imagined they'd manage such a feat. From her point of view, it seemed gigantic. The multicolored structure towered above her.

Both the castle's size and shape filled Rose with pride. She wanted to show it to Mommy and Daddy when they returned home. Determined to see her plan through, she begged for Janice to take a picture. Not that she needed to. The elder sibling agreed with enthusiasm. But before she snapped a shot, Laurence rushed into the room and kicked down their work. The painted blocks collapsed in a thundering crash that haunted Rose's nightmares. She burst into tears, and Janice boiled with rage. The older sister pinned Laurence against the wall despite his superior weight and asked why he would be so cruel. The young man laughed and said he hated Rose. Her sobs were like music to his ears.

***

That event had left a wound in Rose's soul. Not because Laurence had shattered her castle. Not even because of his words. No, the hatred in his deep blue eyes had caused the real trauma. Words might be false, but eyes didn't lie. In search of comfort, Rose clutched her doll, Ms. Penny.

Laurence had such handsome blue eyes. The girls at school considered them dreamy. But that gorgeous gift from God morphed into an ordeal. The color was unique, nonexistent in either his mother's or his father's side of the family. With time, he had come to suspect Daniel wasn't his dad. He deduced he was the son of one of Madeleine's other mates, explaining the strained relationship between him and his father. A ridiculous notion, for this small detail aside, he resembled Daniel like a twin. Regardless, in Laurence's mind, that they weren't related had been an absolute truth.

Laurence and Daniel fought constantly. Rose, however, connected with the old man from the start. Because of this, her brother believed his father loved the girl he had adopted more than him and blamed Rose. As a result, he had lashed out at her. She recalled how he'd uttered dreadful threats in the same speech pattern he had learned from his mom, without using contractions. This mannerism imparted elegance to Madeleine, but from a teenager, it sounded hilarious.

Over the years, Laurence's antics had grown in seriousness. Out of spite toward the alleged prophet, he'd once declared God a fantasy and had professed himself an atheist during a church service. After that incident, the situation had spiraled out of control and Laurence had left. He swore he'd disappear forever. They assumed an empty threat; he proved them wrong. None of them saw him afterward.

To this day, Rose worried about Laurence. She lay on her mattress, unable to sleep, and wondered what had become of him. She hoped he was okay and prayed he had found peace. Laurence wasn't a nice brother, but she understood his pain. May God have mercy on his soul and grant him happiness.

***

Anya didn't mean to spy on her sister. When she entered the room, she had no idea Tania spoke with the president. Once she noticed, Anya almost slipped out, but something about her pink-haired sibling's hunched posture caught her eyes. Whatever discussion they shared failed to please Tania. Out of concern, and a bit of curiosity, Anya stayed.

"—sorry, but I still can't replicate it." Tania sighed. "It's unlike anything I've ever seen." Then she clenched her fist. "But I won't give up! I have a few ideas left. They're unorthodox, but I'm hopeful."

The cyborg on the screen shook his head. "Alas, I am afraid I disagree. This project has been a long shot from the beginning. To be honest, I expected failure. Do not misunderstand, you are beyond talented and produced stellar work. In fact, you achieved better results than anticipated. However, it is now clear that attaining my goal through nanotechnology is a fool's errand. As such, I must cancel this assignment."

Tania bowed her head. "But... Good Doctor..."

"Let me stress again that I asked the impossible. Nobody else could have succeeded. There is no need for shame nor regrets. Besides, I prepared a backup plan. You will receive a new project soon. In the meantime, I suggest a well-deserved rest. Goodbye, Tania."

The monitor went black. A second later, Tania's sobs reached Anya's ears. A wince appeared on her face as her chest grew tight. Rarely did tears touch Tania's cheeks. She was a woman of cold fact and logic, not emotions. Swallowing hard, Anya walked over to her sister and patted her shoulder.

"There, there, Tania. You heard him, it's not your fault."

"So?" Tania sniffed and looked at her. "I had a chance to accomplish the scientific achievement of the decade and I blew it. So many ideas that I won't be able to try out. What a waste, it could have been a ton of fun."

Anya kneeled to be the same height as Tania. "Well, nothing stops you from continuing in your spare time. The Good Doctor doesn't control your hobbies."

"But"—Tania's mouth gaped—"you're right!" She pumped her fist in celebration. "Hooray! Science day and night! Awesome!"

A large smile formed on Anya's lips. This was so Tania.

Chapter 4

Kotar 9, 2134, on the Nirnivian calendar

Since that animal had injured him, Brucie had been on medical leave. While he still had time off left, he showed up in Valardir for a visit one day. Rose was in a meeting when he arrived, so we went for a drink in the cafeteria. As far as I could tell, the near-death experience hadn't changed him. Um, I can't decide whether or not that's good.

—Thoughts of James Hunter, Hocmar 28, 2134, on the Nirnivian calendar

Careful not to spill the azure liquid within, James rested his glass on the table, then sat down. The sweet smell of druikinaka juice tickled his nostrils, and he salivated in anticipation. The equivalent of blended gummies sounded unappealing, yet somehow the result worked. As for Brucie, his goblet contained a thick white concoction reminding James of a milkshake.

"Um, you're looking great, Brucie!" James smiled. "I'm glad you're okay."

The bodyguard shrugged. "Sure, dude, 'twas just a scratch, ya know. Don't need no freaking vacation; I'm doing fine, but they're forcing me." His expression then grew somber. "Gotta tell ya, I dunno what that thing was, but it scared the crap outta me."

"Yeah, I hear you." James scratched the back of his head. "I can't believe Mr. Ricdeau's the one who killed it."

"Ain't that surprising. The geezer used to be a real stud, ya know. Daniel ain't in his prime, but don't ya doubt he got some mad skills! Ah, don't let that worry ya, dude. He has a good heart."

"Yeah, he's a nice man. I like him."

"So you like old men now?" Brucie winked, followed by a chuckle. James ignored the taunt. "Hey, I'm just messing with ya. Don't looka me like that."

"Sorry! I was thinking that if the monster had torn you apart, I, uh, I'd miss your sense of humor."

Not certain I meant it, but I figured he'd enjoy hearing it, so why not?

—Thoughts of James Hunter, Hocmar 28, 2134, on the Nirnivian calendar

"Hey, who wouldn't?"

"Fair enough! I guess we're lucky you made it!"

After a laugh, Brucie leaned back in his chair and linked his fingers behind his skull. "Nothing to do with luck, I survived 'cause I'm freaking amazing; I mean, I'm waaay too cool to die." A sudden shudder disturbed his nonchalant posture. "But that freak—ah, man, it was unreal. I dunno what kinda messed-up universe it came from, but must be a shitty place." Brucie put his lips on his straw and after a loud slurp, he continued. "At least I got scarred protecting something that's worth it, ya know..."

"Janice?" James asked as he remembered the bodyguard had saved her.

"Yeah, man. Damn, that's a real woman." He mimicked the shape of a female silhouette with his hands. "That body of hers—so freaking hot—"

"Don't drool too much: she's here." Janice indeed entered the lunchroom, but she walked at a hurried pace. She handed something to a man James had never met and almost turned away when she noticed them and waved. "Hi, James! Back already, Brucie?"

"Nah, just here 'cause ya can't live without me!"

"Ooh la la, someone has a high opinion of himself! Listen, I gotta go, but try and catch me before you leave."

On that note, she left, and once she exited the room, Brucie whistled. "Man, I wish I could grab that ass. Ain't ready to lose my dick over it."

Well, he was still as disgusting as ever with women. While I tried not to gag, I realized that since Janice had become the subject of our conversation, it was a perfect time to ask Brucie about what had happened between the Ricdeau sisters. I figured he wouldn't have much to say but gave it a shot anyway.

—Thoughts of James Hunter, Hocmar 28, 2134, on the Nirnivian calendar

"Um, hey, speaking of her, Rose, uh, told me Janice is avoiding her."

"No shit! It's damn obvious, ya know."

"It's strange: Rose said they were close until suddenly Janice started acting weird."

"Now that ya mention it, yeah, they used to spend a lot o' time together." Brucie frowned, deeper in thought than usual. "If ya wanna ask why, you ain't talkin' to the right guy. I asked Janice 'bout it, but she brushed it off, ya know. Funny shit is, the gal loves her sister. When talking 'bout Rose, Janice is like 'she's so awesome!' A bit more and I'd figure she wanna marry her or something. I don't get women."

To use his words: "no shit!"

—Thoughts of James Hunter, Hocmar 28, 2134, on the Nirnivian calendar

James raised his glass to his lips, concluding the "investigation" wouldn't progress any further. A pity, but the expected outcome. He had no idea what to discuss any-more, so he chose the first thing that came to his mind. "Rose told me about her childhood. I, um, wonder what she was like as a kid." A funny image then entered his brain. "Better yet: as a teenager, that must've been some-thing."

"Ain't asking the right guy again, dude. When I met Rose, she was legal if ya know what I mean."

Urgh.

—Thoughts of James Hunter, Hocmar 28, 2134, on the Nirnivian calendar

"Teen Rose, huh?" The bodyguard rubbed his chin. "Yeah, I can't even imagine. Maybe she was all moody and rebellious—writing dark poetry and crap. Hey, guess who could tell ya?"

"Uh, her family?"

"Yeah, but also the ultimate iceberg o' coldness, man."

"Who the hell is that supposed to be?"

"Who else but Kristina Dupree, dude? That babe is all business."

True enough, Kristina Dupree wasn't a warm woman. However, she had known Rose for a long time. I wondered what kind of story she could offer. Besides, I'd rather talk to her about Rose than Daniel or Janice—that might appear sus-picious. The problem was, Kristina hated me. If I questioned her about her past, I doubted she'd answer. In fact, she'd probably scream for help instead.

—Thoughts of James Hunter, Hocmar 28, 2134, on the Nirnivian calendar

Chapter 5

One advantage of working in a high-end military complex, Janice had discovered, was access to sophisticated equipment. Work served as the main purpose for these, and in several cases attempting using them for personal affairs would land you in deep trouble. For instance, pity the poor soul foolish enough to borrow a missile launcher to play a joke on their neighbor.

Still, opportunities existed, the easiest to exploit being the video conference rooms. Sure, accessing them during the day required official business, but evenings and nights, most remained unoccupied. And that was why, once a month, Janice stayed late, prepared a beverage, and contacted her friend Bob. They used to work together at the neutral zone's border. In fact, if she remembered correctly, she'd talked to him when her dad had requested her return to Valardir.

Janice missed Bob; they had grown close during their time as colleagues. Thanks to the magic of Valardir's technology, they could see each other, and that beat the crappy phone conversation they'd share through her telephone at home. Phone service lacked quality near the border, when it worked at all. Her only complaint—she had to trade the desired beer for a nonalcoholic druikinaka juice. Smuggling the coveted bottle posed a certain risk she preferred to avoid. Now, Janice's father might have the rank to pull off sneaking in his priceless Uisge, but she hung far lower on the ladder. Then again, he might show mercy and agree to help her. She'd have to remember to ask him next month.

"And that's it for me," Bob said after he shared the new developments at the border. As usual, life there proved uneventful. "How about you? Got any juicy stories for Bobby?"

"Nope!"

"But, what about that special assignment the Commander assigned you?"

Janice shrugged. "Can't talk about it. It's top secret."

"Hey, you can trust an old pal like me!"

"Yeah, I know, but Dad's strict. If he caught me squealing..." She mimicked slicing her throat with her index finger, and Bob scoffed. To be honest, Janice doubted Daniel would go that far, but better to be careful considering the subject. Besides, the task embarrassed her, so she'd rather avoid discussing it.

"No way, you're his daughter."

"Hey, Dad's tough."

"Seriously?" Janice nodded and Bob responded with a grunt. "Damn, the old man has a mean streak."

"He wouldn't be Commander if he didn't. Anyway, you're not missing much. It's freaking boring."

"That's hard to believe."

"Well, it is." Then she paused and her lips twitched. "Hey, Bob, how do you feel about people who say opposites attract?"

"Ah, you found a new conquest!"

"Heh, I wouldn't go that far. It's just a guy I've been hanging out with. Really, I thought nothing would happen between us, but Brucie's convinced I'm going ga-ga for him. I dunno, it got me thinking about the possibility. He's a nice guy, but we're very different. He's so shy and reserved. Then again, dating my type of man never paid off for me. What do you think?"

"Depends. If you ask me, serious relationships work better with someone you have a lot in common with."

"Yeah, makes sense, but shit—at this point in my life, I'm not sure I want serious." Janice moaned. "Dear God, my sex life has been going downhill. I could use a fling. Maybe I should just scout him out and see how it goes. If he's interested, we can have some fun and who knows where it'll go? If not, no biggie."

"Sounds like a plan. So, who is the lucky bastard, anyway?"

"None of your business, bud."

"Ah, come on, Janice!"

"Fine, his name is James Hunter."

"The human?!" Bob's mouth gaped. "You want to bone a freaking human? What, we Gorumars aren't hot enough for you? Damn, we've known each other since the war and you never once offered to sleep together, but that James fellow slips into our universe by accident and you're all over him? I'm outraged, Janice—outraged!"

"Bob, you remember you're gay, right?"

"Oh, so that's it, you won't sleep with me because you're a homophobe! I didn't expect that of you. You disgust me!"

"You're such a goofball sometimes."

"Don't blame me, I learned from you! By the way, rumor has it Rose is spending a lot of time with the human, and your father, the honorable Commander, lets him live in Valardir. No offense, but what's this weird fascination the Ricdeaus have for humans?"

"Ah, buddy, I have no idea whatsoever."

Chapter 6

Kotar 17, 2134, on the Nirnivian calendar

If I was going to talk to Kristina, it had to be without Rose. That made it tricky—they were almost always together. The only chance was breakfast. Sometimes Kristina showed up early at the cafeteria while Rose exercised. No way to predict when, though. For a week, I stopped hanging with Rose when she trained, pretending I felt too tired and needed more sleep. Instead of staying in bed, I went for breakfast, fearing Rose might discover I lied. If that happened, I'd have some explaining to do, and I had no idea how I'd handle it. Sometimes Kristina was there, sometimes she wasn't. That morning I saw her sitting at a nearby table. She poked on her minicomp with a stylus and paused every few minutes to take a quick bite. That woman never relaxed. Still, I couldn't figure out how to start a conversation. We didn't get along, so just asking questions about Rose wouldn't cut it.

—Thoughts of James Hunter, Hocmar 28, 2134, on the Nirnivian calendar

Though the eggs on his plate smelled delicious and his stomach grumbled, James barely ate. He picked at the meal with a fork, tearing the omelet apart, occasionally bringing a piece to his mouth. Instead, he studied Kristina as she worked. More than once, he feared she'd sense his gaze and stare at him, but she proved so deep in concentration that her eyes remained fixed on her device.

After a quick peep at the clock, James nibbled his bottom lip. At this rate, Rose would finish training soon. This was hopeless. He should eat the meal and return to his room. When he was about to, a metallic clink echoed. He scanned the area in search of the source but found nothing. With a sigh, James refocused on his eggs and in doing so spotted an object glimmering on the floor next to Kristina. He squinted and recognized keys. They must've fallen from her pocket. That could be his excuse to talk to Kristina, except how should he proceed? Going from "you dropped your keys" to "tell me everything about your employer" seemed like a stretch. Then again, if he didn't exploit this opportunity, he'd lose it. Gritting his teeth and suppressing a shiver, James got up and grabbed the keys.

"Um, excuse me, are these yours?"

Upon hearing his voice, Kristina lifted her neck. As she spotted the keys, she gasped. "Oh, thank you!"

She seized her keys and returned to her minicomp. So much for a chance to chat. Except, I couldn't leave it at that after how hard it had been to approach her. Besides, there was something I should've said earlier.

—Thoughts of James Hunter, Hocmar 28, 2134, on the Nirnivian calendar

"Ms. Dupree, I, uh, I'm sorry for what happened when we met."

Kristina scowled and her lips twisted. "No, I should be apologizing. I've never liked being touched, so I overreacted."

Shocked, James almost stepped back. "Uh, no, I mean, a random guy grabbed your face. I deserved that slap."

"At that point, sure, but watching you with Rose, it soon became clear you told me the truth when you explained you mistook me for Nadia. It's obvious you don't have it in you to act that way, but I felt embarrassed and didn't bring it up. Because of this, it has been awkward between us, and I'm sorry." She attempted a smile. "If only you kept her picture in your wallet, you could've shown it to me back then."

The sad part is I did, but I didn't think of it. Especially embarrassing when considering I talked to her photo every day.

—Thoughts of James Hunter, Hocmar 28, 2134, on the Nirnivian calendar

After that, the blond assistant adjusted her glasses. "Anyway, you've been so great with Rose. Now that you're here, she's so much happier. I'm grateful for that."

"Really?" Bolstered by those words, James risked pulling the chair opposite Kristina, and she declined to object. "I was under the impression you thought I wasted her time." He bit his tongue, but too late to stop that last sentence. What if he'd offended her again? Thank God, she took the observation in stride.

"Oh dear Ulgorack, I said that once." Kristina winced and blushed. "Again, I'm sorry, Mr. Hunter. Rose procrastinates with her job, and it's part of mine to make sure she does her work. It can get frustrating, and I lashed out. But, Rose has a lot of stress and is lonely, so it's great to see her spend time with you." She paused. "As long as it doesn't affect her tasks, but even when it does, that's on her, not you. Anyway, we got off on the wrong foot. How about starting over? We're both eating alone. Why not change that? I deserve rest too, don't I?"

What good fortune—she'd invited him. James hadn't expected that. Out of astonishment, he hushed, and Kristina misinterpreted the cause of his silence. "It's okay if you'd rather not, Mr. Hunter. I'm not the popular type: people find me boring. I'm used to it."

"Um, no... no... uh, don't be silly, I'd be happy to join you, but call me James. Mr. Hunter makes me feel like an old guy."

A timid smile appeared on Kristina's face. "Sure, but call me Kristina. Women dislike old age even more."

Okay, not a great joke, but for her, it was a decent effort. I decided her attempt at humor was a good sign. I brought my plate over and prepared myself.

—Thoughts of James Hunter, Hocmar 28, 2134, on the Nirnivian calendar

"Oh, James, I forgot something. I'm sorry; it'll only take me a second." Kristina then picked up her minicomp, gave it a few pokes with her stylus and put it aside again. "There, I'm done."

"Work is important to you, isn't it?"

"Yes. You could say perfectionism is in my nature. Back during school, I studied more than necessary. I got excellent grades thanks to my dedication, though my social life suffered."

James couldn't help but notice the sadness in her tone. "Success has a price."

"Correct."

"Well, it paid off—you're the Melkar's assistant."

"Yes." Kristina's cheeks reddened at the compliment. "I have an excellent career and I owe Rose for that. We attended the same school. I won't pretend we were friends, but we knew each other." She rubbed her lips. "When I got my degree, I applied for a job in the government. I figured I'd be rejected because of my lack of experience. Somehow, Rose heard about my application and recommended me." Kristina tilted her head to the left. "When I learned about that, I was astounded. I met with her and demanded she retract the recommendation. Of course, I appreciated the gesture, but I didn't want handouts. I wanted to earn success by merit." A slight giggle escaped her. "Rose refused. She said I was talented, devoted, always gave a hundred percent, and she believed I was the best candidate. Such praise from the holy prophet felt so... nice! They hired me. Rose put herself on the line. I couldn't let her down, so I tried even harder than usual. I impressed my boss and was promoted quickly, but I wasn't satisfied there. One day, Rose's assistant quit, and she asked if I would consider replacing her. I accepted."

"That must be a lot of responsibility."

Kristina nodded. "It is, and while Rose is a nice person, being her assistant can be difficult."

"Yeah, uh, she admitted she's lazy, so you have to push her."

The blond woman shook her head. "That's inaccurate. Rose isn't lazy, she's burned out. Please understand: she's been through a lot. These days, she's sick of it all: the politics, the religion, it's too much." Kristina sighed. "Her energy is gone, but she keeps going for the sake of her people. It's so sad." Then Kristina paused and scowled before continuing. "Sometimes I hate myself for pushing Rose so hard, but that's why she hired me. She won't quit, and I'll stay by her side until the end. I wish things were different: the poor soul deserves to rest. You have no idea..."

"Actually I do. She told me about it."

"Believe me, it's far worse than she lets on. You can't imagine."

The little I knew about Rose's life depressed me, so I wondered how much worse it could get. But I remembered the intense sorrow in her eyes... maybe Kristina was right, and that made me shiver.

—Thoughts of James Hunter, Hocmar 28, 2134, on the Nirnivian calendar

A moment of awkward silence passed before James dared ask, "Um, you've known Rose since she was a kid, huh?" Kristina agreed. "I wonder what she was like. It'd be interesting to travel back in time and see teenage Rose." There, it was out. Adrenaline rushed through his veins as he hoped his nervousness didn't show.

"If you did that, I think you'd be disappointed. Rose was a different person then."

Curious, James leaned forward. On cue, Kristina recoiled for a fraction of a second. "Oh? how so?"

"Well..." Kristina's eyes darted to the upper right as she tapped her chin. "Um, she believed she was a prophet." Kristina lowered her voice to a whisper. "Don't tell anyone this—if you do, I'll deny it until I'm dead—but she was mean back then. She, uh, looked down on people. Acted like she was better than everyone; like she was so special. Okay, so she is, but there's no reason to be hurtful about it. She forced students to do her homework. She chose her targets carefully and preyed on the timid ones who didn't dare refuse. Often, they focused more on her assignments than theirs because they couldn't bear the thought of the Melkar receiving a bad grade by their fault. Rose justified her actions by saying her time was too important for such trivial matters, but she always goofed off anyway."

By Kristina's demeanor, I suspected she was a victim of that scam. That was rotten and didn't sound like Rose. To be frank, she sounded unpleasant, and I doubted we'd have been

friends. When I met her, she had more of an inferiority complex rather than a superiority one.

—Thoughts of James Hunter, Hocmar 28, 2134, on the Nirnivian calendar

"But it wasn't all her fault. We're responsible for our behavior, and that holds true for Rose, but in her case, Nirnivia as a whole shares the blame. All her life, we treated her like a princess. The teachers refused to punish her; other students never dared pull a prank, or even speak behind her back. You can't expect a child raised in such circumstances not to develop an ego."

James shrugged. "Um, I guess not. She sure has changed. What happened?"

While thinking about her answer, Kristina caressed her face, covering her mouth. "Small incidents eroded her faith until she believed she wasn't the Melkar. She became much more likable as a result, but she overcompensated. Now, she hates herself." Kristina's eyes moved to the right. "I suppose what affected her most was Gail Wagner. Rose wasn't the same after that." The assistant blinked twice and brought her fingers to her lips. "Oh no"—she gulped—"please, forget I said that. I shouldn't have. It's a personal matter, and it's not my place to talk about—"

Then a cheerful voice interrupted Kristina. "Hey, you two, I'm so glad you're getting along for once!"

James turned his head and discerned a winged figure approaching while waving at them. Rose had finished her training.

Kristina swallowed hard. "Oh, Rose... uh, I'm sorry, I didn't mean to."

Poor Kristina turned white as snow. Whatever happened with that Gail, it was enough to terrify her. Realizing that im-

plied Rose would be furious, I was afraid myself. Yes, I wanted information on Rose, but not at the price of pissing her off.

—Thoughts of James Hunter, Hocmar 28, 2134, on the Nirnivian calendar

"Why are you sorry for having breakfast with Hunter?" Rose's face lit up, and she clasped her hands. "Unless there's something more going on..." A lock of her hair she rolled around her index finger. "Did I catch you in a romantic moment? Now I understand why you've been letting me train alone, Hunter! But, Kristina, why would I be mad? I'm thrilled!" Then she reconsidered. "Well, I'm sad for Mark, but if he's not your type, he's not your type."

Kristina held her head with both hands and her breathing sped up. "No, there's nothing between us." She whimpered. "We were talking about the past and I mentioned Gail Wagner. I shouldn't have, I'm so sorry. Please forgive me!"

After closing her eyes, Rose let out a deep sigh. Then she crouched next to Kristina and patted her shoulder. "It's fine, don't worry about it."

"I didn't mean to, I swear!"

"I know, it's okay, Kristina. I'd rather not think about Gail, but it's not like it's a secret. What happened is public knowledge."

"You're not mad at me?"

"Of course not." Rose offered a benevolent smile. "How about you go to the office and prepare while I handle this? I should be the one telling Hunter about my sordid past."

"Okay."

With that, Kristina gathered her possessions and Rose took her place. As soon as Kristina left, tears rolled down her cheeks, and she rested her head on the table, sobbing. That

wasn't the anger or sense of menace I'd dreaded, but in a way, it was worse.

—Thoughts of James Hunter, Hocmar 28, 2134, on the Nirnivian calendar

"Rose!" James hopped to his feet and stepped toward her but then hesitated. "Are you okay?"

Through her cries, she ignored the question. "Hunter, have you ever done anything so horrible you regret it with every fiber of your soul?"

"Yeah. I mean, everyone has regrets, right?"

Rose lifted her head, revealing reddened, puffy eyes because of her weeping. "No, not like this." She sniffed. "I'm talking something so terrible, I don't deserve forgiveness. Once I've told you about Gail, it's possible it won't ever be the same between us."

"Um, it can't be that bad."

Or could it?

—Thoughts of James Hunter, Hocmar 28, 2134, on the Nirnivian calendar

"We'll find out." Rose inhaled. "When I was a teenager, I"—whimpers stifled her speech—"was a real brat." Again, tears overcame her.

"Rose, you don't need to do this."

I'm such a good detective.

—Thoughts of James Hunter, Hocmar 28, 2134, on the Nirnivian calendar

"But I do—otherwise you'll always wonder. Besides, now that it's out, I have to get it off my chest." Another deep breath she took. "Hunter, I'm ashamed of who I used to be. They raised me to believe I was the Melkar, and it went to my head. My wings mesmerized the crowd. No matter what I did, they hardly punished me. At worse, I received a slap on the wrist. Teachers didn't dare give me bad grades; my dad—well, Daniel—spoiled me. I also became lazy and manipulated others into doing my homework. This might seem strange to you, I'm not sure if you'll understand, but despite the special treatment, or perhaps because of it, I was angry at the world."

Chapter 7

Fools, they were all fools. Pathetic, egotistical fools filled this world God had created. In tears, Rose flipped one more page in the school yearbook and gazed at the pictures. Be it her fellow students, the teachers, or any random idiot on the streets, they were the same. She was to be their salvation, their miracle. She would save their souls. But did anyone out there care about her? The real her? No.

Rose, study those sacred texts, they are important. Rose, you must speak at the hospital, a sermon of hope will raise the patients' spirits. Rose, yes, you are sick, but this group prayer is essential. Rose, that man wants a confession. Rose, that woman needs your blessing. All their desires they shoved down her throat. But what about her wishes? What about her dreams? Who would save her soul? No one, for nobody gave a damn about her or ever would. In their greed, they each grabbed a piece of her for themselves until all that remained was a broken empty shell.

"You!" Rose whispered at the images, sobbing. "You don't even see me. I'm an invisible girl. All you see is your expectations, the Melkar and nothing else; you use me, then you abandon me." A twisted giggle escaped her lips. "But I'm glad! You're worthless! I want nothing to do with you! I hate you. I hate all of you!"

Except that was false bravado. God, she felt so lonely. She longed for them to notice her; not the holy prophet, but Rose Ricdeau. Longed for them to acknowledge her existence, to treat her like one of their own; to accept and love her. Longed to date boys, and go shopping with the girls; to laugh with friends and live a normal life. Was that really so much to ask? Was that so wrong of her?

Ever since childhood, Rose had been marginalized. The kids refused to play with her: what if she skinned her knee? The scolding they'd receive was a scary prospect. Why risk it? Rose didn't need them. Why would she need imperfect beings when God stood by her side? They couldn't fathom it, and she couldn't explain, but somehow even God wasn't enough.

"I'm nothing! Hollow! Light goes right through me. Hollow, hollow, hollow. That's why you can't see. That's why I'm the invisible girl."

Rarely had Rose been invited to birthday parties; the parents were far too ashamed. They proved unworthy of such a divine presence: their homes were houses of sins. Oh, and no matter, why would she crave cake and cheap paper hats? God stood by her side. They didn't realize that even God wasn't enough.

Another turn of the page, and a photo of Curtis revealed itself. His wavy hair and glimmering eyes awakened passions Rose had never experienced before. In her fantasies, she imagined he'd be the first who understood the real her. He'd take her dancing and sweep her off her feet. At the end of the evening, they'd finish with a tender kiss. She wanted to find love and get married. Was that really so much to ask? Was that so wrong of her?

Despite her reveries, Rose knew Curtis wouldn't date her. Yet today he'd approached, so timid, so shy. Her pulse had quickened, her breath shortened. With a dash of hope, she'd concluded sometimes dreams come true. Then Curtis had begged her to pray for his dying mother. Such a sad request, how could she decline? Rose put on a brave face and fulfilled her role, but inside her heart shattered. Inside, the pain raged. Even if in secret Curtis fancied her, she wouldn't have him. He couldn't recognize how much she yearned for his embrace. Why would she need a high school romance when God stood by her side? Curtis failed to recognize that even God wasn't enough.

"Why would I ever think you'd see the real me? I'm an idiot! You're the same as everyone else. Why would you fall for an invisible girl? You see right through me! That's fine! I don't need you! You're a worthless jerk and I hate you!" If she believed those words, maybe her heart wouldn't ache so, but her lies brought no comfort.

Now she scrutinized Tiara McKay, and envy consumed her. Tiara was the most popular girl in school. So pretty; so beautiful. She wore grandiose clothes, and perfect makeup complemented her features. Every boy courted her, every girl wished to be her. Meanwhile, Rose remained stuck with copies of this single white dress. It looked nice enough but lacked variety. Cosmetics couldn't touch her, for the Melkar had to be a natural beauty. Rules even governed her hair: the braid on the left side, how she despised it. She wanted to feel attractive like teenage girls often do. Was that really so much to ask? Was that so wrong of her?

To console her, Madeleine assured her that appearance is meaningless. It's what's inside that counts! Rose remarked that she should be able to wear whatever she pleased, then. While her mother agreed, she retorted that as the Melkar, Rose's followers expected a certain guise and she should oblige them. Why would she need physical glamour when God stood by her side? Her own mom couldn't comprehend that even God wasn't enough.

"Tiara, you're not so pretty! You're hollow! Hollow, just like me! You paint yourself so the light reflects on you. But

I can't, so I'm stuck as an invisible girl. That's all right! I'm strong, I can face reality! But you? You hide behind fancy clothes to delude yourself! You're pathetic and I hate you! I hate everyone!" On that note, she rested her head against her desk and she cried. "Why won't you look at me? Why won't you see me? Why do you make me an invisible girl?"

Perhaps Rose's image in the mirror believed she'd asked her, for she answered: "Poor child, your path is difficult. Being the Voice of God implies great sacrifices. You must be strong, for your own sake and theirs. They cause you sorrow, but do not blame them: they don't realize what they are doing."

As she heard those words, Rose straightened and stared at her other self. "Oh, that's rich. I'm so hollow, the only one who sees the real me is my reflection! What do they want from me?"

"Hope and salvation."

"But... I'm trying... doesn't that count for something? Why can't they see me?"

"It isn't their fault: they are intimidated by your holy blood."

"Holy blood?" Rose's voice resounded with folly. "Holy blood?!" She forced a maniacal laugh. "That's it, huh? Don't they understand it's the same as the blood coursing through their veins? Don't I bleed red like the rest of the world?" Rose shook her head. In doing so, she spotted the drafting compass on her desk. The tool served well during her geometry homework, and she had forgotten to put it away. Her lips twisted in a deranged smile as she seized it. "What if I showed them? Huh? What then?"

With that, Rose opened her left hand and brought the metal prong toward her skin. About an inch from her target, she wavered and stopped. A slight tremble assailed her as she sobbed and a few deep breaths she took. Before her nerves relented, Rose gritted her teeth and plunged the point into her palm before sliding it sideways, causing a scratch. She positioned the injury above the yearbook. A few drops of blood dripped on her fellow students, staining the page crimson.

"There! Holy blood! Isn't it as red as any other? There's no goddamn difference! Now that I showed you, will you see me? No—no, you won't! I'm the hollow girl! I'm giving you my damn holy blood and you don't care!" Rose sneered. "As far as I'm concerned, you can drown in it!"

Then she fell silent. Blood kept seeping into the pictures when a voice echoed from behind: "Sis! What are you doing?"

Rose turned around and discovered her dearest sister Janice. With clear panic on her face, she sprinted toward Rose, gripped her hand and inspected the wound. Had it finally happened? Was she visible? "Oh dear Ulgorack, you've cut yourself! It isn't deep. Why would you do this?"

"Um, I... I know it seems crazy. It's, um, a Melkar ritual. Don't worry. But please, don't tell Mom and Dad about it. It's important, but Mom doesn't like the idea of me getting hurt. That's why I'm doing it in secret."

Janice winced. "I don't know... this is... freaky."

"Janice, please... don't tell them. I know what I'm doing. Ulgorack speaks to me, remember?"

Despite her appeal, Rose desired nothing less than to be discovered. She prayed her sister would run to Daniel and disclose everything. But Janice played along. How could she miss the fact it was a huge cry for help? Like everyone, Janice didn't see the real her. She remained the invisible girl. All she wanted was for them to notice she required assistance. Was that really so much to ask? Was that so wrong of her? Why would she need support from mortal beings when God stood by her side? No one understood that even God wasn't enough.

Chapter 8

Holy shit, that was messed up.

> —Thoughts of James Hunter, Hocmar 28, 2134, on the Nirnivian calendar

After a short silence, Rose exhaled and continued, "It was during that awkward period I met Gail Wagner."

"Um, you did something bad to her?"

Rose nodded. "Yes, but without meaning to—that's the worst part. Gail and I spent a lot of time together. She pretended to be a friend, but she didn't really like me. In fact, I doubt Gail ever liked anyone. Rather, she kept me around so I'd cover her back. I showed her how useful I could be right from the start."

***

A few days after the compass incident, Rose walked down a hallway in her school. Around her, life went on as usual, oblivious to the cesspool of emotions raging within her. Voices talking about banalities reached her ears. From homework to prospective dates, the words mixed into a cacophony. A few parts of each story she caught, but not the whole, rendering the narratives incomprehensible. The constant chatter gave her a headache. Not improving matters, it appeared many students didn't believe in deodorant.

Despite the large crowd, forging a path posed little problem for Rose. As she stepped forward, people moved out of her way without being asked to. Should a distracted fellow fail to notice Rose, causing her to stop for a fraction of a second, they offered a pitiful glance begging for forgiveness. Such a show of respect from so many, yet none saw her. None realized the shadow weighing on her. None reached out. Invisible till the end, it seemed.

That morning, Rose had woken up in a bad mood, as usual, and what she stumbled upon worsened it. There, near the cafeteria, Curtis chatted with Tiara. As if her twinkling eyes filled with desires and giggles didn't prove her interest enough, she performed the classic hair flip. Rose gasped and covered her mouth with her fingers as tears formed in her eyes. A sickening sensation crushed her heart. The pain wouldn't have been greater had she been stabbed. Still, she refused to cry in public, though she realized she couldn't hold her sorrow at bay for long.

Gritting her teeth, Rose headed for the bathroom. There, she would lock herself in a stall and recuperate. Why him? Tiara could have any boy she yearned for. Why did it have to be him! As she advanced, the sadness morphed into anger. Oh, she would weep, but out of rage.

Or so she assumed. When Rose reached the bathroom door, she spotted a peculiar group nearby. A bunch of people surrounded a lone figure. Curious, Rose approached and recognized Gail Wagner along with her cronies. Thanks to her hair, dyed pink and cyan, identifying Gail demanded no effort. That girl had a reputation. A total bully and troublemaker. So much so that rumors claimed the scar on her left cheek had come from a knife battle of all things. If true, Gail refused to divulge.

Gail and her gang encircled Emily, an introvert devoid of malice. No matter what had happened, there was no way the petite redhead had provoked them on purpose. Gail and the others towered above Emily as she held the notebook she carried like a shield and stared at the floor. Now close, Rose noticed a single braid on Emily's right side. It resembled the one she sported, though hers was on the left.

"Got a new hairstyle, huh, punk?" With a sneer, Gail pointed a menacing index finger at Emily. "What's with that braid? You impersonating the Melkar? You think you're freaking holy now?"

"No! Gail, please, I swear. I'm sorry."

"Bullshit!" With that, Gail shoved Emily, who crashed into the lockers with a metallic bang.

Rose shuddered. That blow must've hurt. Shocked by the violence, her instinct ordered her to spring to Emily's defense. Even Gail wouldn't dare harm the Voice of God. And if she did, she'd regret it. Rose's devout followers would ensure as much. But somehow, her body refused to budge, and she remained standing there watching. With horror, she realized a part of her enjoyed the cruelty she witnessed. Rose suffered, yet nobody helped her. Why should she assist the fools who ignored her pleas? They didn't care about her. No one else stopped Gail—why did it have to be her?

"Please, I'll never do it again; I swear!"

"I don't know...," Gail mumbled while rubbing her chin with fake hesitation. "I think you need a lesson!" With a laugh, one of Gail's friends grabbed a pair of scissors from her bag and handed it to her leader. Meanwhile, the other two accomplices pinned Emily. The terrified youth screamed and begged for forgiveness. Her tormentor approached and cut her hair strand by strand.

This was so wrong. A voice in Rose's mind implored her to end this madness, but she ignored the plea. Emily's distress brought her pleasure. Somehow, it was cathartic. To see someone else's suffering dulled her own pain. Shame crept inside her. This wasn't right. Such a horrible scene shouldn't make her happy, yet it did.

In a mere minute, Gail finished her demented grooming. Emily looked grotesque: Gail had botched the haircut. If only the victim had been Tiara. Rose indulged in discreet giggles. What had happened to her? Was she going insane?

A teacher, Mr. Armandis, suddenly arrived. He loomed toward Gail with a severe expression. "Ms. Wagner, you've crossed the line yet again. When the principal hears about this, you'll surely be expelled!"

And then, Rose acted on impulse. By doing so, she sealed Gail's fate and her own. While she raised her hand to draw Armandis's attention, she said in her sweetest tone, "Sir, please do not blame Gail. She has done nothing wrong. It's my fault. I told her to do to it."

The teacher's mouth gaped, and he recoiled. "What? But why, Your Holiness?" His skin whitened.

As a prophet, Rose always had to appear radiant and hide her sorrows at any cost. As such, she practiced her drama skills daily and now she applied all she'd learned. Her eyes dripped with innocence and purity. Mr. Armandis ate it up, as she had known he would. "I'm sorry, poor Emily committed a sin of pride. Ulgorack spoke to me; he said she needed a lesson in humility. I... I tried to obey his directions, but I couldn't bring myself to do it, so I asked Gail. In retrospect, I suppose I made a mistake."

"Oh... I see..." Armandis's lips twisted as he pulled at his collar. "Your Holiness, I... we have rules. This isn't the kind of decision you should make by yourself."

Rose blushed and lowered her head in mock guilt. "You are right, of course. God's ways are mysterious; sometimes it's hard to understand his wishes. I try my best, but... I'm so sorry. Still, Gail isn't to blame. She didn't dare deny my request. If you must punish someone, then punish me. I'm the guilty party."

Rose claimed victory before he replied. Even Emily apologized for her sin of pride in tears. She'd manipulated these fools and had gotten away with no reprimand. A grateful Gail thanked her. The bully was shocked: she'd never expected the Melkar would come to her aid. Thus began the strange and unsettling relationship between Rose Ricdeau and Gail Wagner.

Rage overwhelmed Rose, but she couldn't bring herself to harm someone directly. Instead, she observed Gail torturing her prey and she arranged for the tyrant to escape unscathed. The grief she caused lessened her own burdens, but at a price. After the fact, her behavior always disgusted her. Rose's self-revulsion increased and she ended up ever more miserable: the brief respite turned into more sadness. She wasn't that stupid—she realized she was poisoning her psyche, but she couldn't stop herself.

Chapter 9

Again, that was messed up.

—Thoughts of James Hunter, Hocmar 28, 2134, on the Nirnivian calendar

"From the start, I knew Gail was trouble, but hanging out with a bad girl felt so glamorous. She didn't care what people thought, and she did whatever she wanted. If her actions hurt someone, she didn't give a damn. That intrigued me. Rules overwhelmed me; Gail had none. And she was older. School wasn't Gail's forte. They held her back a few times. Those days, age seemed so important... she was eighteen, practically an adult. And I did appreciate the pain she caused." Rose shuddered. "What can I say except I had issues? As cruel as I could be, Gail was far worse. I don't enjoy speaking ill of the deceased, but she was a mean bitch and beyond toxic. Still, I'm to blame for my failings. I headed downhill before I met her. Eventually, my mother realized I was walking down the wrong path. I didn't behave as the Melkar should. Mom understood that even the Voice of God wasn't above temptation, and she feared the special treatment I received had corrupted me. Nobody else saw things her way. In this battle, she fought alone. Mom tried to open my eyes but failed. Now that I'm wiser, I'm thankful for her efforts."

***

It was so pointless. Why her mother insisted on boring her so, Rose couldn't comprehend. She was the Voice of God; Ulgorack spoke to her. No need for sacred texts when he taught her everything in a more direct manner. Yet her mom constantly read those ancient dusty books aloud and offered extensive commentary. Rose loved her, but Madeleine Ricdeau was merely the head priestess. A prestigious position, but nothing compared to the holy prophet. What could her adoptive mother offer her given this fact? Therefore, Rose's mind focused on more important matters, such as the slumber party at Gail's house that evening. Soon, the old woman noticed her lack of attention and shouted, "Rose! You are not listening."

"Huh?" Rose blinked twice. "Oh... I am, I swear."

A lecturing finger Madeleine waggled. "Child, one should not swear so lightly. You of all people should understand this."

"But—but I heard everything you said!"

"Is that so?" The senior stared at Rose cross-armed. "Then would you mind telling me what passage I quoted?"

"Sure. It was about the plights of Gregory Elbanestor."

After a disapproving shake of the head, Madeleine replied, "Incorrect. Besides, you are thinking of the plights of Gregory Elvonastar. Not only do you ignore me, you forget your past lessons. This is important. Nirnivia puts its faith in you. You cannot fail."

"Mom, I mispronounced a name! So what? I'm the Melkar, I know what I'm doing!"

"Do you, dear? I doubt it. Your path is challenging. You must be vigilant, for your gift can become a curse. Your visions will confuse you. Should you interpret them falsely, the entire world will suffer the consequences. I must teach you, so you can decipher Ulgorack's messages."

With a scoff, Rose rolled her eyes. "Really? You're not even a prophet, just a priestess!" She stood up and rested her hands on her hips. While Madeleine gritted her teeth, she held her tongue. "How can you teach me? You know nothing! Ulgorack chose me! How about having faith in him?"

With those words, Rose turned around and started to leave. The old woman's volume doubled. "Young lady, come back here this instant!"

"You've wasted enough of my time, Mother! I have to prepare for the slumber party."

"That Gail is a bad influence. Perhaps I shall forbid you from attending."

Unfazed by the threat, Rose faced Madeleine and glared at her with a wide smirk. "That's an interesting idea. How about I ask Dad for his opinion?"

That card she'd played before, and she intended to use it often. Dear Daniel always caved in and granted her every wish. That had proven useful since Madeleine had increased discipline. The poor fool claimed Rose was headed down the wrong path and attempted to rectify her course. Her mother's lecture still echoed in her mind: "Oh, child, holy prophet or not, you are also a teenager. It is an awkward period of life and so you need guidance." How ridiculous. Who could serve as a better guide than God? Good thing Daniel undermined Madeleine's authority each step of the way. When she reprimanded Rose, he annulled the punishment. Should she resist, a bitter fight ensued, a truth Madeleine was well aware of. Rose expected that explained why she now sighed and lowered her neck in acceptance.

"Fine, child, but I offer a final warning. You are arrogant and foolish. Deep down, you have a good heart, but we spoiled you. It is our fault, but if your behavior continues, you will pay for our sins. I beg you, come back and study. If you refuse me as a teacher, eventually Ulgorack shall run out of patience and take my place. For all his compassion, he is far stricter than I am. Do not test him."

Stifling a giggle, Rose exited the door.

Chapter 10

Still sitting at the cafeteria table with James, Rose now held her head with both hands. "Unfortunately, I ignored Mom's warning. Back then, I didn't realize how much I'd regret that decision."

Her voice faltered and her skin grew pale. James even noticed a slight tremble in her arms. While he had no idea what she planned on revealing, it took a toll on her. He swallowed hard. "Um, Rose, you don't have to tell me."

"I'm fine." The prophet forced a nervous laugh. "Okay, I'm not, but I will be once I'm done." Rose paused for a deep breath. "In a twisted way, it's funny. Mom feared Gail was a bad influence corrupting me. The bully sullying the prophet. And really, why wouldn't she be? It's the logical conclusion. But life isn't logical. Life isn't a perfect narrative thread. Sometimes, the obvious villain ends up being the victim and the alleged hero is the executioner. There was this weird boy, Yangil Fergal. He looked strange, dressed stranger and didn't speak to anyone. Even the way he moved felt unsettling. Gail and I always made fun of him." Rose's lips twisted. "Well, everyone did, including the good kids. One day I received a vision, or so I thought. Pictures popped into my mind. Gail and Yangil dated, got married, formed a family and lived happily ever after like in fairy tales. Convinced Ulgorack had sent a message, I rushed to Gail. At first she assumed I was playing a prank, but I insisted. She eventually believed me, but she doubted my vision because she had nothing in common with

Yangil. I joked that they were the same age. That didn't impress Gail, but I kept pushing.

"Two weeks later, Gail reluctantly agreed and organized a date with Yangil for the next Saturday. That evening, she came to me and she was a mess. She'd hung out with Yangil and had a bad presentiment. He'd scared her. Unwilling to admit I could be wrong, I explained her initial repulsion was a test. The Voice of God had to be right—Yangil was Gail's soulmate." Rose sobbed. "The poor fool listened. She should have trusted her instinct instead. Gail went on the 'date.' Police found her dead the following day. Yangil had mutilated her. Thank Ulgorack I never saw the body, but the news said she was barely recognizable. The cops arrested Yangil. The trial ended with the judge sentencing him to jail for life. Gail wasn't a good person, but nobody deserves that! It was all my fault!" screamed Rose in tears before resting her brow on the table, using her arms for support.

James reached out and patted the winged woman's hand. "Um, no, Rose, it was Yangil's fault. You didn't kill Gail."

"I know that, but... but I sent her to him. When I learned what had happened, I locked myself in my room and wept. After a while, my parents worried."

***

Rose prayed for death, but it refused to come. Why? She deserved it. Gail was dead, and Rose was to blame. Lying in bed, she wept into the pillow. The moment she'd heard the news, Rose had locked herself in her room and cried. Intense shame filled her heart.

Every fifteen minutes, either her mom or her dad checked on her, attempting to talk through the door. Rose ignored them, and due to what she assumed to be respect for her grief, they let her be. To them, she was a teenager mourning a lost friend. They didn't know the role she'd played in Gail's demise. Nobody did. Gail had kept Rose's false vision secret. Had the consequences of her failure not been so drastic, she might have appreciated the gesture. As it stood, it felt like she'd avoided a well-deserved punishment, and that increased her guilt.

As Rose wallowed in misery, knocks once again reached her ears before her mother's muffled voice said, "Rose, my dear, will you at least let me bring food? You have not eaten for the whole day and we are concerned."

Stifling a sigh, Rose peeked out the window. The darkness outside confirmed the sun had set long ago. By now, she should be starving, but her stomach refused to complain. In truth, she expected she'd never eat again. No matter, starvation served as a far lesser sentence than the one she'd earned. For a moment, Rose considered answering that she wasn't hungry, but she lacked the strength for a response and remained silent.

Soon, Daniel said something, but she couldn't make out the garbled words. Then her mom replied: "I would prefer to avoid drastic measures, but I suppose we have no choice. Very well, Daniel, you have my blessing."

Two seconds later, a loud crash echoed through the chamber and Rose gasped. She sat up and gazed at the smashed door. Her dad's silhouette filled the entrance. "Princess!"

Madeleine's hand patted his shoulder. "Now, dear, I shall handle the girl." With a frown, Daniel opened his mouth, but no words came. In the end, he acquiesced and left. Then Rose's mother approached and joined her on the mattress. The priestess attempted to wrap her arm around Rose for comfort, but Rose recoiled. While a wounded expression formed on Madeleine's face, she accepted the rebuke. How could Rose explain that it wasn't out of anger toward her, but rather the fact that she didn't merit sympathy?

"My child, I have heard about your friend Gail. I am so sorry. While I cannot pretend I liked her, it is a tragedy."

The news had spread quickly; everyone had learned of Gail's murder, but not the cause. If her mom discovered what had happened, she'd be furious. Rose didn't dare imagine what she'd do. If Rose kept her mouth shut, she'd be safe. Yet she couldn't do that. "It... was my fault."

Madeleine rested her palm on her heart. "Child, of course not. Why would you believe that?"

A few tears dropped on Rose's cheeks as she yelled, "You don't understand! I told Gail to date that boy! I"—the few drops of water morphed into a torrent—"had a vision, or maybe it wasn't; I'm not sure anymore." Then Rose flinched, expecting a scolding.

Instead, Madeleine smiled, nodded, then said, "I see." The clemency stung worse than the anticipated reproach would have. Rose stared at her mother in shock.

"You see? You see?! Mom, I killed Gail! I've been bad! Punish me! Scream at me! Hit me! Hate me! Dear God, I don't care what you do, but punish me! You warned me, I ignored you, and now I... why are you so calm? Tell me 'I told you so, you spoiled little brat!' Scream at me! Please, punish me!"

Shaking her head, Madeleine exhaled and offered a sad smile. "And why would I do that? You are far better at it than I would ever be. Any reprimand from my hand would dull the torments you inflict upon yourself. I tried teaching you, child, but you refused. Now, Ulgorack has made you teach yourself instead. Such was your decision, and I will not obstruct your progress. Gail was hardly innocent, but it is unfair that she died for you to learn a lesson. However, it is reality and we must accept it. If you will take advice from a mere head priestess, I suggest that you right your wrongs so your friend's death does not end up being in vain."

"Gail wasn't my friend!" Rose formed a fist and punched the mattress. "She... used me. Only kept me around because I protected her. I was a convenience, nothing more."

"I realized that from the beginning, but I did not expect you to."

Rose whimpered. "But I can't judge her. I used Gail too. Mom, I'm so messed up. So... angry. When I saw someone filled with more rage than me, it made me feel better about myself. When I watched as Gail tormented others, I was on top of the world. Until I crashed down due to the realization that I've become a monster. Gail wasn't my friend at all: she was nothing to me but a crooked crutch. Somehow, that makes it worse! Mom, please, I swear I'll try to be good from now on. I don't know if I'll succeed, but I'll try. Please, help me. How can I take the pain away?"

"Poor child, I do not know that you can." Rose shrieked and her tears doubled as her hands covered her face. With a touch of pity, Madeleine caressed her hair. "All I can offer is this: I forgive you and love you now and always, no matter what. However, that will not stop the anguish. For that, you must forgive yourself, and that will not be easy." Her mother's words proved true, for Rose never completely did. Madeleine sighed. "That is a fact I am well aware of, for I am unsure I will ever forgive my own sin."

"Your own sin?"

Madeleine nodded. "Indeed. I have been so worried about your education as the Melkar that I failed you as a daughter. Never have I realized the anguish you endure. And yet the signs were there. That you ended up befriending someone like Gail in itself was, in retrospect, an obvious call for help, and I ignored it. I foolishly assumed she was a bad influence, when in truth the pain you endured had already corrupted you long before you met her. Perhaps the vision Ulgorack sent you was not only to remind you not to trust too much in your interpretation of them and to pay attention to the lessons I teach, but also to show my own blindness."

"Wait." Rose blinked twice. "You still think it was a vision? That Ulgorack tricked me?"

"Well, I did warn you that if you refused me as a teacher, he would teach you himself."

"Yes, but..." With a gasp, Rose shook her head. "No, it's impossible. God wouldn't destroy a life just to teach a lesson."

"Dear child, the ways of the gods are mysterious and beyond our comprehension."

"Maybe so, but I refuse to believe Ulgorack would be that cruel. No, it wasn't a vision. I fooled myself into thinking it was."

Madeleine shrugged. "Either way, in this tragedy we share the blame, though I do not know if that shall be any comfort to you."

***

"Mom was so understanding, but that wasn't what I wanted." Rose's voice trembled. "I wanted the hate I deserved. In desperation, I revealed the truth to Gail's parents in person. For a moment, I thought her father would strangle me, but he walked away in silence instead. Even they wouldn't provide the penance I craved." A sob escaped Rose's lips. "The important part is, Gail's death changed me. I questioned whether I really was special. I had been so wrong—maybe I wasn't the Melkar. Maybe everyone was mistaken. While I wasn't pushed enough to believe it then, my traumatic experience planted a seed of doubt that would eventually grow until I became certain I am nothing more than a random mutant. I cleaned up my act little by little, starting with doing my own homework. Also, I tried to be nicer to people and apologized to those I'd mistreated in the past. First, I went to Emily, but she assumed the apology was a test. The poor girl was convinced I tempted her to see if she would repeat her sin of pride." A sad laugh Rose produced. "I suppose undoing one's evil isn't that simple. What happened to Gail saved me. I fear who I'd have become without that wake-up call, but it's horrible that this had to happen for me to open my eyes."

James nodded. "Um, yes, it's a tragedy."

And that was putting it mildly. A long time had passed since Rose told me about Gail, and thinking about it still gives me shivers.

—Thoughts of James Hunter, Hocmar 28, 2134, on the Nirnivian calendar

"So, that was my darkest hour. I hope you don't think less of me for it," Rose said, averting her gaze. "But I wouldn't blame you if that's the case."

I mean, it was quite a revelation and didn't put her past self in the best light; I'll admit that.

—Thoughts of James Hunter, Hocmar 28, 2134, on the Nirnivian calendar

After a short pause to regain his bearings, James sighed. "Um, Rose, let me tell you a story too. One day, I ate at a fast-food joint and a homeless man searched a trash can for scraps. I'd ordered two burgers but only ate one, so I gave the man the second burger. Imagine my surprise when he flung it in my face. Then he walked away screaming that he didn't want my pity."

"Strange story"—Rose scowled—"but I don't see the point."

"Oh, uh, the point is: sometimes we want to help, but it doesn't turn out like we expected. It's hard to predict the results of our actions. Everybody makes mistakes."

"Yes, but a man throwing food isn't comparable to murder!"

"No, your story is far worse, but in a way we did the same thing: you tried to help Gail, I tried to help that man. We both failed. We can't read the future."

Unless she was a prophet; then she could, but she wasn't good at it.

—Thoughts of James Hunter, Hocmar 28, 2134, on the Nirnivian calendar

"Rose, your biggest mistake was pushing Gail to give Yangil a chance despite her bad feeling, but you didn't put a gun to her head. Gail made a choice. You were wrong and something terrible happened, and yeah, that makes you responsible in part, but it doesn't mean you're a monster. As they say at home, the road to hell is littered with nice guys with good intentions."

"I know little about the concept of hell, but I understand your meaning. Even if you don't blame me for Gail's death, that doesn't change the fact that I did rotten things during my youth. That doesn't bother you?"

James rubbed his chin. "Uh, a bit, I guess."

Mostly because Doctor Death messed with my head.
—Thoughts of James Hunter, Hocmar 28, 2134, on the Nirnivian calendar

"But it was ages ago. Everyone has regrets. Listen, I'm not proud of my teenage years either, and I doubt anyone is. Angsty teenagers acting like assholes are a dime a dozen, aren't they? I wouldn't be friends with the old you, but I like who you became, and that's what counts."

Tears of joy replaced the tears of sorrow in Rose's eyes as a smile formed on her face. "That's a huge weight off my shoulders. I'm so glad I confided in you. Thanks, Hunter. I don't deserve you." She giggled. "That was quite a round of our game. You owe me a major story, but I must take a rain check. I should've started my workday already, and Kristina is waiting."

Chapter 11

Kotar 18, 2134, on the Nirnivian calendar

Since I'd talked with Kristina, I went to the gym with Rose again in the morning. Though, no worries, I remained my dear old lazy self and stayed on the sidelines. With Brucie gone, Rose exercised without a trainer. While she managed fine, she believed she slacked off and decided to change that. Boy, she wasn't kidding. She pushed herself beyond what Brucie asked of her. Even the stoic soldier NISDA sent as a replacement offered a few impressed nods as she worked out.

—Thoughts of James Hunter, Hocmar 28, 2134, on the Nirnivian calendar

Conversation proved sparse during the intense session Rose imposed on herself. The required physical prowess demanded too much energy, and so except for a few encouragements on James's part, he remained silent. The situation changed once she arrived at the cool-down phase of her training. Now, a short-breathed Rose paced in place at a low speed, which James had learned lowered her heartbeat and temperature.

"Not too shabby, huh, Hunter? Sorry for tooting my own horn, but I'm pleased with my 'performance' today."

"Um, yeah, you did great!" James said, acquiescing. "I guess you don't need Brucie's help anymore, but I kind of miss him. It's not the same without his insults and random unfunny jokes."

"Yes, that's true, but don't worry, he'll be back soon." A short pause emerged as Rose wiped off beads of sweats rolling down her brow. "Well, Hunter, I'm ready to cash in my rain check."

James frowned. "Huh?"

A giggle escaped Rose's lips. "Remember when I told you about Gail? I was in a hurry, so I asked for a rain check. Time to pay up!"

"Yeah, that's right. What should I tell you?"

"Hmm..." Rose tapped her chin with her index finger. "Oh, yes, here's a good one! How did you meet Nadia?" A glimmer of curiosity flashed in her eyes, and James blushed.

That was a fair question, and easy too! I smiled like an idiot as I remembered what had happened. I must've daydreamt about Nadia for a while: Rose brought me back to reality by snapping her fingers.

—Thoughts of James Hunter, Hocmar 28, 2134, on the Nirnivian calendar

"Come on, Hunter, don't leave me hanging! I need my dose of romance!"

"Huh? Oh, um, Nadia... we met while waiting for the bus."

"Wow, love can bloom anywhere. So, you ran into a cute girl and wooed her with your words? No offense, but you're so shy I'm surprised you'd do that."

James dismissed the notion with a wave. "Nah, I didn't dare talk to her. I did notice her, though. She was stunning. Um, I had to remind myself not to stare at her."

"Ah, so she made the first move. You must've made a great impression."

"Nah, she didn't care at all about me. Nadia didn't look at me once."

"Okay..."

"But then, there was this boy who crossed the road without checking both ways and a truck approached fast. Before I realize what I was doing, I jumped, grabbed the kid and protected him with my body. Um, I guess my instincts took over."

After a gasp, Rose covered her mouth with her hand. "Oh my God! Hunter, you saved that poor child's life! You're a hero!"

James scratched the back of his head while he forced an embarrassed laugh. "Well, no, not really... the truck stopped before it hit me. The boy would've been fine."

"So what? You still put yourself at risk to save a child. That it ended up being unnecessary doesn't change your bravery."

The warmth in James's cheeks increased. "If you say so. Nadia felt the same. She rushed to check if I was okay. We started talking, and when the bus arrived, she sat beside me."

"Now it's getting interesting!" Rose clutched her fists in excitement. "I can see where it's going. You asked her for a date just as she reached her stop."

James averted his gaze. "Uh, other way around actually."

"Thank Ulgorack Nadia's a woman who takes what she wants or you would've been out of luck. Oh, Hunter, she practically begged you to ask her out."

"Maybe, but back then it seemed inconceivable. A hot girl like that interested in a total loser? Impossible. When it was clear I wouldn't make a move, Nadia did. I couldn't believe it! I still don't understand what she saw in me."

After a sigh, Rose sat next to him and rested her palm on James's shoulder. "She saw a good man willing to risk everything to save an innocent life, and that's special."

"No, it's what anybody would do."

"No. It's what everybody should do, but they don't always." She hesitated. "Nadia didn't." James remained quiet and responded with a shrug. "You're so hard on yourself, it's depressing." She exhaled. "At least it worked out, and you seduced Nadia."

"Um, I guess."

To be frank, I didn't think I was so lucky. Sure, I won Nadia's heart despite myself, but fate took her away in a most cruel manner. Not that it changed anything. Even if I'd remained on earth, she'd have left me sooner or later.

—Thoughts of James Hunter, Hocmar 28, 2134, on the Nirnivian calendar

Chapter 12

It had been a while since I'd played Rubarg, so when Janice asked if I'd be up for a game, I accepted. And that was the right call—I enjoyed myself. Besides, the break had made me rusty, so it was about time I got back into it. There was something off with Janice, though. She had difficulty focusing and missed a ton of easy shots. Hell, I almost won for once.

—Thoughts of James Hunter, Hocmar 28, 2134, on the Nirnivian calendar

"Nice one, buddy!" Janice said as she rested her stick on the rack.

"Thanks!"

Then she turned and faced James while tilting her head. "Hey, I've heard you went to a library." She ran her hands through her hair. "Since you're going outside now, how about catching some grub this weekend? Valardir's cafeteria gets the job done, but it's not exactly the finest cuisine Nirnivia offers."

And, yeah, that sounded fun! Ever since I'd arrived in this universe, I'd only eaten Valardir's food and, while not horrible, it tasted bland.

—Thoughts of James Hunter, Hocmar 28, 2134, on the Nirnivian calendar

"Sure, that'd be a nice change of pace."

"Great!" Janice snapped her fingers. "Oh, and it's my treat! I know the perfect place, it's so freaking good." She winked. "Trust me, you won't be disappointed."

Chapter 13

Kotar 19, 2134, on the Nirnivian calendar

Inside the war room, Daniel sat in his chair, fingers joined in a pyramid. The main screen displayed camera footage from a grocery store. Not the material one would expect NISDA's officers to be watching on the job, but closer inspection helped understand the incongruity. Armed men invaded the shop. They shouted for the customers lingering in the area to raise their hands and stay out of their way. As they performed crowd control, another group of thugs filled carts with products at a rapid pace.

"The video contains several spots where we can see Stalker, sir. The best one is coming up," Nicky said, pointing at the monitor. "There, in the lower-left corner."

The video slowed until they distinguished individual frames. Thanks to Nicky's instruction, spotting the strange color pattern and distortion demanded little effort from Daniel. "Are you sure it's not just an artifact caused by bad compression or faulty equipment?"

She shook her head. "Not according to the techs."

Daniel nodded as he processed the facts. Such a coordinated assault against a grocery store proved beyond unusual, especially since the crooks stole only food and not money. Even then, this would fall under the jurisdiction of the police, but they'd spotted an anomaly. On further inspection, the cops had deduced the cause might be that Stalker was involved, which implied BBR was the culprit. Handling those terrorists was NISDA's responsibility, so they'd sent the recording to Valardir for review. Given the police faced a wave of child kidnappings, perhaps they appreciated not having to deal with this.

Upon hearing Nicky's words, Ron Tigh crossed his arms and sneered. "What the freak are those bastards thinking?"

"They're probably desperate for supplies. I'm guessing the attack on the apartment complex cost them some of their benefactors, whoever they might be." Daniel sighed. "That also explains why they attacked a military convoy."

"That makes sense." The Koporal rubbed his chin. "That means stealing from Ostark isn't enough anymore. We can't let the sons of bitches get away with this crap."

A nod came from Daniel. "No, we can't. We must step up our efforts in the neutral zone."

"Yeah, but that's always a pain in the ass. The treaty with Ostark is freaking restrictive. Think our good old pal Doctor Death will collaborate?"

"No idea, my friend." Daniel forced a sad smile. "But we'll find out soon." Then he reached for the special pager that allowed him direct communication with the cyborg. "I'll set up a call with him right away."

Tigh rolled his eyes. "Oh goody." Sarcasm dripped from his tone. "I'm looking forward to it."

Chapter 14

Kotar 20, 2134, on the Nirnivian calendar

I didn't have much to do, so I read the books I borrowed from the library. One of them was a novelization of the original Melkar's life. I figured that'd be less dense than an actual historical account and hoped it'd be accurate enough for my purposes. I doubted it'd help, but I might learn a couple things about the Melkar. And, hey, it passed the time. Progress was slow, though; I'm not a fast reader.

Like Rose, Misha was born with wings, but in her case, the Melkar didn't exist and there weren't any mutants. People were confused. Other than that mystery, she seemed normal at first but became weird when she turned three. Misha made cryptic predictions and most happened. Strangest of all, she foresaw an epidemic in a country she'd never heard of. Sounded far-fetched, but if true I understood why they believed her to be a prophet.

Just when I was getting drawn into the story, my door opened. I gasped and dropped the book. Visitors had to ask permission to enter. What was going on? I turned around and saw two huge soldiers approaching. They ordered me to follow them. I asked why, but they refused to answer. As we walked down the corridor, I felt like a child escorted by a pair of angry daddies. A voice in my head urged me to run. I resisted—no good would come of it. Before long, I realized they were taking me to Daniel Ricdeau's office.

—Thoughts of James Hunter, Hocmar 28, 2134, on the Nirnivian calendar

Daniel sat at his desk, fingers joined in a pyramid. At first his eyes appeared closed, but James noticed barely opened slits. He'd witnessed the Commander adopting a similar posture earlier. Once the soldiers pushed James forward, Daniel lifted his head and smiled. "Thank you for bringing him. You can go now."

"Yes, sir!" With that, the soldiers saluted and departed as instructed.

"Is something wrong, my boy? You seem tense."

That pissed me off. I mean, he'd sent armed guards to get me without warning. Of course I was tense. I glared at him but didn't dare speak.

—Thoughts of James Hunter, Hocmar 28, 2134, on the Nirnivian calendar

"Oh…" The old man's lips twitched. "Were they rough with you? Sorry, James, I must've given them the wrong impression." He frowned. "Did they hurt you?"

After scratching behind his ear, James said, "Um, no, nothing like that."

"Good, otherwise I'd have to discipline them. Again, I apologize if they were brusque. Armed forces aren't always polite when on duty. I should've explained this was meant as a friendly invitation."

"That's okay… I guess."

Then Daniel snapped his fingers. "Oh, I have an idea! This should perk you up!" He opened a drawer and fished out two small glasses along with a bottle. Without delay, the Commander popped the cap off and poured the golden liquid within. "Priceless uisge, completely against regulation, but a geezer like me deserves a few indulgences." He winked before raising his glass. Grasping the implication,

James imitated the gesture, and a clink echoed upon contact. "Go ahead, gulp it down."

James obeyed, and the alcohol burned his throat. Several coughs escaped his mouth. Strong, yet possessing a certain sweetness.

Really, it tasted great. I hadn't done shots in a while, so I guess my body wasn't ready, but it calmed my nerves.

—Thoughts of James Hunter, Hocmar 28, 2134, on the Nirnivian calendar

"Packs a punch, eh?" Daniel said after a chuckle.

"Yes, but I enjoyed it!"

"Oh, no surprise there, it's quality stuff!" He leaned forward. "My boy, you must wonder why you're here." A scowl formed on his brow. "There are rumors circling around that you've been talking about Rose lately. Like to Kristina Dupree, for instance, and Brucie too. Don't be so shocked, there aren't many secrets in Valardir that don't reach the Commander, even when it's not my intention. At any rate, I was wondering if you'd mind telling me why. That's not an order, I'm just a concerned father who worries about his adult daughter too much. Rose went through rough patches in the past, and she didn't always talk to me about them."

"Uh, no, it's nothing like that, sir."

No way I could be honest, so I had to think fast. Thank God I came up with something.

—Thoughts of James Hunter, Hocmar 28, 2134, on the Nirnivian calendar

"It's, uh, because of Janice. Rose told me they used to be close, but now Janice avoids her and Rose doesn't know why. She misses her sister a lot. It's not my business, but I was hoping I could help Rose fix it."

After a sigh, Daniel nodded. "Ah, my boy, that's a mystery I also tackled without success. Janice has been acting weird for a while, and not only with Rose. She ignores the whole family! Outside of the job, we rarely speak. She hasn't visited home for months and avoids family gatherings. If forced to attend, she sulks in a corner. I don't know what's wrong, but it's torturing me and everyone else."

Now that he mentioned it, he had a point. Take the New Year's Eve party. Janice had sat between Brucie and me on purpose; she'd hardly chatted with her parents. When Daniel hugged her, Janice almost pushed him back. I figured it was because of their professional relationship, but maybe there was more to it. It seemed Rose wasn't being singled out. Interesting... still, Janice acted odd around her sister.
—Thoughts of James Hunter, Hocmar 28, 2134, on the Nirnivian calendar

"I haven't known Janice for long, but that doesn't sound like her."

"It's not. Before, she visited us almost every day, and she loved family gatherings. Then she changed. I can't recall any incident. Problem is, she's a grown-up; I can't run her life." Daniel shook his head. "Laurence is part of it, but that can't be the main reason. The situation deteriorated years after he disappeared."

James recalled hearing the name before, but he couldn't pinpoint where. "Laurence?"

"Oh, you haven't met him. Laurence is my son and eldest child. I'd introduce him, but I have no idea where he is."

With those words, James realized Rose had revealed her brother recently. She'd claimed he'd vanished, and they had received no news since. "I'm sorry, that must be difficult."

"Yes." Ashamed, Daniel averted his gaze and focused on the desk. "The worst of it is I'm to blame. I couldn't save him. Laurence was a troubled child; he got that from me. I was the same in my youth. The boy hated Rose with a passion you wouldn't believe. Even when she was little, he'd stare at her with such animosity. He felt she'd stolen his place, that his mother and I only loved her. No matter what we tried, that never changed. He was so rough with her, we didn't dare leave them alone together.

"Poor Rose thinks she split us apart, but the fact is Laurence wanted to be angry: if Rose hadn't been there, he would've found a different reason. He had problems before she showed up. He attacked anyone who looked at him funny. On occasion, he assaulted guys thrice his size. That often landed him in the hospital, but Laurence refused to learn his lesson. Eventually, the school expelled him and we had to find another. Then another. And another. Because I was the same as a kid, I understood his rage. Yet that didn't help at all.

"I reasoned with Laurence, but to no avail. What fixed me was a special disciplinary camp. They made me into a respectable man, and I owe them everything. Heh, they expelled Laurence after two weeks. Then again, the mentor who cured me wasn't there anymore. In the end, Laurence had to drop out: all the schools rejected him. He ran away not long after and I haven't seen him since." He took a short pause, then continued.

"Thankfully, I did better with Janice. Rose was harder. She was a good girl, but she is the Melkar and that's a lot of pressure. Still, she turned out okay, so I must've done a decent job. With Laurence, though, I was a total failure."

"Um, nobody said being a father is easy, sir."

"That it's not." Daniel groaned. "At least I think he's alive. He was when Rose caught Alcharia. I contacted him through a third party. Laurence wouldn't meet in person or even talk on the phone. I hoped that Rose's condition would soften him, but he was as mad as ever."

"I'm sorry, sir," James whispered again. "Maybe... maybe it's not too late, and he'll come around."

"Oh, I doubt it, but I'll keep praying," Mr. Ricdeau replied with a sad smile. "I'll never understand how someone can be jealous of an abused child. Am I really that bad?"

"What?"

"That's right, you wouldn't know." Daniel sighed. "Rose had a complicated childhood from the start. Her wings caused a complication during her birth, and her mom died. As for her dad, he blamed Rose for his wife's death. The bastard beat her. The cops arrested him when Rose was five, but she'd already endured so much."

There are no words to describe the disgust I felt. I pictured Rose as a child. She must have been so cute: a small angel with miniature wings. How could anyone hurt her? How could someone harm any kid? I wish I could pretend it's inhuman, but it happens all the time back home, doesn't it? Unfortunately, such tragedies weren't restricted to my universe. It was so depressing, yet so common.

—Thoughts of James Hunter, Hocmar 28, 2134, on the Nirnivian calendar

"He... that's... oh dear God, Rose... I..."

Daniel shrugged. "As you can imagine, he was found guilty in a court of law. A few days later, he hung himself in his cell. It's strange nobody noticed his suicide attempt before it was too late. In fact, how did he get a rope?

There's something fishy about the whole deal. Some speculate the guards let him do it. Some even suggested they murdered him, then disguised their sin. There wasn't much of an investigation: everyone hated his guts after what he did, so people were happy."

A scowl formed on the Commander's brow. "Perhaps that was wrong, my boy. I won't deny he committed a heinous crime, but prison guards aren't only there to prevent escape. They're supposed to protect the convicts. If I had been the one in charge, I would have made sure those men did their job properly." He groaned. "Anyway, Rose was freed from a life of abuse, but she was now an orphan. That wouldn't do. The Melkar needed suitable parents. We were among the many candidates and came out on top. With Madeleine being the progressive branch's head priestess, Rose would have spiritual guidance. And while I wasn't the Commander yet, I had a prominent position in the military, so money-wise we did great and could provide for her. Of course, the centrists and especially the orthodox complained, saying Madeleine would teach Rose progressive doctrine and ignore the other two branches. Madeleine promised she'd teach Rose all three viewpoints as impartially as possible. I doubt they believed her, but she did."

A nostalgic smile formed on Daniel's lips. "When the Council proposed we adopt Rose, we were honored, yet terrified. I won't lie, James, raising the Melkar was a challenge and brought some grief, but Rose was and still is a wonderful daughter. I'd do it again without hesitation."

Crushed, James struggled to organize his thoughts. He yearned to condemn Rose's father, insult him with the harshest possible pejoratives, but nothing seemed appropriate. He'd denounced him over and over but couldn't convey the vileness of his actions. Both men remained silent for a moment and then Daniel said: "Well, thank you for answering my question, my boy. Consider yourself a free man! Unless you have anything else you'd like to ask. I should go back to work soon, but I can spare a few more minutes."

James grimaced. "Thanks, but it's enough for today. Rose's past tends to be... gloomy."

"Yes, it does."

So I returned to my room. I didn't learn much, but I got a clue. Janice distanced herself from her whole family. As I left Mr. Ricdeau, I didn't care about that mystery anyway. I couldn't stop picturing a tiny angel being beaten again and again.

—Thoughts of James Hunter, Hocmar 28, 2134, on the Nirnivian calendar

Chapter 15

That evening, Rose and I played Kuhard in the garden. Let's just say I wasn't great, which is normal, but it didn't help that I couldn't focus. Looking at Rose, I remembered everything Daniel had revealed about her biological dad. I imagined Rose bloodied and battered as the bastard mercilessly beat her. How could he? She was his daughter. This world is a sick, sick place. A part of me wanted to talk about it, but I wasn't sure it'd be appropriate. Besides, I was afraid I'd put my foot in my mouth.

—Thoughts of James Hunter, Hocmar 28, 2134, on the Nirnivian calendar

Again, Rose achieved victory. In this instance, she secured James's defeat by slaying his Commander with a bomb, an obvious mistake on his part. Twelve losses in the span of an hour; on average, that meant a five-minute match length. A pathetic display, even by James's standards.

"Poor Hunter, I win again."

"That's okay." James scratched the back of his neck. "I'll improve, eventually."

Rose moved a strand of hair aside and said in a suspicious tone, "What's the matter? When you think I'm not paying attention, you're staring at me as if I have two noses. Is there something on my face?"

"Uh, no, it's nothing."

That look... Rose could've squeezed the truth out of anyone right there. Gulp.

    —Thoughts of James Hunter, Hocmar 28, 2134, on the Nirnivian calendar

"Ah, um, it's just your dad—well, Mr. Ricdeau—told me about your biological father and how he blamed you for your mother's death and hit you. I... I feel horrible ab—"

"He said what?" As Rose uttered that question, she stood up so fast she flipped the board. It collapsed on the ground with a crash. The pieces flew through the air. Now on her feet, Rose rested her hands on her hips and glared at James. If the situation hadn't been so tense, he might've joked about how she was lucky she'd already won or he'd suspect her of cheating à la Brucie.

I'd never seen Rose so mad before. Sure, she got angry on occasion. The closest was when Jade had tried to open a discussion on legalizing euthanasia, but this was worse. That incident had made Rose rave like a lunatic, but she hadn't turned violent. This time, I had the impression that if Daniel had been present, she would've strangled him.

    —Thoughts of James Hunter, Hocmar 28, 2134, on the Nirnivian calendar

"I'm sorry!" James flinched. "It came up during a conversation, please don't ki—"

Before he finished, Rose inhaled a deep breath and shook her head. "No, I'm the one who's sorry; it's not your fault, Hunter." She sat again, touched her brow as if enduring a brutal headache. "I hate when people... how my real father..." Unable to express her emotions, Rose sighed. "I'm tired of hearing about how Dad was a monster. He was a good man, Hunter. I was young and remember little, but he never blamed me for Mom's death. In fact, my first childhood memory is of asking if Mommy left because of me, and he assured me she didn't. Was he a perfect father? No, but he wasn't abusive."

"Why would Mr. Ricdeau lie about that?"

"That's a complicated story," Rose whispered after a groan. "Dad was nervous and lacked experience with children. Back then, even I understood he felt uncomfortable with parenthood, as if he had no idea how to handle it. But I also knew he loved me and tried his best. Overall, he did well. I missed him a lot when I moved in with the Ricdeaus."

"So he never hit you?"

Rose's voice trembled. "Once." Before James even attempted to open his mouth and comment, Rose presented her palm to hush a potential rebuttal. "Please let me finish the story. We were in a supermarket..."

***

So many types of food, on such tall shelves—little Rose gazed at them, mesmerized. She'd visited the supermarket before, but the wonders of the place still astounded her. Why they needed this variety, she couldn't understand. Why would one crave bread or nasty vegetables when chocolate or yummy cakes were available? Unfortunately, her dad insisted she eat those disgusting things. Why? She didn't know. Though she disliked his insistence, she forgave him, for she loved him so.

The shelves were so high that, even if Rose jumped, she failed to reach the top. Her father assured her that someday she would grow. Why? She didn't know. It seemed inconceivable, a mere fantasy, but her daddy wouldn't lie.

Such a mysterious world, filled with magnificent things. Nothing to do but explore and learn. She couldn't comprehend, but she sure tried. Maybe one day she'd wake up enlightened; then she'd understand the truth of existence, and the meaning of life.

As they strolled down the aisles, people pushed carts around. They picked up boxes and bottles filled with unknown contents. As young Rose stared at the food, amazed, they watched her in admiration. Why? She didn't know. What made her so special? What made her so strange? The boy with three arms, everyone ignored. Why did wings matter more than a tail or claws?

Even at her young age, Rose noticed that Daddy acted different today. His smile had turned into a frown. Why? She didn't know. He was always so anxious and worried constantly. But this was worse; he almost wept. What was a child to do? To cheer up Daddy, what was a child to do? As Rose considered that question, she spotted them in a corner. Those delicious candies she so desired. She begged Daddy, but he refused. Why? She didn't know. She pleaded, but he stayed firm, saying she ate too many sweets. She disagreed. Finally, his patience ran out, and he scowled while raising his voice. Oh, Daddy, why so angry? Oh, Daddy, it was only candy.

Little Rose could be stubborn and wouldn't give up so fast. She grabbed a bag, but Daddy took it back. Furious, the girl felt insulted. Daddy had gone too far! Without thinking, she put her hands on her hips as she often did when provoked. Why? She didn't know. A simple habit without ill intent, yet innocence sometimes begets tragedy.

Such a mysterious world, filled with magnificent things. Nothing to do but explore and learn. She couldn't comprehend, but she sure tried. Maybe one day she'd wake up enlightened; then she'd understand the truth of existence, and the meaning of life.

Daddy hated the posture. He'd asked her before not to do that. It made him so sad and depressed. Why? She didn't know. Still, Rose promised she wouldn't do it again. For her daddy, it was the least she could do.

Often she broke her word. Oh, she never meant to. Her head forgot: it wasn't her fault. So much information overwhelmed her tiny brain. It couldn't process all the rules, all the laws. Thankfully, Daddy proved merciful. He didn't punish; rather, he reminded her, and being a good girl, she apologized. But not this time: Daddy's eyes flashed with rage. He slapped her on the left cheek. Why? She didn't know. In truth, he barely touched her. The blow brought no pain but, surprised, she fell on her bottom. Rose wanted to ask why, but only tears came.

Then everything changed forever. Her cries destroyed her life. The people in the store became violent. They tackled Daddy; some punched him. A few comforted her, vowing the bad man would never hurt her again. They took Daddy away; she begged for him to stay, but they disregarded her pleas. Why? She didn't know. Rose shrieked in terror. Where had they taken him? Would she ever see him again? She swore if he came back, she'd never eat candy. She swore she'd never ever adopt the cursed posture. Please, Daddy, please come back! Please! Daddy! Daddy! Please come back! But he'd never returned. No, Daddy had never returned. What was a child to do?

Such a mysterious world, filled with horrifying things. Nothing to do but scream and cry. She couldn't comprehend, but she sure would. After a few days, she woke up enlightened. She'd learned so many new words: *abusive* and *prison*, *suicide* and *death*, but most of all, *orphan*. She now understood the truth of existence: blessed is ignorance, blessed are the fools, for knowledge does nothing but shatter your dreams.

***

"And so his fate was sealed," Rose continued while sobbing. Tears ran down her cheeks. "Dad was arrested for child abuse and assaulting the Melkar. There were plenty of witnesses. Based on the testimony, I was lucky to be alive. How ridiculous. I had no injuries—not a single mark. But Dad had attacked the holy prophet, even if it was just a little slap." Rose's voice had trembled before, and the tremors increased from that point. "They wanted revenge. They wanted to keep me away from him for fear he might hurt me in the future. I tried to explain that I loved him, that he was nice... to no avail. The judge sentenced him to jail for life without parole and dared imply he had shown lenience. Nowadays, I think it was all a setup. Those in charge had determined my father couldn't raise the Melkar properly and used the incident at the market as an excuse to assign me to a suitable family. Either way, the outcome was the same. A few days later, Dad committed suicide, and so I never saw him again and never will, for he denied himself the afterlife by doing so."

Grimacing, James leaned forward. "Rose—"

The alleged prophet dismissed his plea with a wave. "I'm not done yet, Hunter. The big question is: why did Dad slap me? For years, I wondered, until a distant relative enlightened me. Did you notice I put my hands on my hips when I'm angry?" James offered a timid nod, but Rose proved so enthralled by her own tale that she didn't realize. "Mom did the same. When I took that stance, I was like her double. Dad wasn't quite the same after she died.

When I imitated Mom's posture, I reminded him of her, and that saddened him. That's why he begged me not to. That day at the supermarket, if Mom had been alive, it would have been their wedding anniversary. Dad was depressed. I can sympathize. I suffer the same pain every year. So when I... he... lost his temper. It only happened once. So, Hunter, that's the whole truth." A devastated James opened his mouth, but Rose interrupted. "Maybe you feel Dad was a good man treated unfairly; that's fine. Or maybe you believe he was a terrible person deserving his fate; that's all right too. I'd rather avoid moral musings, so please spare me your opinion. All I ask is that if you must judge Dad, then do so for his real actions, not the fantasy others imagine."

Rose clearly wouldn't appreciate my outlook, so I kept it to myself. Whether her father deserved punishment or not, he received a harsh verdict. I don't know how it is in Nirnivia, but at home, there were people who did far worse to children, only to get ridiculously short sentences. They were freed soon after and found new victims. Life imprisonment for a slap seemed drastic in comparison; not that I condone hitting a kid. Perhaps this universe is different, but I expected her dad wouldn't have been in as much trouble if Rose had been wingless. It appeared striking the Melkar resulted in extreme retribution, but that's not surprising. I figured I should remember that in case we ended up enemies. That sounded implausible, yet I had to face the possibility.

—Thoughts of James Hunter, Hocmar 28, 2134, on the Nirnivian calendar

Awkward silence fell over the room. James realized the revelation had exhausted Rose. She needed time alone, he recognized that. Without a word, he got to his feet and prepared to leave, but Rose stopped him.

"Oh no, Hunter, you're not going anywhere. It's your turn."

James blinked twice in rapid succession. "Huh?"

"I satisfied your curiosity and told you about my biological father. To use your term, it felt like hell. You know the rule: you owe me a question now." James gritted his teeth in dread; whatever Rose planned, he suspected it wouldn't be fun. "What about your parents? Who are they? What do they do? How was your relationship with them?" That was more than one question, but James decided he'd oblige without protest.

There wasn't much to say. My parents were average in most respects. Average parents for an average loser. Rose didn't care about the information. She hoped to wash away the unpleasant memories. Thing is, I didn't want to talk about my parents because I'd probably never see them again. I wished she hadn't asked, but after what she'd gone through, I couldn't refuse.

—Thoughts of James Hunter, Hocmar 28, 2134, on the Nirnivian calendar

"Um, my mother is Michelle Hunter, and she's a schoolteacher. My father is Henry Hunter. He repairs cars. There's not much more to say. They were good parents overall. I can't complain. And I wasn't too hard on them either. I've never been a troublemaker. I guess they had an easy job, ha ha." James paused for a minute while considering what more to add. "Dad owns a garage, and he's disappointed that I won't be taking over the family business. I can't repair cars for shit—maybe I could learn, but the real problem is I have no business sense. I'd bankrupt the place in a month or two. Too bad, it'd be interesting to take over. Sure as hell would beat working at that convenience store."

What I didn't mention is how Nadia and I had fought about this subject. Nadia thought I should give it a shot. The way she saw it, I hated my job, so why not? She had a point, but it's difficult to move forward when you're convinced you'll screw up.

—Thoughts of James Hunter, Hocmar 28, 2134, on the Nirnivian calendar

"Hunter, not everyone is cut out for business. I couldn't do it either. It's not your fault." Rose's concern moved James. The winged woman was a wreck, but she still tried to make him feel better. How touching.

"Um, I know, and so does my dad. He never forced me to follow in his footsteps or anything. We got along well. Anyway, they weren't perfect, but who is? They welcomed me back home when I couldn't pay rent. That's cool."

"Why wouldn't they?" Rose winked. "You're such a sweet boy." Then a yawn escaped her lips. "Well, Hunter, this conversation drained me... I better call it a day. Sorry for cutting our time together short."

Frankly, I was drained too. Rose's story disturbed me, and chatting about my parents didn't help either. Part of me wondered if she'd done that on purpose. Like, I made her recall some sad memories, so she did the same to me. But, nah, Rose wouldn't do that, at least not on a conscious level.

—Thoughts of James Hunter, Hocmar 28, 2134, on the Nirnivian calendar

Chapter 16

A slight tremble assailed Gareth Stevenson as he stepped out of Dr. Nigel Crane's office. Back when he had expressed a desire to return to field duty, the therapist had shown concern. That proved especially true when Gareth had revealed the date he chose for his psych exam. Nigel warned this was unrealistic, a fact Gareth was aware of. He deemed that tight goals eliminated procrastination and thus helped achieve success.

Despite Nigel's reticence, he agreed to help and doubled the amount of sessions they shared. This one demanded considerable strength. The memories Gareth recalled... the mere thought brought shivers. Perhaps he had been too en-thusiastic. Still, he wasn't a quitter and didn't intend on becoming one. Though he might fail, he'd try.

***

Rose's story about her dad left me shaken and disturbed, but I didn't have a chance to recuperate. The time came to leave for the restaurant with Janice. Since I wasn't in the mood, I somewhat regretted accepting, but canceling at the last minute felt like a dick move.

—Thoughts of James Hunter, Hocmar 28, 2134, on the Nirnivian calendar

The instant James passed through the door, a delicious aroma tickled his nostrils, and his stomach grumbled. Thanks to the recent encounter with Rose, his appetite had vanished, but the odor of food reminded his body of its hunger. No question, this kitchen served superior-quality food compared to Valardir's cafeteria. As for appearances, James had difficulty making out the décor. Like many similar establishments he'd visited on earth, the owner favored low lighting. James had never understood this trend. He'd heard that, according to science, the relative darkness encouraged people to eat more. That might've been true, but the only effect he noticed was an increase in his annoyance.

One thing was for sure, guests sat at every table James spotted. That crowd plus the line at the entrance suggested they might be in for a long wait, though he supposed that didn't matter. When you have nothing to do, delays are of little consequence. When a lull in the intense chatter permitted it, faint violin music tickled his ears. A nice classy tune, but no match for Rose's skills. At least the host performed his duties at a decent pace. Sooner than expected, it was their turn and Janice explained she had a reservation. No waiting after all, and James's belly thanked God for it.

Once the host confirmed Janice's statement, he led them to a table and handed them menus. As he took his place in his chair, James caught a glimpse of Janice. She looked stunning. The touch of makeup she'd applied accentuated her features and concealed the rare blemishes. In truth, James couldn't remember if she wore cosmetics in daily life, but if so she put more effort into it than usual. Most days, Janice kept her hair braided or in a ponytail. For this occasion, however, she let it down and that style suited her. As for her eyes, they glimmered in the candlelight. And the outfit—what a beauty. One could count on one's fingers what James knew about women's fashion, but no doubt it had cost a pretty penny. The red dress fit Janice to perfection and achieved a perfect balance of showcasing her natural assets and leaving enough to the imagination. Sexy, but sophisticated.

In hindsight, her appearance should've clued me in on Janice's true intentions. But I was so preoccupied with Rose and her father that it flew over my head.
—Thoughts of James Hunter, Hocmar 28, 2134, on the Nirnivian calendar

Self-conscious, James peeked at his T-shirt and jeans. The other men wore elegant jackets and dress shirts along with ties. To be fair, he lacked an extensive wardrobe in this world, but he was still underdressed by quite a margin. In fact, he thought the host, as well as a few of the waiters delivering plates, fired snobbish looks of disapproval at him. A slight blush tainted his face at this realization. Yet none dared complain, and James wondered if perhaps Janice's status as the NISDA Commander's daughter granted her special treatment.

The moment they sat, Janice leaned forward and, keeping her volume low, said, "This place is freaking stuck-up, but they got the best cooks in town. Trust me, I'd never come here if the food wasn't awesome." Then she rested her palm on James's menu, preventing him from opening it. "Hey, buddy, when you check that thing out, you might get sticker shock. No worries, it's my treat."

After a moment of hesitation, James replied, "An evening with a beautiful woman and a free lunch? I guess I caught a lucky break." As he finished his sentence, a lump formed in his throat. What if Janice misconstrued the statement and became offended? In the end, he had no cause for fear: she giggled and winked.

"Who knows how lucky you'll get!"

James's cheeks reached a darker shade of red. Of course his previous words wouldn't upset Janice. How could he forget he spoke to someone who rivaled Brucie in terms of questionable remarks? Okay, that was a stretch, but still. "Um, Nadia wouldn't approve—"

"Relax, bud, I'm just kidding."

To reduce awkwardness, James opened the menu. While most items had unfamiliar names, photos helped to understand their nature. He had no idea how Nirnivia's currency worked, but the numbers below each entry sent a shiver down his spine. "Thanks for paying." James scratched his neck. "I, uh, feel cheap, though."

Janice dismissed the notion with a wave. "That's ridiculous. You're not cheap, you're poor!"

"Yeah, fair enough! I only have thirty dollars to my name and they're worthless here."

That's when a waiter came to ask what we wanted for drinks. Janice ordered a blue paradise, and I figured I'd follow her lead. Once the waiter returned with our glasses, I tasted a sip. Delicious, and so sweet... it was druikinaka-flavored all right. We kept chatting, but my heart wasn't in it and it must've shown.

—Thoughts of James Hunter, Hocmar 28, 2134, on the Nirnivian calendar

"Are you okay, James? You're a bit off tonight."

"Yeah, it's just, uh, Rose told me about her father."

Janice grimaced. "Oh boy."

"Your dad said he beat her, but Rose denied it. Do you believe her?"

"I dunno, bud. I was a kid then, so I didn't follow the news. Rose isn't a liar, but it sounds far-fetched." Janice shook her head. "Either way, Rose's life is messed up."

"Yeah, I mean, she told me about Gail too and—"

Janice winced. "Please, don't go there. That was so hard on Rose, I don't think she ever recovered. How about changing the subject?"

"Sorry."

"No worries."

An awkward silence filled the air, and then a new voice emerged. "Are you ready to order?" And so we did.

—Thoughts of James Hunter, Hocmar 28, 2134, on the Nirnivian calendar

"If you don't mind telling me, what did you do back home, bud?"

James shrugged. "I was a clerk in a convenience store. I always had dead-end jobs—that's the latest one."

"No shame in that, bud."

"Yeah, but it sucked. At least I didn't lose a career along with my family. What about you, why did you join the military?"

Janice rubbed her chin for a second. "I guess I followed in Dad's footsteps. I was fascinated by his work." She ran a hand through her hair. "He didn't want me to, because of the danger and all that crap. Nothing else interested me, so I ignored him. Dad wasn't happy with the decision, but he accepted it. It was mine to make, and he respected that."

"Military life must be tough. I couldn't do it. Have you ever been sent on a dangerous mission?"

"Yup, especially during the war. Actually, I got my share of injuries." She then locked eyes with James. "I don't get special treatment if that's what you're wondering."

"Um, no, uh"—James sighed—"you're so courageous. I'd be too scared to do anything like that."

"And with good reason! It's not for everyone, but I can handle the pressure. What helps is, if I die on a mission, it'll be for Nirnivia. I'm proud of that." Janice chuckled. "I guess that makes me a patriot, huh?"

"Yeah..."

Another giggle escaped her lips. "It's funny, people say war is like Kuhard, but I can't stand that game."

"Maybe you should give it a chance. Rose has been teaching me. I hated it at first, but it grew on me. Rose always wins, though."

"Not surprising, buddy. Dad taught her when she was a kid."

"Yeah, she's great with a violin too. Have you ever heard her? Uh, you grew up with Rose; you must've."

Janice didn't reply immediately. Instead, she took a sip of her drink. He might've imagined it, but James noted her arm trembled. "You're close to my sister, aren't you?"

"Um, yes, we live together and I owe her so much. She even saved my life. I don't know what I'd do without her."

"Yes, that's only natural." Janice's pupils darted upward, then she frowned. "You know, we had a rough start. I was a jealous kid."

"Yeah, Rose talked about that."

"Really?" The gigantic woman tilted her head as her scowl intensified. "Did she tell you anything I should be embarrassed about? If so, it's all lies." She giggled. "Except for the truths."

"No, no, she likes you a lot."

"Same here! Rose's a kind, gentle soul without malice. You can kick her down again and again; she'll forgive you. I respect her for it."

And I believed her. Janice sounded so genuine it was hard not to. But then, why did she avoid Rose like the plague?

Normally, I wouldn't have dared to bring it up, but somehow when I heard her say that, I couldn't stop myself.

—Thoughts of James Hunter, Hocmar 28, 2134, on the Nirnivian calendar

"Um, she misses you."

"What do you mean? I work at Valardir."

"Well, Rose said you guys don't talk anymore. She thinks you're mad at her."

"What?" Janice threw her hands in the air. "I'm not! I don't care who her biological parents are, Rose is my sister and I love her." She rolled her eyes. "But she can be a total drama queen. Ooh la la."

I considered pressing on and mentioning how I had seen her avoiding Rose myself, but I sensed her frustration growing, so I chose something safer.

—Thoughts of James Hunter, Hocmar 28, 2134, on the Nirnivian calendar

"Okay. It's not my business, but if you're angry with Rose, you should talk to her. I'm sure you guys can work it out."

She forced a laugh. "I'm not, buddy, I told you!" Janice almost shouted. The other patrons gawked at them. She proceeded at a more reasonable volume. "Listen, you're trying to help us make up, and that's cute, but there's no need: I'm not mad at Rose."

"Um, great!"

The funny part was, despite how defensive she acted, I believed her. Back then, I couldn't make sense of it. I forgot one simple possibility... anyway, the waiter served our food, and Janice hadn't exaggerated. It was delicious, some of the best I ever had! The rest of the evening went well. I found out nothing about Rose's past, or what was going on between Janice and her, but I had fun.

—Thoughts of James Hunter, Hocmar 28, 2134, on the Nirnivian calendar

Chapter 17

Now that had been pointless. Brucie had been correct. As Janice entered her house, she pondered whether she should reveal that fact to him. He'd be insufferable. The quasi-date had left her far more exhausted than expected. She must be getting old.

With a sigh, Janice headed for the master bedroom. She wished to crawl into bed, forget the whole evening and drift into sleep. First, she had to remove her makeup—not to mention the dress. Janice began with the latter and slipped into pajamas. As she finished donning the garment, footsteps echoed in the distance and she froze. An intruder...

Used to surprise thanks to her military career, Janice recuperated in a flash. Without hesitation, she headed for the gun safe next to the mattress. In a rapid motion, she input the code, opened the door and reached for the pistol within. Then a male voice echoed: "Hey, babe, are ya here?"

Janice mumbled a curse and shoved the weapon back inside the metal box before closing it. She recognized the trespasser, and he posed no threat, though he'd better provide a valid explanation for breaking and entering unless he fancied a well-placed punch.

"Brucie, what the freak are you doing here?" Janice yelled while walking toward the living room. As anticipated, she found the bodyguard standing there with a dumbstruck expression.

"Heard 'bout your date with James and thought I'd ask how it went."

With a scoff, Janice crossed her arms. "That's none of your business. And what's wrong with you? Fancy yourself a burglar now or what?"

"Nah, ya left the door open. Figure I'd check on ya to be safe."

Janice sighed while closing her eyes and shaking her head. "Goddamn, I must be even more tired than I thought. Well, anyway, if you're bothering to check on me, you must be getting better."

"Oh yeah, top shape. Ain't be long till I get back to work now."

"Good. That monster could've have torn us apart." With a hard swallow, she remembered that many had suffered that fate. "We're lucky." A shiver assailed Janice. "God, I hope I never go through something like that again."

"Ain't gonna disagree with ya there."

Then a realization hit Janice and she frowned at Brucie. "Wait! You show up the second I come back. Amazing timing, how did you...?" A groan escaped Janice's lips. "Brucie, you asshole, you were there."

The bodyguard shrugged. "Yeah... sorry, babe, wasn't planning on doing anything. Was just curious, ya know."

"You deserve some dick punching right about now."

"Guess so, but ya ain't gonna 'cause I'm a lovable scamp. Plus, I saved yer life; gotta gimme some leeway."

Janice waggled a menacing finger. "Don't push your luck, buddy."

"Gotcha." Then Brucie smiled. "So, how did it go?"

"About as well as you expected." By Brucie's confused stare, Janice deduced he didn't grasp the hint. "Ooh la la, you're so dense. James kept bringing up Rose. A lot. And here I assumed Nadia was the competition, but turns out it's good old sis as you said."

"He ain't gonna get Rose, ya know that."

Janice forced a giggle. "So what? The guy's hot for my freaking sister, that's a major turn-off. I'm not taking this any further. You must be so happy."

Brucie shook his head. "Nah, babe, ya got me all wrong. Yeah, I'm jealous as freak but I want the best for ya. Ain't saying James is the best—sure ain't a stud like me, but ya want 'im, so..."

"How sweet." She failed to conceal the sarcasm in her tone. "Or it would be if I believed that."

"Ouch!" Brucie winced. "But seriously, are ya okay? I can stay with ya for the night if ya like."

"I told you: I'm done being your booty call. Get out of here!"

"Ain't what I meant, babe!" Brucie held his opened palm in front of his body as if wielding a shield. "I can keep ya company, ya know, crash on the couch. No touching involved, I swear."

"Ooh la la!" Against the odds, Janice burst into genuine laughter she didn't expect in her current tired state. That man could be so ridiculous. "You're really worried, aren't you?" Brucie nodded. "Bud, I have a tiny little crush, it's not like I'm in love. Come on!"

The bodyguard's mouth gaped. "You ain't?"

"No! And even then, you caused my crush. You put ideas in my head, Brucie. I figured, why not try it out and see where it goes? I thought maybe we'd sleep together. It's been a while since I've had some action. From there, who knows what'll happen, but I'm a long way from dreaming of marrying James or anything serious."

"Ain't ya done with booty calls?"

"Psst!" Janice dismissed the notion with a wave. "With you, sure!" She paused for a moment, then smiled. "So, you felt bad because my date didn't go well and checked on me. No plans for sexing me up?"

"Yup."

"Whoa, Brucie, you've grown more mature."

He winked. "Now I ain't saying that, but part o' me's growing if ya know what I mean!"

"And he's back! Forget I said anything. Get out of here, Brucie!"

"Fine!" He mimicked a phone with his fingers. "Call if ya change your mind."

"Won't happen, but thanks!"

On that note, Brucie departed and Janice exhaled in relief. In truth, she would've enjoyed company, but it would've been a mistake. An innocent night spent with Brucie easily led to more. In fact, it seemed quite possible that was the reason he'd suggested staying with her. Somehow, she doubted it, though. She had the impression he'd displayed genuine concern. Perhaps a foolish notion given their past, but still, she preferred to give him the benefit of the doubt.

Chapter 18

Once I got back to Valardir, I went through the security procedures and returned to my room. Since I arrived five minutes before eight p.m., I avoided that jail Rose had warned me about long ago.

—Thoughts of James Hunter, Hocmar 28, 2134, on the Nirnivian calendar

Once inside his chamber, James walked to his mattress and sat down. Then he reached inside his pocket and pulled out his wallet, from which he grabbed Nadia's picture. "Hey, babe. Sorry it's a little late. Janice invited me to a restaurant. Oh, don't look at me like that, Nadia. It wasn't a date, I swear. Just two friends hanging out." He forced a chuckle. "No, really, honest to God! Heh, I mostly went because I thought I might learn something about why Janice ignores Rose. That went nowhere fast." A groan followed. "Same could be said for this whole"—James performed finger quotes with his free hand—"'investigation.' Not sure it's worth continuing. It's pointless."

I kept talking to Nadia's photo for about ten, fifteen minutes. When I finished, it was still early for bed, so I figured I'd continue reading the book about Misha, the original Melkar. As I picked it up, I wondered if Janice had had an ulterior motive for inviting me to dinner. She'd dressed fancy... was it possible she wanted something to happen? After considering it, I decided that no. Her clothes matched the dress code, and she knew I had a girlfriend. Besides, why would an active woman like Janice be interested in a lazy couch potato? I couldn't be her type.

Convinced there wasn't anything strange in Janice's behavior, I lay in bed and read. Misha's story became even wilder. Forget random predictions, people claimed she stopped a robbery while shopping with her parents. According to witnesses, she transformed into a creature of light and immobilized the thief without harming them. That shattered my suspension of disbelief, but things got interesting, and I was excited for the next crazy twist. I turned the page, and that's when I heard a beep. Surprised, I stared at the source: my minicomp sitting on the desk.

—Thoughts of James Hunter, Hocmar 28, 2134, on the Nirnivian calendar

With a frown, James approached the device. As he reached for it, the screen flashed in rapid succession. Soon, Doctor Death's ravaged visage appeared. As usual, his electronic eye displayed a joyful smiley. "Hello, James, and good evening," said the mechanical man with his constant tone. "I apologize for the intrusion. If this time is convenient, I would like to resume our previous discussion concerning the first human."

Speaking with the Ostarkiran president spiked James's anxiety and sickened him. How he wished to avoid the conversation, but he realized he lacked any other source of info, and his own research had produced no results. Of course, it'd be impossible to determine whether the new information was accurate, but beggars can't be choosers. Besides, excitement for the prospect of more details on the first human had already doubled his heart rate. Should he refuse to listen, his curiosity might end up killing him.

"Um, yeah, sure."

"Excellent! However, before we reach the main attraction, I must offer a warning. Based on what I have heard, you are living dangerously." James tilted his head and furrowed his brow. "By that, I am referring to how you have been inquiring about Rose's past. That bravado resulted in Daniel Ricdeau bringing you to his office to intimidate you."

Okay, that was freaky. The bastard was really well informed, and I wondered how he managed it. Still, I preferred not to show how much he impressed me.

—Thoughts of James Hunter, Hocmar 28, 2134, on the Nirnivian calendar

"Uh, no, he, uh, just worried about Rose."

The Doctor's smiley changed from happy to pensive. "Perhaps, but having large armed men with a threatening demeanor escort you must've been intimidating."

"That was a misunderstanding."

"That is possible, but I doubt it. The use of passive-aggressive methods to threaten someone subtly is in line with Daniel's behavior, I assure you. But enough of that—you've had considerable time to ponder about the first human. In truth, it is a simplistic riddle. His identity must be obvious to you by now..." While James remained silent, a ball of embarrassment formed in his throat. "I see that is not the case. I am disappointed, James. You proved before that you could use your head—it is an activity I encourage. Nevertheless, I shall spell it out for you. The first human is alive and well. In fact, you met him already." The cyborg's stare intensified. "His name is Brucie Garland!"

With a gasp, James stepped back and almost dropped the minicomp. "What?!" Then he covered his mouth with his hand. The walls were thick and soundproof, but he shouldn't risk drawing attention anyway.

"Is it not evident? Contemplate his rude manners and idiotic behavior: only a human being could display such a lack of class." The president's arm parted from his body as his palms pointed upward. "Brucie is the only realistic suspect." On those words, the smiley simulated a laugh. "Oh, wipe that ridiculous expression from your face: I attempted humor. You are so tense; I merely tried to lighten you up. James, you should relax: it will help you live longer. Alas, you did not appreciate my jest." That wasn't a question. "Fair enough, I shall provide the correct solution: James, I am the first human."

Every fiber of my being screamed out not to believe him. I was sure he lied. He wasn't from earth. Don't ask me why, but the possibility revolted me. Maybe because deep down I viewed him as a disturbing creep I'd rather not have anything in common with. Thanks to him, I doubted Rose, but I trusted him less. And I'm ashamed to admit it, but his physical appearance played a part. Rose looked like an angel from heaven; he looked like a grotesque sci-fi reject. That alone made it so much easier to trust her.

—Thoughts of James Hunter, Hocmar 28, 2134, on the Nirnivian calendar

"No!" James slapped his desk and a loud thud echoed. "That can't be! Rose was right: you're manipulating me."

"Why in hell would I? Please forgive the insult, but you are completely useless."

That was true—I couldn't imagine why the Doctor bothered with me. Yet I wasn't convinced. He had reasons, even if I had no idea what they were. Eventually, I realized he'd mentioned hell. That was odd: it's a concept from Christianity that meant

nothing here. Nobody used that curse, except me. Plus he wasn't the kind of person who swore, so he said it on purpose.

—Thoughts of James Hunter, Hocmar 28, 2134, on the Nirnivian calendar

"I cannot fathom why you are outraged. It was predictable." The Ostarkiran president shook his head. "The clues pointed straight toward me. Examine the evidence and you will find my assertion beyond coherent. Think of the day you arrived here. The instant it was revealed you were human, people wished to murder you. I am not talking about savage criminals, but average citizens who would normally never entertain such violence. The only human they have ever met was I, the most hated person in Nirnivia." He bent his neck. "Alas, they misunderstand me. In any case, they feared that you would be another version of me. A preposterous notion. Humans vary in personality; the same holds for Nirnivians. However, irrational fears trump logic."

In his mind, James recognized this explanation appeared more credible than Rose's. Yet it wasn't proof. "There is more," the cyborg promised as he discerned James's skepticism. "How about your current living arrangements? Daniel keeps you in Valardir, a military complex. Why is that? The answer is surveillance. I will concede that 'visitors' are dangerous, but do you not agree their caution seems a tad excessive? Granted, I cannot establish that a nonhuman 'visitor' would be treated otherwise, so perhaps that argument is lacking."

Doctor Death paused for a second, then proceeded. "Consider how BBR kidnapped you to run some twisted experiments. That demanded substantial effort, and for what? They have a single goal: annihilate me for the sake of vengeance. Humans should be of no significance to BBR unless I am one. Diabo planned to study your physiology and psyche in the hopes of discovering a weakness they could exploit against me. Even better: why do you think Mr. Pierre Garland calls himself Diabo? While Nirnivia and Earth share far more than logic would dictate in terms of languages, people here have no concept of the devil. I suppose Diabo could be a word with a different meaning in this universe, but I assure you it is not the case. Pierre chose that moniker specifically for me. I am half Brazilian on my father's side and half French on my mother's. When Pierre was my prisoner, I once mentioned my grandma would believe him to be a 'diabo' and he adopted the name. It was a pathetic attempt to scare me, but for an atheist, such religious concepts are meaningless; thus, his endeavor failed. On a lighter note, how about coffee?"

James blinked twice in confusion. "Coffee?"

The mechanical man acquiesced. "But of course! Is it not strange that this land also has coffee? It is the only beverage we share except water. And beer, I suppose, though what they call beer is fairly different from our own version."

"Um, I guess, but it's not as weird as the same language thing."

"Ah, yes, that is indeed a mystery. I could not solve it, but coffee is another story... I missed that boost in the morning. This world lacked an alternative. After a while, I yearned to replicate it and came fairly close. The taste and effects are comparable, though not the ingredients. In the end, I determined that I'd worked so hard for a cup of coffee I deserved one—hence the identical name. The general population prized my invention, and it spread across the country. Rose despises it, however. Ah well, that is her loss."

His points made a ton of sense. I searched for a contradiction that exposed his deception.

—Thoughts of James Hunter, Hocmar 28, 2134, on the Nirnivian calendar

"Wait!" James clutched his fists. "Something is fishy. They, uh, call you Doctor Death. Mr. Ricdeau said that's because when it comes to medicine, you're a real genius."

"That is correct."

"Then you're lying! A human might be an amazing doctor on earth, but not here!" Impressed by his logic, James beamed. That should stump the cyborg. Except he shrugged off the argument.

"A fascinating yet flawed conclusion. Discounting the mutants, have you noticed how Gorumars could pass as humans? They could stroll down our streets and none would be the wiser. That is eerie, not to mention unlikely; however, it is a fact. As it turns out, their insides are similar too. There are differences, but my previous experience served me well. Based on my research, a human and a Nirnivian could even mate and have a child together. I never tested that theory, but I am confident it is accurate. Back home, I was a surgeon, a superb one. At the risk of sounding egotistical, I was among the best. When I arrived here years ago, I could not bear to be torn apart from the profession I loved, so I studied. At first, they denied me a medical license. As you can imagine, the Nirnivians were uncomfortable with having a visitor operate on them. With time, I proved my worth, and the demand for skilled doctors trumped their reticence. Eventually, I earned respect and was responsible for several medical breakthroughs. I have met Rose, you know; we became quite close. I never was a religious man, but when I saw her wings, I had no choice but to reconsider my views and asked if she was an angel. That confused Rose, so I explained the concept."

The cyborg's voice hadn't changed, since that was beyond his capacity, but his remaining blue eye glimmered with nostalgia. "And that is why, when you asked the same question, Rose understood what you meant."

"That somewhat makes sense." James groaned and slammed his fist into his left palm. "But it doesn't add up! Why would a human start a holy war against Nirnivia?"

"Holy war?" The mechanical man's smiley burst into laughter. "Is that what they claim happened? How ridiculous: I have no interest in a holy war. I am a rational being and as such reject the existence of God. Nevertheless, I do not care if the Nirnivians or anyone else deludes themselves with a nonsensical dogma. Oh no, I am merely trying to save Nirnivia, or rather the world, from NISDA. I inadvertently uncovered their dark secret; the result is my broken body."

James gritted his teeth. The account grew more and more plausible. Sweat dripped from his forehead. Though his heart begged him not to, his curiosity demanded he inquire further:

"What dark secret?"

"As I have revealed earlier, it is Project Ekelon. For your sake, it is best if you stay unaware of the details. Besides, I am running out of time." Annoyed, James moaned. The Doctor ignored him. "I understand this omission costs me credibility, but I cannot jeopardize your safety. Regardless, I survived the impossible odds and in an improbable twist of fate, I reached Ostark. I became a prominent member of their society, and in another unlikely turn of events, they chose me as president. It is a long story. One day we might be able to discuss it thoroughly. Ostark was already engaged in battle against Nirnivia. The reason that President Laforge, my predecessor, started this conflict felt irrelevant to me, so I derailed the ongoing struggle toward an alternative goal: exposing NISDA."

James grimaced. "That's so far-fetched..."

"I realize that, and it is unfortunate. While I do not blame you for your wariness, I hope in the future you will accept that I am your only ally."

I spent the majority of the night thinking about what I'd learned. Doctor Death being human resolved several mysteries. On the other hand, his account was filled with holes. The whole deal about him surviving an assassination attempt and ending up as the president of Ostark seemed so... stupid. It was possible the part about him being the first human was true, but in that case, his explanation for how he became a renowned surgeon felt like a fairy tale. It sounded too easy. Then again, what Rose told me was far from rock-solid. I debated with myself until I fell asleep from exhaustion.

—Thoughts of James Hunter, Hocmar 28, 2134, on the Nirnivian calendar

***

The next book, The Cyborg's Fortune, is available for preorder and releases on June 3, 2024.

Do you want a free short story that serves as a prequel to The Cyborg's Crusade? Then, join the cyborg's fan club on my website,
https://thecyborgscrusade.com/fanclub.html

Please consider leaving a review. Those help a lot. Note that you can buy books, and follow me on social media with this link:
https://thecyborgscrusade.com/hub.html

Thank you for reading, I hope with all my heart you enjoyed The Cyborg's Riddle.

ABOUT THE AUTHOR

My name is Benoit Lanteigne and I'm a French Canadian (outside of Quebec) who's trying to write in English. That can be tricky. I'm a computer programmer and I enjoy it. I see many inspiring writers who hate their day jobs and hope to quit someday, but that's not my case. Mostly, I've worked on websites and web applications.

Back in school, I enjoyed writing and according to my teachers and classmates; I had a talent for it. Well, not so much for grammar and spelling, but they liked my stories. Once I went to university, I dropped writing as a hobby. There were other things I wanted to focus on, such as my career. Then, in the early 2000s, around 2006 I'd say, I had a flash of inspiration. At first, it was a single character: a winged woman with red hair. I didn't even know who she was, but the image stuck with me. From there, I began figuring out details about her origins and her world, but I only started writing for real in 2009. After over ten years of hard work, books of The Cyborg's Crusade are finally ready for release.